Praise for

WONDERLAND

"Exquisite . . . *Wonderland* is a striking evocation of the artist's quest, as inspiring in its way as Patti Smith's memoir *Just Kids*."
— *Los Angeles Times*

"Richly interior . . . Much of [*Wonderland*'s] force comes from Anna's struggle to navigate both the contrived, semi-magical world of touring and songwriting and the real world clamoring just outside it . . . What makes Anna such a powerful narrator is her seductive desire to keep her options open."
— *Washington Post*

"In Brundage, D'Erasmo has created a wry, questioning, sensual artist."
— *The New Yorker*

"[A] questing, questioning, melodic narrative . . . Sentence by sentence, Stacey D'Erasmo is a gorgeous writer . . . [She's] given a vibrant, idiosyncratic voice to her heroine."
— *Minneapolis Star Tribune*

"*Wonderland* is addictive fare . . . D'Erasmo's fierce, inventive prose . . . is on full display . . . No, D'Erasmo isn't a rocker. But her book? To risk another cliché, it's worthy of at least one encore, if not more."
— *Oregonian*

"Heartbreakingly intense . . . [A] dramatically satisfying, philosophically complex novel."
— *San Francisco Chronicle*

"The world of *Wonderland* is authentic, vibrant, and genuine. D'Erasmo explores the delight and terror of second chances. A great read."
— **Michael Stipe**

"[A] profound and impressionistic novel, in which a rock star's comeback tour becomes a meditation on performance, ambition, loves lost and found, the passage of time and the sparks that create art . . . *Wonderland* pulses with the magnetic beat of second chances." — **BBC**

"*Wonderland* is a witty and unflinching novel about life, love, art, and sound checks. A deep howl and a bittersweet song, this is D'Erasmo's best yet." — **Sam Lipsyte, author of *The Ask***

"When Anna Brundage is in the zone, she pulls songs from the air; she showers her fans and collaborators in pain and beauty. *Wonderland*'s insight into how a woman inhabits, feeds, and sometimes undoes her own artistry is rare and profound." — **Ann Powers, author of *Weird Like Us: My Bohemian America***

"Like Anna, her unforgettable narrator, Stacey D'Erasmo has found a new sound here: a voice so gorgeous and raw that it captures what it means to be human. D'Erasmo's prose is lyrical and alive – this is a vital, powerful novel – and *Wonderland* will strike a chord with anyone who's ever dreamed of getting a second chance." — **Elliott Holt, author of *You Are One of Them***

"[D'Erasmo] really outdoes herself . . . You read with highlighter in hand, ready to underline amazing phrase after amazing phrase." — *Paste*

"Meditative, beautifully crafted . . . *Wonderland* is built of fragments – scraps of memory, of the peripatetic life on the road, of sex and drugs and rock and roll as art – as it must necessarily be, to convey its hero's passage into maturity. In chronicling [Anna's] journey, D'Erasmo has again given us a wise, wonderful gift." — *The Rumpus*

"This isn't a book about the music industry so much as an evocative exploration of universal themes: the anxieties of middle age, the bittersweet freedom of the creative life, the burden of the legacy a daughter inherits from her father. It's difficult to make territory as familiar as rock stardom feel this fresh, but *Wonderland* is a breakthrough in the style of an early Brundage — a novel that takes what we think is solid, and splits it open at the seams." — *Bookforum*

"D'Erasmo gives us an inside look at a world most of us will never experience. As Anna strives for perfection in her music, you get the feeling she just might make it." — *Oklahoman*

"As Robert Mapplethorpe told Patti Smith, this one, *Wonderland*, has the magic." — *Washington Independent Review of Books*

"[D'Erasmo] combines the delightful worlds of literature and music while bringing out the best in both mediums . . . A rich and exquisitely crafted novel." — *Lambda Literary*

"Highly entertaining . . . D'Erasmo's prose makes the story so absorbing . . . I found myself going back over, trying to savor each word of lyrical prose like one would with each note in a song they love." — **The Sun Break**

"[A] rhapsodic portrait of a rock-and-roll diva . . . Anna is an irresistible narrator. D'Erasmo brings us inside the music and the musician's psyche in this transfixing song of a self evolving through discovery, loss, and renewal." — *Booklist,* **starred review**

"Commanding . . . Spellbinding . . . Meticulously crafted." — *Publishers Weekly,* **starred review**

WONDERLAND

ALSO BY STACEY D'ERASMO

Tea

A Seahorse Year

The Sky Below

The Art of Intimacy: The Space Between

Wonderland

WONDERLAND

Stacey D'Erasmo

MARINER BOOKS

HOUGHTON MIFFLIN HARCOURT

BOSTON · NEW YORK

First Mariner Books edition 2015

Copyright © 2014 by Stacey D'Erasmo

www.hmhco.com

Library of Congress Cataloging-in-Publication Data
D'Erasmo, Stacey.
Wonderland / Stacey D'Erasmo.— First U.S. Edition.
pages cm
ISBN 978-0-544-07481-1 (hardback)   ISBN 978-0-544-48389-7 (pbk.)
1. Domestic fiction. 2. Psychological fiction. I. Title.
PS3554.E666W66 2014
813'.54 — dc23
2013019523

Designed by Chrissy Kurpeski
Typeset in Mercury

Printed in the United States of America
DOC 10 9 8 7 6 5 4 3 2 1

For all my fellow travelers

The obvious analogy is with music.

— LYN HEJINIAN, *My Life*

COMING BACK

Christiania

THERE IS A man fixing a bicycle, or attempting to fix a bicycle, in the lane. I am sitting by the bluish window of a borrowed apartment in Christiania reading a paperback mystery badly translated from Italian. I bought it in the Copenhagen airport. It has something to do with boats – someone was murdered on a boat, salty types haunt the harbor – but I don't care about boats.

I do find that I care about Christiania, which, though I've never been here before, feels familiar to me, as if I've dreamed of it many times. A good-sized island in the center of Copenhagen, surrounded by a river, it was taken over by hippies in 1971 and declared a "free state," with communal property, no cars, and drugs openly for sale on the main drag, helpfully named Pusher Street. It has been a free state ever since. Now it is a leafy, semi-occluded place, with dirt roads, peculiar hand-built houses – some look like shacks, some look like spaceships – a few streets of stores selling crafts, and a climate all its own: it is warmer and damper here than in Copenhagen proper, as if one has stepped into a vast terrarium. Christiania, shaggy and rural and utopic, is a collective wish, under constant threat of being torn down by the government or turned into condos. There was a riot last week, apparently; a building was set on fire, it isn't clear by whom, the anarchists or the cops. Christiania's signature, its export to the unfree world, is innovative, handmade bicycles. Some of them look like the bicycles people, or aliens, might ride on Jupiter. Some of them look as if they were made by Dalí. Some appear to be anticipating a time when people will be much taller.

Christiania's melancholic hope loops around my heart. It is the ruins of the future. As soon as we got here, the very first stop on the tour, my comeback tour – coming back from what to what, anyone might well ask – I wanted to stay. But we're all leaving in the morning. We're taking the train to Göteborg, whatever that is. In the living room of this borrowed apartment, five enormous windows made out of salvaged glass look onto the dirt road below. The light blue of the glass makes me wonder if it was salvaged from a church. Otherwise, the room is all bookshelves, a long curve of modernist red sofa, and two enormous, identical sleeping hounds with coarse gray fur. The old man with pink gauges in his earlobes who let me in told me not to worry about them, which I don't, but I wish they would wake up. Instead, they lie on a chartreuse blanket on the floor, paws twitching in twin dreams. It's cold in here. I would like to wrap a sleeping dog around me for warmth, but settle for a pair of fingerless knit gloves that I find on one of the bookshelves.

The bicycle wrench goes *cling clang . . . clingcling clang*. A loud screech, a ping. The man swears. I don't speak Danish, but by the propulsive sound of the word he makes I know he's swearing. I look out the window. Short, choppy yellow hair; tools and a sweater on the ground; a bicycle turned upside down, gears to the sky; his round face; a bit of a gut on him, though he's young. Young*ish*. He drinks from a dark brown beer bottle, a slender wrench dangling from his other hand. He has stripped down to a T-shirt in his exertions; the indigo-blue edge of a tattoo is visible on one upper arm. He is handsome – almost too handsome.

My new young manager, Boone, looking, as usual, like he died two days ago, clatters up the wooden stairs and into the room carrying a small velvet bag. "Are you ready, Anna?" he says. "Sound check in an hour. Why did you turn off your phone? You should see where the rest of us are staying – this is *nice*." Boone has a face like a chipped white plate. Small, round, questioning dark eyes. An ambivalent beard. A concave chest.

He can't settle, doesn't sit down, hovering a few feet away. I would like to put him in my pocket and feed him crumbs.

"It's cold," I say.

"Not really," he ventures. Boone is still trying to find his way around me. "Take a look at this." He opens the velvet bag, unwraps tissue paper from a porcelain figurine – a vaguely Turkish-looking man who appears to be singing, smiling face uplifted, and playing a tiny porcelain guitar – which he sets on the coffee table. "Only a hundred fifty euros." He rocks on his heels.

"Huh," I say in what I hope is a neutral tone. Something about the figurine makes me uneasy – its uncanniness, its exorbitant price, its sentimentality. What is actually going on in the world if this kitschy thing is valuable?

"There was another one there, a Schiffener, but it wasn't nearly as good. Why did you turn off your phone?"

"I don't know," I say, because I don't. The jet lag makes me feel a beat or two behind myself. I pretend to go back to reading my book. Sardines, a bloody handkerchief. The pensive, hard-drinking, salty-tongued detective. It smells like licorice in this room; where did I leave it? I'd like some licorice.

"Anna," says Boone. "I've been trying to call for an hour. What are you *doing*? Whose dogs are those? They look like van Stavasts – do you think they could be? It's a really rare breed."

"I don't know." I turn a page. I hate Boone, I think. "It's too cold in here."

Boone sighs. "Anna. Are you freaking out?"

I don't respond. I'm not exactly trying to torment him. It's just that, for one thing, I'm cold. I hate being cold. For another, I resent the implication, which underlies every exchange we have, that I should be grateful that he agreed to take me on. He's said I must know how major I am, but we both know I went to him. All of Boone's other acts are much younger, their beardless pallors glow, they have some sort of Icelandic/Ber-

liner/post-polar-ice-cap handcrafted glamour, they wear peculiar Amish-like outerwear and badly fitting pants, only
maybe two of them are junkies. They are all, of course, very
serious. Brilliant, even. Their music is the music of the new
world, coming over the waves, half translated. If you told me
that they cobbled their own shoes out of scrap leather made
from the tanned hides of cows they had butchered themselves
with knives made in their own smithies, I would believe you.
Many of them claim to be my lifelong fans, too, to have the lyrics from *Whale* engraved on their hearts, to be unreasonably
devoted to my very shadow, but I can't help feeling that if I
were taxidermied and tied to the front of their tour buses, I'd
be equally as lovable to them.

In my darker moments I feel like the Queen of England,
bound and gagged by reverence. Tin-crowned and irrelevant.
Perhaps I should stay here in Christiania, take up my other
life, pass through the hemp-scented membrane of this place
and become another Anna Brundage, maybe a better one. An
Anna on a distended, futuristic bicycle. Also, for yet another
thing, this entire idea was along the lines of a disaster. Music
is quicksilver, gossamer; careers are measured in butterfly life-
times. My butterfly life ended seven years ago in Rome. No one
gives a shit about what I do anymore. I'm on a tiny label, albeit
a tiny one with some cachet, but I paid for *Wonderland* myself. I begin to feel queasy. What have I started? I eye the sentimental porcelain figurine, singing so witlessly. Why did Boone
agree to take me on? Am I a novelty act?

"I'm just cold. It's too cold in here," I say. "How's the
house?"

He scratches at his chin, grimacing. "Online sales are all
right so far. It was a holiday yesterday, everybody was out
drinking, we're expecting more at the door. I mean, given who
you are it's going to be great, but it is the first one, and there's a
big World Cup match on TV tonight, you can't—"

"Isn't there any way to turn the heat up?"

Boone zips his sweater up to the neck in the way of a man who would like to strangle someone and is strangling himself instead. He puts the terrifying figurine back in its wrapping, its little velvet bag. "I have no idea. It isn't my house." He's so aggravated that he's barely speaking above a whisper. "I don't even understand where we are. Is this island some kind of commune deal?"

"But I can't sing if I'm too cold. You know that."

"Anna. Darling. Put on a sweater. There will be heat in the theater. This place – it's dirt roads, did you see that? It's not so surprising that the heat doesn't work that well." He shifts his weight from one foot to the other. "But everyone is playing the Bee Palace right now. Right?" He regards me. "This is good." How young he is. His beard barely on his face, he might scratch it right off one day. But he does work hard, he does.

"Christiania is a free state," I offer as an olive branch of information. "The last one in the world, I think. We're in the ruins of the future. Can you check on the heat at the theater?"

"Yes," says Boone. "If you turn your phone on. Anna, it's *nice* in here. You have the best one." He gives me a significant, managerial look and clatters out. Also proving my point about the gratitude thing.

Beyond the salvaged blue window, the man is squatting next to the broken bike, smoking a cigarette and drawing lazily in the dirt with a stick. He is definitely almost too handsome. Daring myself to open the window, I open the window. I whistle. He lifts his face. "Hey. Want to come up for a beer?"

Apparently he speaks English, and he's thirsty.

He does have a gut, it turns out, but in a while I discover that over his belly button, unafraid and rather large, are the letters *AMOR*. "Who was this for?" I say, tracing them with my forefinger, still in the cut-off gloves, my hand just beneath the hem of his rucked-up T-shirt. I am nervous, not nervous, nervous, making my way down the steep slope into the first valley of the *M*. This is where the tour properly begins, right here, where the point of the *M* is lost in a fold of this stranger's skin. This is the way in. I like the way he smells. My pulse quickens. I used to do this; it was part of it, part of the mystery of it. Not a dare, not a conquest, more like heading down an unnamed street.

He shakes his head. "No one. Long story." I ask him, my forefinger moving slowly around the *O*, which team he's rooting for in the World Cup, and he tells me, and I instantly forget. Ohio? Oostan? He watches my face, holding still, while my finger coasts around the belly of the *R*. He pulls his shirt all the way over his head, smiling.

We move to the borrowed bed. There, on his back, his eyes change. I can see the wolf in them. He doesn't ask me who I am or what I'm doing here or why I called out to him. When I kiss him, he puts his arms over his head, looking me in the eye. The scent of him wafts up. He has a small, old scar just above his left eyebrow. His expression is cool, appraising – partly as if he expects this, but also as if he might believe that the world is like this, it can kiss you or kill you at any second, and you must never turn away from either possibility. If a woman whistles to you from a blue window, you go up, no matter what might be waiting at the top of the stairs. Perhaps he has his unnamed streets as well. Or maybe it's because we're in Christiania; in the ruins of the future, you do whatever. Or maybe he knows this house, knows who lives in it. Maybe it's his house. Maybe they're his sleeping dogs. Or maybe he grew bored of not fixing the bike. I am pleased that I remember how this goes, that I can still do this, the ride is starting, though before – before, everything moved much faster somehow, things were blurrier.

Now the clock ticks in the cold room. The moments unfold with each tick. His hands are large, warm. His breath smells of beer and tobacco and of a spice I don't recognize. I am naked, but I keep the gloves on. The sheets are rough. His belly is still cold. He turns us over and I get a shock. His feet are Simon's feet: wide-toed, flat. I bite my lip, getting goose bumps. I stop, then I rally. Fine. Is this Simon's joke on me? He's got Simon's feet. I'll give him Simon's fuck. The thought seems to warm me up a little.

He pauses, looks into my face. "You're on the poster," he says. "In the square. Wonderland." His *r* is so soft, buoyed on a long bridge of air, it all but disappears.

"Yes." I see now that he is older than I thought, perhaps in his late thirties, early forties. Like me. Small lines around his eyes, smoker's teeth. Is that Simon's tooth, too, that pointy, faintly yellowed one? I try to pull him closer, but he holds himself away, looking at me.

"You are the singer?"

"Yes. I guess. It's been a while."

"I used to sing, too," he says. "It's been a while." He smiles. His hand cups my breast, he puts his mouth there as well; his fingers are chapped, one thumbnail is black-and-blue. Simon's feet churn at the bottom of the bed, too far away. I try to touch Simon's pointy tooth with my tongue, but I can't find it. I look harder, getting warmer. If I can't have Simon, I want the wolf, though the wolf keeps darting away, turning into the bicycle-fixing man, then back into the wolf, then back into the bicycle-fixing man. I chase the wolf, biting his ear, his shoulder, a kind of whistling for the animal, the animal arrives, he springs. *AMOR* skims my belly.

But just then, carried by the wolf, I am pierced by sadness. As if the wolf has bitten. My knees shake. I grip this other man's shoulder blades with my half-gloved hands.

He turns back into the bicycle-fixing man. The wolf is gone, Simon is gone. He rolls over, sighs. "Maybe I will come to your concert," he says.

"Sure," I say, though I don't want him to. I want him to leave now. I feel tired. What time is it in New York? What time is it here, for that matter? "What's your name?"

"Mads." He spells it, but it sounds like *maaas, moss, mass,* an exhalation, a conjunction.

"I'll put you on the guest list, Mads. Listen, I'm already late."
I kiss him. Animal scent. The smell of coffee from downstairs
subsumes it. I sit up, wrap the blanket around myself. It is soft
and finely woven – someone's indulgence. It smells faintly of
Mads's sweat.

Mads puts his shirt on last, disappears down the stairs.
Shuffling to the kitchen in the blanket, bare feet on the cool
floor, I empty what's left of the beers into the sink, set the bottles on the wooden counter. There is the licorice on the counter – black twists, loose, like flower stems. So unlike the far
more slender, never entirely straight white lines of the past.
I take a black twist and put it in my mouth. The long gray
hounds haven't woken up this entire time, as if enchanted. Are
they van Stavasts, as Boone said? Schiffeners? If they have another special name, a special breed, I don't know what it is.
A utopian breed, I guess. I kneel down to stroke them, feel
their heavy, rough paws. One wakes up and licks my hand. Not
wolves, either, these two. Are there wolves in the free state?
In the thickets of trees somewhere? Are they happy? When I
stand up and look outside a few minutes later, the bicycle is
still there, upended, solitary. The front wheel, spokes shining,
turns slowly in the breeze. It occurs to me to take the bike, box
it up and send it to Jim, my ex. A little girl with blond hair leads
a white horse, bridled but unsaddled, down the dirt lane. The
horse flicks his tail. I feel jittery, skittery, unsatisfied, though I
am not, technically, unsatisfied. I wish I were as round as that
wheel, but instead I am like the seeking line of a graph, graph-
ing something that is rising and falling unevenly. If Mads is
Amor, does that make me Psyche? She went on the road, too.
She had a journey to make.

What if I just stopped now, before the inevitable losses, the
bumps that are sure to come? Wrapped in the blanket that
smells of the stranger I just fucked, standing at the blue window salvaged from somewhere else, I see it: if I lived here, if
Mads were my husband, if this were our house, if I dwelled

here, with him, in the ruins of the future. I would know where and why he got that Gothish tattoo over his belly button, maybe I was even there when he got it, a little annoyed, it was taking forever, just wanting to go home, bracing my legs against the wall in the cold tattoo parlor in Munich, both of us drunk. In the days when we drank together, too often. Those gray hounds – Igor and Elgor – are our hounds, one of them had a thyroid operation last year, the other is afraid of mice. Right now, our daughter, our son, are at what passes for a school in Christiania; our son, half feral and with hooded gaze, is never off his skateboard. That bicycle is mine; Mads was supposed to have fixed it weeks ago; I need it to get across the island to my job at the bakery construction site. I'm the site manager. That's why I have these fingerless gloves, I need to be able to write and handle tools, and even in this other life I get cold easily. The indulgent blanket was my extravagance. And yesterday was a holiday and today the lumber didn't arrive, so. A beer, an afternoon fuck; later, maybe, we'll walk down to Pusher Street and get a plate of noodles. We like it here in the ragtag remains of this big, failed idea for humanity. At night we sleep face to face in our wooden bed, his arm heavy on my hip, as if, even now, he's afraid of losing me to the wind. I've had my troubles; so has he. This island is our agreement about something, our aging optimism.

I reluctantly take off the blanket and wash between my legs, dress. For my comeback tour, I have an outfit, constructed by my friend Fritz, that makes me look like a knowing stork. It is a tight black sheath of a skirt, quite short, to show off my long legs. I am to wear this with black stockings or striped stockings or, if it's hot, no stockings. The shoes are made of thick black straps with fetishistically high white heels. They grip my feet, heavy as horseshoes, cleverly weighted in the front; they weren't cheap, but it is almost impossible to fall in them. The top is also tight, very, blue-black, and it covers me from wrist to neck to hip. Fritz told me months ago to keep growing my red hair, and now that it is well past my shoulders, I have three styles: a tightly banded braid; entirely loose; and a flowing arrangement that involves ten bobby pins and pomade that comes in a little raspberry-colored tube. Fritz, who looks like a sensei and dresses in small, extraordinarily expensive rags that clear his ankles, is always right about these things. I wrap myself in this outfit (black stockings): swaddling cloth, armor, brace. I go with the braid. When I look at myself, done, in the long mirror in the bedroom of the borrowed apartment in Christiania, I see a woman who looks as if she could vault into other people's dreams and vault out again before daybreak.

The blue window darkens, dulls. Glancing at my watch, I see how very late I am. Boone will be furious. I don't feel queasy anymore, but I do wonder if I am ready for tonight, if I am ever ready, if I have ever been ready. I wonder if I should stop, but then I remind myself that I did stop, for seven years, and it wasn't better. In fact, it was much worse. This is my second chance. I won't get a third. I head down the stairs, relishing the strong black licorice, following a dirt road overhung by trees toward the center of what remains of the future.

My Sister and I

MY SISTER AND I had matching felt coats. Our mother made them. They were like the coats of little hussars, with strong shoulders, nipped waists, and deep, elaborately embroidered cuffs. The full skirts of the coats tapped the backs of our knees. Lila's coat was red – the red of tulips – and mine was blue – sky blue. Her long blond hair fanned out over that tulip red, wavy and luminous at her shoulders, then trailing away into ever smaller, fainter, wiggling golden threads, the same shade of gold as my father's hair, disappearing halfway down her back. My hair, like my mother's, was red and thick, pirate's hair, which she cut short all over my head. In my coat I looked like a sky-blue stalk with an exploding red flower stuck on top: surreal, scrawled, perturbed. In her coat, my sister looked like one of the lost daughters of the Czar. The felt coats weren't warm, but they were extravagant, which had its own sort of heat. We were living in the Wellfleet house then, it was winter, and we liked to roll down the dunes in our extravagant coats, whirling spirals of red and blue in the sand, sand in our mouths, sand in our hair, the coats' skirts flying, dizzying ourselves. Lila was a fearless, tireless roller-down-of-dunes; she would stagger up again and again, dizzier each time, and hurl herself willy-nilly in any direction. "Run, Anna!" she'd yell at me over the beach's ceaseless wind. "Run!" That was what we called it, *running the dunes,* like ski runs, maybe that's what we were thinking. Though we had never skied, knew nothing about it except what we had glimpsed on the tiny, terrible black-and-white television that our father kept in an upstairs closet, taking it out and plugging it in perhaps once a week, to watch the news that we cared about not at all. When we pouted, he said,

"You don't need television, you have your amazing brains. Use them."

A mixed blessing, that one. I sometimes think that Lila would like to forget about her brain, that she feels she has been superbly trained for some life she'll never live, doesn't want to live, but that fine brain of hers ticks on relentlessly, unstoppable. Where is the dune in Wyoming – where she and her husband have built an environmental wonder of a house, complete with composting toilet, and hand-raised two strong and sensitive boys – to turn that off, dizzy it into insensibility, or at least give it something impossible to work on?

Our father loved us, both our parents loved us, but there might be such a thing as too much visual pleasure. It leaves you with an appetite for something the world doesn't necessarily have to offer – you know the door is there somewhere, it's a perceptual plane, but it might open if you press on the air just here, if you tilt sideways to a particular degree and close one eye, if you go down that alley, if you follow that sound, if you sleep too much or don't sleep at all, if you give up this lover or take on that one, if you spend all the money, if you hoard the money, if you make a sacrifice, if you wait, if you rush forward as blindly as possible, if you come to a full stop, dumbstruck. If you push harder. If you give up pushing. Our parents spent all their time visualizing things that didn't, at the end of the day, exist. Tearing holes in the world. What were we supposed to think?

Two little girls in hussar's coats, one tulip red, one sky blue, holding hands at the top of a dune. A Czarina and a pirate silhouetted against the sky, the empty beach their demesne, the wind rippling the full felt skirts of their splendid coats. My sister tugs me forward, and before I know it I'm already off my feet, whirling down a hill of sand.

The Interior Motion of the Wave Remains

IF ALL ENERGY and matter is made up of particles and waves, think of it as a wave. Something that leaves me and rolls to you, leaves you and rolls to me, over and over. You change, from you to you. I change. But the interior motion of the wave remains, moving between us. Everything matters. Everyone matters. Think of me, if you like, as a person who can't ignore the wave. A radio that is always on. I've never slept enough, either, I don't know, my parents weren't big on organized bedtimes, maybe that has something to do with it. But, anyway. I'm not sure I can explain it any better than that. Maybe it's also that, in bed, everyone reminds me of everyone else, some endless corridor of doors always opening and shutting, and me, like Alice in Wonderland, running from door to door, some tiny, some huge, looking for you, as you change from you to you.

The Broken Train

HERE IS MY father, sawing a train in half. This is the famous picture, the one they always use at the entrance to Roy Brundage retrospectives in New York or Mumbai or London: my father wide-legged on top of the still train, his long blond hippie hair blowing in the breeze, his bad foot curving inward, the silk vest over the T-shirt, the power hacksaw he holds over his head, his upraised arms, surprisingly muscular for one so slender and apparently frail, the pale blue sky that seems to be everywhere, excessive, promiscuous. His blue eyes: light-struck, wide, almost angry. As if he is looking at something no one else can possibly see, as if he has pierced the veil momentarily. He is thirty-two. It is 1972. He is crazed and beautiful. He is, though no one except him knows it yet, reinventing sculpture.

In the less famous picture that follows this one, he has on a thick pair of safety glasses and enormous gloves, and four men are on top of the train with him, arguing. It will take them five days to saw the train in half crosswise and even after they've sawed down to the rails, arguing the entire time and snorting speed to stay awake, they will have to bring in a massive winch to pry the train from itself, to open it up to that abundant pale blue sky, to topple the halved seats, to push the train's divided weight over gravity's edge until it gives, crashes, one half of the enormous machine twisting onto its side and sliding sideways into the field, one half remaining upright on the rails, gaping, as if waiting for the other's return. This is the really famous picture, the one on the postcards still on the racks at MOMA: the twisted half of the train, torqued metal, the great mechanical beast down. At the same time, in the same frame, light falling into the upright half on the nonexistent passengers, the light like ghosts peering out the windows, wondering why they haven't reached their stop yet. They are late. Where is the conductor? The peculiar, tympanic space between, the prairie in that in-between space, spreading out to the horizon.

Here is my father, in a picture no one took, lying down in that space, on the tracks between the train's jagged halves. It looks dangerous: the weight of the broken train has to fall somewhere, doesn't it? Opened up like that, the weight is wild. But it isn't literally dangerous, of course; the train can't run. The tracks had been abandoned long ago; they disappeared altogether about half a mile away. But to be in that gap, to lie down in that space—he said later that the old rails were burning hot, that they had absorbed the energy of the power hacksaws that had been going for five days—to put yourself in the center of the fresh injury, the broken metal, the weight, the yearning of one half of the ruined train for the other: that was dangerous. It was. And yet he lay down there.

I am in love with him in this moment. As if he is not my father, as if he is a stranger, a man I might be just about to meet, or have met, briefly, in the past. I see him as clearly as if I had been there, been hovering near him. His bad foot quivers. His hands sickle. He closes his eyes. His heart slams. His skin, pale on an ordinary day, is paler now. His eyelids flutter. He smells the seared metal, old cloth, earth, his own stink. The train, ripped apart, looming over him, seems to exhale heavily as it releases the winds of its mechanical insides, torn open by my father, who has dared to lie down in the terrible opening he has created. I am in that opening. I want to trace his face with my fingers. I want him to tell me what it is like to lie down there. I want to lie down with him, I want to feel the unspeakable weight of the torn train hovering over him in the instant that he's feeling it. It is as if I were born twice: once from my mother's womb, and once from my father's mind, right then.

In reality, I was three at the time. I wasn't there, nowhere near there. A small girl, in no danger. We were living in the Chicago house, of which I remember staring out a narrow window as the El rounded a curve. The smell of paint. A huge, dim closet, with one old brown ice skate in it, not ours. The cold; maybe that's when I began to dislike cold so much. Did I know what my father had done? Did my mother explain it to me? My mother was an artist, too; she painted strangely ominous, strangely exposed, strangely linked groups of women on glass. I thought they were pretty. Maybe my mother told me what he had done, maybe she said, "Your father finished sawing a train in half today. For art. He has become a hero, though no one knows it yet." I don't remember.

And how would I have understood her, anyway? Trains were the wooden boxcars on a string I pulled *clackclackclack* over the floors of the Chicago house, or the flash of silver as the El pulled away around a heavy curve. I understand the sawed-in-half train only as everyone else understands it, in retrospect, in retrospectives, as a photograph that exists and several more that don't, as a moment in a field in Nebraska that, when it was happening, no one cared about at all. It wasn't until later that anyone knew what he had done to sculpture. The moment that the train was torn open existed only for him, for the four other sweating, speed-addled guys, for a jackrabbit or two, for the astonished prairie: they felt the immediate impact. The rest of us have felt it as the endless sound waves of a moment we didn't experience, didn't know about when it was happening. We weren't there, and we didn't care. I pulled my wooden train *clackclackclack* around the house, up and down the stairs; my mother was pregnant with Lila. The rough of her corduroy maternity jumper against my cheek, its gray-green. That I remember. I didn't hear the crash, didn't see the train go over, just as I didn't know how the baby got inside, or how it would get out.

And yet. It tore me open, too, in its way. It made an opening for me. I have had the conviction for quite some time that if I could do in music what my father did in space by sawing the train in half, then I could solve the mystery of my life.

Rome, the Last Last Time

IN ROME, THE last time – he insisted it was the last time, the last time after the last time in Arezzo, *This has to be the last time* – the crash occurred in the silence. Simon was across the room, playing with the cord of the blinds. I was sitting on the bed. I had just told him, finally, what happened three years before, before we had properly started. That I got rid of it. What else could I have done? When it happened, I said, I thought I would never see you again. Anyone would have done the same. The only reason, I said, that I was sure it was you is that I had always been more careful. You were the one who wasn't. I knew I was being cruel, because it was the last last time. Wasn't it? He didn't look at me. He shook his head. Three years composed of stolen days and nights that, all told, added up to perhaps a month. This was the last day of that long, long month. One half of whatever we were a heap of twisted metal, the other half still patiently, foolishly standing, eagerly peering out the windows, expecting to arrive at the next station. We were the only two people present at the moment the train fell open, the paint hit the canvas, the note sounded. For everyone else, for anyone else, the event is retrospective, the shock waves spreading out from a moment that is already past. Seven years of bad luck followed that quiet conversation. In Rome, I already felt the moment passing, I could practically see us, the too-tall woman and the too-short man, marooned on opposite corners of a hotel room, as if I were remembering it even as it happened. It could be the case that, for me, all art is retrospective as well. The ripples extend outward until they disappear.

The Bee Palace

GITTE LIGHTS THE galaxy of little candles scattered over
the floor. Here in the Bee Palace, in the green room that is actually painted black, the candles are white, star-shaped. Gitte
is slender, wraith-like, barefaced, with deep-set eyes, in a long
white woolen shift and motorcycle boots: she looks like some
figure out of a fairy tale, the woman whose job it is to light
the stars every night. The Bee Palace, like many structures in
Christiania, is a whimsical wreck, not palatial at all; the roof
hangs very low on one side, where two-by-fours are nailed
willy-nilly to the outer wall as dubious braces. They look like
weather-beaten drunks leaning against the building. Inside,
it's drafty, graffiti-spattered. Colder even than the apartment;
I can feel my throat constricting. I need a scarf. From somewhere – where? – comes a sound that seems to be skateboard
wheels on concrete. Pietr, my imaginary son with Mads. Gitte
touches the flame to the waxy stars set here and there in the
small, beer-scented black room. A little grouping on the floor,
in a corner. She can make a match last through one, two, three,
four, almost five candles. Is that a Danish thing? A Second
World War skill? Gitte lowers the overhead lights, smiles lov-
ingly at us, and, having prepared the room as if for our collective wedding night in a meat locker, leaves, saying, "Forty minutes." I wonder if Mads is coming, now I want him to. I stroke
my throat, blow on my fingers. I knew how to do that, but do I
still know how to do this? They're connected in some way I've
never been able to understand, maybe never wanted to understand. Out of the corner of my eye, a flicker, as of something
rustling in leaves. Though there are no leaves here, only a sofa
covered in peeling black vinyl, a herd of star-shaped candles,
and a plug-in coffeepot on an old folding table. I imagine for

a moment that the hounds, Igor and Elgor, have followed me, or that their ghosts have followed me. I turn my head to see their long, grave, furry faces, but there's nothing in any corner. I summon my breath, cough on the chill.

"It's too cold in here," I say to Boone, who is sitting next to me with an earpiece on, tapping on his iPhone, here on the peeling sofa in the green room that is actually black.

"I told them," he says softly, tapping. "They're working on it."

"Are you growing a mustache now? What is that?"

"Stop." He brushes my hand away from his face. "I needed a project. And it's lucky. I'm going to have a full beard by Rome."

"What does it mean, 'working on it'? I can't sing like this." That flicker – what *is* it? I turn my head, can't catch it.

Boone removes the earpiece and looks up from the iPhone, the surface of which is broken into at least four bustling squares; in one of the squares a bearded man is talking. "Listen, Anna, you know I worship you, but –"

Mercifully, Zach, Tom, and Alicia – my band, it seems – burst in, smelling of night air and cigarette smoke and garlic. They lean against the chilly, crumbling black walls, still laughing at some joke from dinner, eyeing one another, whether as allies or rivals or lovers, I'm never quite sure. The candles send their shadows far up the walls, unnaturally tall, like a premonition of their onstage presence. Who are they, I wonder. Who will they be by the time we're done? I've known them only about a month. Boone put them together for me, like a hand of cards. Ten of diamonds: Alicia, with porcelain skin and platinum hair, plays the cello. At home in San Francisco, she is part of a new music ensemble called Minerva. Jack of spades: Zach, he of the shaved head and muscular arms, plays the bass. He's toured with Beck, which he told us in the first breath of meeting him. Eight of clubs: Tom, squinty-eyed and wry, plays the drums. He's probably in his late thirties, but he looks older because of his paunch and the stoop of his shoulders, the fisherman's hat he always wears that comes down to his ears. He carries Purell everywhere he goes and applies it religiously. He is, in fact, applying it now, spreading it over every rounded finger with great concentration. Boone assured me that Tom was a brilliant drummer, and in fact he is, which is why he's toured with so many bands over the years. The Purell smells like rubbing alcohol and lemon. Onstage, these three veer between listening too closely to one another and not listening at all. It doesn't help that Alicia is high only nearly all the time. If she would stay high, the other two could meet her there, but as it is she's always careening awkwardly halfway into sobriety about midway through the first set, like a car suddenly thrown from third into first gear. The entire band bucks. During our all too few rehearsals back in the States, I felt them behind me, jolting and choking; sometimes I turned around and made faces. It didn't help.

"I have the set list," I say, sliding the folded-up sheet of notebook paper out of my tight skirt pocket, and we all huddle around to look at it, by the light of the wax galaxy on the floor.

Zach leans forward, nodding. "Man, I feel like I'm back in high school. I played this shit until it wore out." He pumps his fist in the air. "You're a badass, Anna."

"It's a mix of new and old," I say. "Denmark was always good for us before."

"Right on," says Zach, "Denmark!"

The others gaze at me, the light of their faces on the peeling black sofa glowing in the shadows. Boone glances at the time on his iPhone. It occurs to me that Boone does look ever so slightly like the White Rabbit, though with a scruffy brownish-reddish beard penumbra instead of whiskers. Always telling me I'm late, I'm late.

Alicia touches my knee. "How do you feel, Anna? This is such a cool moment." Alicia likes to look like Tinkerbell crossed with a cancan girl from outer space, and most of the time she succeeds. Tonight she appears to be wearing a very short, Mylar, upside-down lily from which her white shoulders and platinum head emerge like a miracle; with the lily she has on hot-pink spike heels.

"I feel all right," I say quietly. Actually, I feel much better than all right, even in the cold. I feel like the future.

"This is how it's going to go," I say. "'The Orchids,' 'Waiting for a Sign,' 'Smoke and Mirrors,' 'Going, Going,'" and down the list I go until the last song, "'Wonderland.'"

"You don't think you should start with 'Wonderland' or maybe put it in the middle?" asks Boone. "It's actually been getting some downloads here, and that's the one Pitchfork posted –"

"No," I say firmly. "'Wonderland' last. Always. We'll do the cover for the encore."

Boone bites his lip. "All right, Anna."

The flicker flickers provocatively. Shadow of a flame, of a sound. I don't turn my head this time, trying, and failing, to snare it in the corner of my eye.

Gitte wafts in. "It's time," she says, smiling, like Glinda the Good Witch.

We all stand up – me, Boone, Zach, Tom, and Alicia – and take hands. Boone's hand in my left is light; Zach's hand in my right is heavy, gripping, already sweating. He gives off a subliminal hum of energy, like a power line. "Okay," I say. "You guys are the best, I'm so lucky." I squeeze the hand in my left, the hand in my right. "Here we go. Good show."

"Good show," they echo, and we hug, we kiss, we walk out, me in the lead. The light hits my eyes.

And then here is what happens at the Bee Palace: shivering, even in my armor and the fingerless gloves I have borrowed from the borrowed apartment, I take a few breaths and spiral into the opening notes of "The Orchids." I am there. I blow the song through the back of the rickety concert hall and out into the night, folded, gleaming, fast, faster, unbroken, alive, whirling inside the secret chamber, rose and gold, unstoppable, irresistible, straight into the veins, hair-raising. I take another breath. I am the train, I am the tracks, I am the whistle on the train. I am speeding down the prairie. I heat up. Almost, almost, the train breaks in half this time. I get very close. Very close. I take another breath. Out of the corner of my eye, I see Boone, eyes closed, face uplifted to the choppy, eerie, syncopated sound I make. I take another breath. "Waiting for a Sign."

There are many things — most things, really — that I can't do. But I can do this. It is far too much, and not nearly enough.

An hour and a half later, we reach "Wonderland." The song has reindeer in it, great sadness, a city, an atonal bridge, whispering, buzzing, searching, crying, more questions than answers. As I bow, drenched in sweat, in my shirtsleeves, I glimpse Mads toward the back, standing with a tall woman in dark braids who I immediately know is his wife. At first glance I think Mads is Simon, that he's come to Christiania for the opening concert of the tour. But Simon's wife isn't tall, doesn't wear braids, and she wouldn't be here, of course. Nor would Simon. Though Mads's wife can't see it, I wink at her, at what we both know Mads hides under his shirt. But if those letters weren't written for her, or for anyone, what were they for? I'll never know. She must know. Even so, what must that be for her, to see those letters every day and know they aren't for her, that they never will be, no matter how many times she sucks his cock, no matter the children, no matter the shit and the tears and the endless worries about money, no matter all the bicycles he fixes and doesn't fix, no matter the ruined future they believed in and still believe in, no matter that she'll probably bury him one day. Bury him and his *AMOR:* a letter read by many, but never sent.

Mads is standing up, clapping heartily. He is standing on Simon's feet, Simon's feet are there, inside his shoes. Where is the rest of him? Everyone is standing up. Boone, in the wings, is smiling, his hands still folded under his armpits, rocking gently from side to side. Zach, Tom, and Alicia are laughing, glistening. I am damp, flushed, blissed. Mads's wife is looking down at a cell phone in her hand, a small square of light. We do the encore, Ezra's most famous song, "Burning Horse." My private tribute to him. Though Mads's wife is looking straight at me, the position of the lights in my eyes renders her face obscure, a dark, attentive curve. Flicker, rustle: as if an animal had darted across the wings. But when I subtly turn my head, there's nothing there.

What Happened Next

THE WALLS WERE green; the bathroom tiles were Moorish. It was morning in Arezzo. Outside the window, the swifts were darting above the church in crazy arcs and uneven parabolas—I couldn't find a pattern in their motion. We were grainy from the night before; Simon pawed through the minibar, found a lemon soda, popped the tab, came back to bed. I pressed my mouth to his belly, just above the hairline. He put his hand on my head.

"I don't know," I said. "The room was flat, didn't you think? Cold." It was the *Bang Bang* tour, and everything was opposite. All that had happened for *Whale* now unhappened, in reverse, undoing all that had been done. Pretty soon we would probably all be children, playing toy instruments in a rec room somewhere.

"No. You were fine. I'd like to see the Vasari house. We have time, don't we?" His glasses, narrow-lensed with heavy black frames, arms folded, on the bedside table. The lines between his eyes. His impatience was beginning; his clock was ticking faster. Most likely his stomach was beginning to hurt. It was the last day. We were always fractious on the last day.

"Sure." I didn't know yet that this was, in fact, our truly last day, that he had decided two cities ago to end it. The swifts flew up, up, up, endlessly. They looked like shadows of some larger, stranger creature invisible to the human eye, or like cursive, exploded, electric. Below his hairline, movement. The shift inside me, like a shovel emptying. How is it that those two motions could cross, enfold each other, what could one know about the other—anything? everything? nothing? Is that always the question? And how that could have happened. I almost told him that day about the baby, about what had happened, that I was sorry, because I loved him, now I would have kept it, I would have taken that leap. I thought I might tell him then, as the swifts traced their wild, unchartable trajectories over the church.

I didn't. And anyway, something else had already happened, and I hadn't known it at all. It had happened within him, silently, in Düsseldorf, which doesn't have any swifts, any famous church, not much of anything, really, except an aquarium. It was already happening. Not during the fucking. The fucking, as it turned out, was aftermath. Maybe that's always the case. That day, I thought that if I truly loved him, I would tell him what had happened. And what would he have told me if he truly loved me?

Say it, I thought, as he rose and fell inside me, say it, say it, say it, say it, say it.

Who I Used to Be

FROM THE WINDOW of the train to Göteborg, peak-roofed wooden houses that look miniature, as if miniature horses live inside. Didn't Pippi Longstocking live in a miniature house like that? The sun is bright on the little roofs. Another one of my lives, the one where I live with a little horse in a little wooden house, ticks by. Out the window, the trees look folded, coming to neat green points on top. The bulk of our equipment and luggage is piled up in the bay at the end of the car, but there are bits left over. My feet rest on one of my guitar cases, which is on top of Zach's guitar case. He tends my three guitars and his bass guitar meticulously, his small team of precious creatures. Boone, next to me, is looking at the singing-man figurine; to it he has added another, a porcelain drummer with a red hat. When did he have time to get that? How much did it cost? Is he putting together a band of figurines as well? We all have our totems, I suppose. Mine is the big, cashmere, green and black scarf I bought near the Copenhagen train station which I can't afford and is now wrapped around my head and throat as if I were trying to disguise plastic surgery or some sort of hair disaster. I have to protect my voice; Jim would have made me vats of ginger tea by now. I took the fingerless gloves with me and am wearing them, too; they are connected in my mind to Mads and his loveless love. It doesn't make sense, it wasn't his house. Maybe they're just a trophy, or a wish. Warm me up.

Zach, Tom, and Alicia are across the aisle, tired and dressed in clashing, random layers. Things went late last night; Gitte took us to a bar somewhere across Copenhagen, near a bridge. Alicia is eating chocolates, thumbing her iPhone, earbuds in. Tom, in his fisherman's hat, his Purell sticking out of his pocket, is doing a sudoku. Zach, serious as a Talmud scholar, is bent over a Danish newspaper, trying to translate via Google. His head is perfectly smooth; does he shave it every day? I'm not sure why he's bothering to puzzle out the newspaper. Denmark is already behind us, already gone; we won't be back. The Bee Palace whirls away, broken corner over broken corner. Mads, with his bicycle wrench, grows smaller and disappears. Boone strokes his figurines. He winks at me; he is happy about last night; we're all happy, hung over from schnapps. I am hungry. I have given up the badly translated mystery – who cares whodunit? – for Colette, *The Vagabond*. That coquette's problems seem so easy, no mystery there. Marry him, don't marry him, whatever. I close Colette and open my tour journal, a black-and-white composition book on the front of which is written, in ballpoint pen, *Wonderland*. I've kept a journal for all my tours. *Wonderland* will join *Whale* and *Bang Bang* and *The Pillars* on my bookshelf at home. I put scraps of local newspapers in them, write down my dreams, tape in photos, stolen menus, smear swaths of lipstick. To remember. Because the minute it's over, it's so hard to remember exactly what happened, and where and when and how. The moments collapse into a shiny heap. Tom's head drops onto his chest as he gives up on sudoku and falls asleep. But I find I don't feel like writing in my journal now; I close it and stow it back in my bag.

As the train chugs on past neat Scandinavian towns, I try to make sense of the facts of my life. Fact: I was once a certain kind of famous for what was, in reality, not a very long time in most lives – perhaps four years, before I crashed, flamed, disappeared, walked away from Rome feeling like Godzilla, defeated by buzzing forces no one else could see, a squadron of tiny, blinding airplanes of paralyzing doubt. It felt much longer than four years. Though in music time that's more than long enough to leave an impression, a stain, on the airwaves. A ghost. I may well be chasing not Simon's ghost – the ghost of who he once was to me, since the man is still alive, I'm pretty sure – but my own around these grab bag of European cities, trying to frame some sort of question. What is my question? Was that my ghost, my former incarnation, last night, flickering in the corners of my gaze?

And why was I famous, anyway? Fact: I wasn't famous to everyone. I was famous only among certain people. The smart people, the people who pride themselves on being smart. Part of it – let's be honest – was the glamour of my pedigree, and the history to which that pedigree alluded. Everyone knew who my father was. Or maybe it would be more accurate to say that everyone who loved my music also loved who my father was. You can't separate the dancer from the dance, and anyway, I never tried. When you don't even have a high school diploma to your name, you need credentials. My parents were mine; they seemed to explain everything, all the jagged edges, the awkward gaps, the indeterminacy; later, the bad behavior, the drinking, the drugs, the disarray, and so on. Because there was my father, with his famous sawed-in-half train, but there also was my mother, who painted on glass. They divorced, of course, by the time I was twenty – glass derails train, it turns out – but the iconic part is the two of them together, we two little girls with wild, uncombed hair, a gypsy family floating on the strafed margins of the Reagan years, kitchens filled with poets and artists, borrowed apartments in London and Rome and Istanbul, studios, a donkey in Spain, a swing in the living room on St. Mark's Place, Lila and me in and out of various educational institutions, haphazardly becoming slightly less than savage.

Until Lila, at thirteen, demanded to be sent away to boarding school. Our parents, half amused, half bewildered, complied, so from Morocco Lila wrote away for the application forms. Paterson-Birdcliffe in Maine, no less, took her on gratis as a special case, a darling curiosity, and she more than fulfilled their expectations, graduating at the head of her class, a sensible beauty, freshly painted in exact representational detail, hyperrealist. I stayed loyal to the family business of being outsiders, drifters; I got bored easily in any school and cut classes to go home and draw or paint or write epic novels. Uncle Matt, my mother's brother, who'd played in bands around Portland, Oregon, for years, gave me my first guitar when I was six; I rode it constantly, obsessively. They found me guitar teachers in Spain, in Norway, even in Florida, during that miserable eight months we lived near Orlando. Everywhere we went, I followed my dark thoughts, my light thoughts, wherever. I read adventure stories, travelogues – Tintin comics, a little paperback biography of Amelia Earhart, *The Swiss Family Robinson*. I imagined that we were like them: the Brundage clan, travelers, artists, adventurers, modern saints. I couldn't understand what Lila was doing, and I felt contempt for her, which I didn't bother to conceal. Since I didn't finish high school, I had no desire to go to college. When Lila enrolled at Oberlin, to me it was as if she had entered the convent. What was comparative literature? Compared to what?

And why would anyone leave us for the convent? We were our own royalty. My father's three sisters: strange birds, all of them. My mother's incandescent roseate beauty, the beauty of the artist's wife. We were heroes in certain circles. Even Lila, the golden absence that reinscribed what it was to be us, how impossible, how unusual, how necessary. Timothy Greenfield-Sanders took her picture. Despite our pity, or maybe because of it, we visited Lila often; we wrote her all the time; we sent her videotapes. She and I spent the entire summer when I was nineteen and she was fifteen camped out in a half shack on the Irish Sea. We were those girls, the artist's daughters, the mermaids, the ones with long, tangled hair who did what they wanted. Inside, always, she knew she was free. *You can't take it back,* I want to say to her, as if we were still children. *No do-overs.*

But isn't that what I'm doing out here, chugging along on the clean regional train to Göteborg? A do-over? As one who had it, a piece of it, and then dropped it, hard. Got rid of it. Burnt it. Fact: I burnt it. But now, though it may be too late, I want it back. Instruments piled in the tidy compartment between cars, I can see them from here. Anyway. The point is that, while I wouldn't say I was arrogant – though maybe I was arrogant, probably I was – or even more confident than most, I did have the sense that I was, in a way, expected. That there was a room where people were waiting for me, their faces blurry maybe, but definitely there, they were already there, they were listening for me, that sound just in the other room. So that when I arrived, and I did arrive, I wasn't entirely surprised that they would say, in effect, Ah, it's you. My parents being who they were, it was expected of me that when I opened my mouth I'd have something to say, and, astonishingly – though I didn't know then how astonishing it was – I did.

For five years or so in my twenties, I had my own band, Anna and the Squares. Daisy, Vikram, John, and Miguel. And me. Daisy and Vikram are married now, God help them. John and I stay in touch, barely, with blackened fingers. No one knows where Miguel is, raising the question: did we know where he was then? Did he? Long nights, cigarettes stubbed out in what was left of the pancakes, the sausages, the stew: *No, what I'm saying is . . .* We sounded smart, but not much more, I see that now. Clever, pretty, vaguely titillating, but only vaguely. We bitched about it all the time then, the unfairness of it all, but what were we giving, really? What were we willing to give or be given? Fact: we were all so wrapped up in one another that there wasn't much room left over for an audience. Driving petulantly around the frayed, secondhand alternative zones of the East Coast in Vikram's station wagon, all the equipment stuffed into the way-back, Daisy's perfect cameo head on my shoulder, John riding shotgun, scribbling figures that never added up on his little pad. Fact: it was impossible. We were doomed from the start.

Now Tom is waking up, lifting his face from his chest. "Where are we?" he mumbles.

"Germany?" says Alicia, taking out her earbuds.

"No," says Zach. "It's Sweden. Göteborg is in Sweden."

VALBURG is written in black letters on a narrow white sign-post. A woman wheels a cart with chocolate and sandwiches down the aisle. I have a coffee taste in my mouth, a buzzy feeling in my head; I think I am getting a cold. I bury my nose in the scarf, which is like burying my face in a hare. It cost a stupid amount of money, but tour money is different, tour debt is different, tour time is different. It has no edges, no top, no bottom. It is a series of present moments. And if my voice goes, we're all lost.

"It's Germany," says Alicia.

"That field is so totally Swedish," says Zach, almost accusatorily. The field is solid green, coated with veils of bright, bright yellow dots.

"It's a field," says Alicia. "How Swedish can a field be?"

"It's Swedish," says Zach, with a peculiar air of authority.

"I think the field looks anxious," says Tom, squinting at it.

I turn on my phone, consider texting Simon, which I definitely shouldn't do, then turn it off. It makes a strange and beautiful sound as it turns off, a swirling, tinkling, crunching sound, like a cloud disappearing into a volcano. Where does the cloud go? I would like to make a song that sounds like that, the edge of the cloud tipping into the volcano.

Boone murmurs in my ear, "You should keep your phone on. And Billy Q wants to hang out. He just texted me."

"Wow. Okay." Billy Q is the headliner at the festival we're playing, the reason that thirty thousand Swedes are making the pilgrimage to some field somewhere outside Göteborg, wherever that is, which I still haven't figured out.

"He's a fan." Boone winks. "Do you know him?"

"No."

"What the fuck are you talking about, Tom?" says Zach. He

has already appointed himself leader of the three of them, the translator of foreign newspapers.

The train slows, pauses on the track. Scraps of talk in other languages, the sigh of brakes, the ring of cell phones. I think I hear a familiar voice, then it's gone. Alicia pushes her face against the window. "We could be, like, anywhere."

Zach returns to the newspaper and his iPhone, having settled the Swedish question.

"Or maybe it looks sad?" says Tom, still squinting. "I think the field is having a crisis." He pulls his hat down to his ears.

Zach says, "She insulted the Pope."

"Which Pope?" says Alicia, scrunched into the window.

"The *Pope* Pope," says Zach. "The Queen of Denmark. She forgot herself. That's what it says: 'The Queen forgot herself.'"

"Did she say that?" I ask. "Who said she forgot herself?" I didn't even know Denmark had a queen. Does it have a king, then, too?

Zach frowns. "It's just written like that, I think, as a statement: 'The Queen forgot herself.' The verb is weird. I'm not sure."

"And has she remembered herself now?"

"I guess she has," says Zach. He runs his hand over his shiny head. "I guess so, yeah. And you know what else? There was a flood in Nicaragua. Over a hundred people died. It's all over the news. Beck is doing a benefit for it."

Tom unwraps a chocolate bar. "Beck is a little fucker."

The train doesn't move. Outside, the field remains empty. It's hard to see evidence of its crisis, if it's having one. The yellow veil on the solid green is serene. Inside, the air is growing warm, almost humid. I take off the scarf and curl it in my lap, like a fluffy pet. I tap the top of my guitar case with my toe, just to hear the dull sound. Talk to me. There is the scent of coffee and chocolate. Someone whispering in German, rhythmically, as if reading aloud. A light, warm, female laugh. That flicker, a bit darker today, like a lick of dark lightning.

Letter to Lila

SAME THING, DIFFERENT year. You're there, I'm out here, roaming around with a band of gypsies. I can't do the math on the time difference – Sweden to Wyoming, what is that? We must be ahead, but we might be behind, and maybe the aurora borealis gets involved somewhere, I don't know. Lila, it's the long days here now. What that means is that every note of the sunset is held for hours instead of minutes. It does something to you, some kind of feeling on the edge of happiness and sadness. That summer by the Irish Sea was like this, not that we noticed, busily engaged in who knows what with the books and papers and records everywhere, the loose tobacco you rolled into cigarettes, the lumpen soda bread that never came out right, the starfish drying on the window ledge. We saw the gray curve of dolphins more than once. That was also the summer they did the retrospective on Dad at the Whitney, and it was weird. We said to each other that it was weird. In the clippings Mom sent us, and that we picked up at the post office in the little stone town, he looked thin. A tawny young woman with buck teeth and big eyes on his arm, no comment from Mom on that one. It was weird, because the three of us were the only ones who knew, in all the world, that it was over. Had been since Rome.

Rubble

I SOLD THE bit of rubble from the perforated lighthouse in Ireland, along with the sketch of same, to pay for the making of the CD, a good chunk of the touring expenses, my time away from my job. My father gave me the bit of rubble and the sketch when I turned twenty-one. He gave a fragment of ruined temple wall and a sketch from the Berlin project to Lila when she turned twenty-one. These talismans, pocketed by him, had some kind of juju, marked and embodied moments of . . . what? Revelation? Despair? Triumph? He didn't like to say. Since nothing else remained of the big work, they had become valuable to the art world. My bit of rubble was about the size of my palm, surprisingly heavy, dark gray, jagged from where it had been smashed out of the wall, pitted from years of salt and weather. Lila's looks like the most ordinary shard of concrete, perhaps six inches long or so, with a faded red stripe, but it's two centuries old. She keeps it in a safe-deposit box. I felt guilty when I signed my precious rubble and sketch over to that soft-voiced dealer, but there was nothing I could do. I didn't have anything else to sell. I was down to it. Jim and I had reached the last act, we were done; he left his bicycle when he moved out – the kind of odd, potlatch gesture that was both why I fell in love with him and why I fell out of love with him. Or why I thought I fell in love with him, and so on; I dreamed of Simon often.

I don't know what it means that my time away from the music scene coincides with my time with Jim. It should have been the opposite. He was a musician, too, a good one; he came from a family of folkies, diehard lefties; none of his demons had anything to do with making music, a core that remained as pure as clean water in him. His wide gaze was earnest, and that felt like a lifeline at first. My self-imposed exile had started just before I met him, it was a cloudy thing. *The Pillars,* my third record, had been a dead end; unlike *Bang Bang,* which I had loved, I never loved *The Pillars,* not really, which only made the whole thing more shameful. I was working on something, I said, if asked. But it kept on not coming together, and then its absence grew, year after year; it was like an animal. A broken animal. The people from that time went away; some got famous, some died, some slid down into ragtag lives like mine. I stay away from Facebook. What I've finally made, *Wonderland:* it's more disassembly than assembly, but you can kind of dance to it, in places. Jim, though his bicycle was all that was left of his presence in my apartment, did the arrangements and played half the instruments, grim-faced, his knit cap pulled down low over his ears. Another potlatch, but I needed the help. I overpaid him. He donated the money to Greenpeace.

I had to sell the bit of rubble from the perforated lighthouse because after seven years away, I'm not bankable. I was never all that bankable anyway, however well regarded I may have been in certain circles. Moreover, from thirty-seven to forty-four, in music years, even the kind of unhit-making music I make, is impossible. The Atlantises of a hundred careers as bright as mine, brighter, have sunk since then. It was my own fault, to be sure. I was the one who choked, and the price has been steep.

Here's what I've been doing to make a living for the past seven years: I teach carpentry to girls at a private elementary school on the Upper East Side. Jim knew someone whose girlfriend, a poet, taught English there. I learned carpentry from my father; so, five days a week, I am faced with a hundred little girls in safety goggles, holding hammers. We make benches and tables, birdfeeders and bookcases. They call me Miss Brundage. They have no idea that I have ever had any other life than this, that I am not simply that too-tall red-headed woman with bangs who rides her bike to school from the East

Village and reminds them about *Safety First*. Their parents, of course, remember me – they stop me outside the school to tell me about listening to *Whale* in their dorm rooms, on their road trips, on the mornings after their raves, how they came out to see me at Irving Place, how closely they listened. They tell me I look great. I'm hoping that the mystery of my absence will put a thumb on the scale, that people like this will show up for concerts; I'm not above selling back to them their memory of their younger selves. I was always bigger in Europe, anyway.

I wonder if the faces of the hundred little girls holding hammers will be more or less dear to me when I get back, and why. If the sound of the small saws sawing badly will be a comfort or a torment, and why. I suppose that would be the least of what I wonder, but it's what I think about often: how it will be to walk back into that not unpleasant room in a few months and see all those small pairs of eyes, rendered strange and aquatic by the goggles, looking at me. What will I say? Where will I tell them I've been?

Göteborg

A NARROW ROOM with a high ceiling in a little hotel on a side street. A double bed wedged into the room, leaving just enough space for a chair opposite. Umber wallpaper, imprinted with sprigs of some charming, unshowy, flowering branch, that stops halfway up the wall. My black roller-board suitcase open on the floor, the *Wonderland* journal tossed on top. A tented bit of cardboard on the bed encouraging me to reuse towels. *WE ARE GREEN*, says the cardboard. No, we are not: my checking account balance, my computer tells me, is already sinking into the red. For instance: two hundred dollars gone before the plane even left Newark. Good thing I put the scarf on a credit card. I shut the computer, lie down, and set the tented card on my chest, like one of those pyramids that give you pyramid energy. *WE ARE GREEN*. We are also jet-lagged, broke, broken-up, unsure; we are developing a twitch in our left eye; we were once almost pretty famous in certain circles before we blew it; we have everything riding on this; we are hungry, we are sad, we miss him, we are not going to call, because we know he won't answer. We wish one of those hounds from Christiania, Igor or Elgor, were here. We need a drink. I turn my hand over on the bed, palm up, as if that's how you send an email, a letter, a smoke signal, an invitation.

Hello?

My fingers curl of their own accord, like a baby's grip, or maybe they're looking for the rolled-up dollar bill — or the lira, the five-franc note, the deutsche mark, all the different colors, the badges of our ambition. But that was another, more reckless hand, a hand that would have called, but won't call tonight, from another time. I'm not sure what time it is now, or if the time has changed since we came north. I think north is the direction we came, or was it east? It could have been south. But why are we going north, anyway? Will we end at the Arctic Circle? Note to self: ask Boone where we are. The concert is tomorrow. Tonight there is a party, someone Zach knows from another band. The party is in a castle. I wonder if the castle has a moat. The Queen of Denmark steps lightly over the floodwaters in Nicaragua, trying to remember herself. The woman in white lights the stars. The guitarist tunes up in the castle. Outside, it is ten o'clock at night, or 22, and the light is the color of an eggshell with a candle inside it.

I turn my phone on. There is a text from Boone, sent an hour ago. *U R late hry up.*

We are in wonderland, we think. We are back in wonderland.

Wonderland, or, Why I Was Famous

AFTER THE SQUARES broke up, I played with so many different bands, some folky, some punky, some who knows what. I was whatever anyone needed me to be. I played bar mitzvahs. I told myself I was free, which mostly meant free to be very, very poor. This went on for years, or possibly centuries. I went on a U.S. tour with a band called The Sweet, which was more or less some guys who had grown up together in Iowa. They made cheerleader jokes I didn't understand and went drinking in dive bars without me. They thought they needed a girl with long legs and long red hair singing backup. Midway through the tour, they decided they didn't need that girl, but it was too late by then. Pittsburgh, Avenue A, San Luis Obispo, Chicago, Tucson, a few linty folds of the universe. Places where guys played darts while we sang. Places where fights broke out. When I wasn't bored or pissed off, I was trying, and failing, not to call Daisy and Vikram, just to say hi, you know, it's been a while, how are the kids?; not to smoke; not to drink too much, especially alone; not to surrender to the bleakness of four in the afternoon in whatever Bates motel or someone else's drafty house scattered with kids' toys or while drinking the third cup of coffee in some diner, down to reading the real estate listings in the local paper. Could I live in that bungalow? Out by the river on that horse farm? Rent the room over the hardware store? It's cheap. Sound check not until six. What do you do with those two hours? Try not to ask the big questions. Fail at that, too. The sunlight on any wall, for instance the wall of a cruddy motel room in a fifth-rate city, at four in the afternoon, is beautiful, unquestionably. Lemon, butter, daisy, illuminated eggshell, seraphic, gilded, color of a duck's wing or a Tuscan hillside. Which should be comforting or even inspiring, but generally isn't. Sometimes it makes things worse. In the midst of such beauty, how dare you decline?

I had my reasons. Such as: Daisy and Vikram, reconfigured as a tremulous duo called Whether, were opening for R.E.M. in Asia while I was still back in the States alone, in pieces, with a bunch of morons who made jokes about the cheerleaders who wouldn't fuck them, or would, and who was a bitch (everyone). The van smelled of gas fumes and beer-soaked indoor-outdoor carpet. We slept on floors and sagging sofas, or, worse, in the van itself, in sleeping bags. Also: the part where Daisy and Vikram had broken up with me. Also: the part where they kicked me out of my own band. The Squares had been staying in someone's house in Brussels; it was always miserably cold in that house, even to everyone else. We all wore shirts layered over other shirts, several pairs of socks. I also wore a parka. My hair was canary yellow with black dots in it. As we sat around someone else's plexiglass dining room table wearing all the clothes we had, Daisy kept drawing a little pattern on her hand, maybe the shape of my stolen soul. She was already pregnant with their first kid, though she wasn't saying that yet, of course. Also: being bewildered. Also: feeling murderous. Also: knowing it was over, our *Conformist* period had come to an end. Vikram, who used the word "reframing" at the plexiglass dining room table in Brussels, never did have any balls, not really. He mistook his narcissism for having an imagination. John and Miguel, like Tweedledum and Tweedledee, said nothing, swathed in multiple T-shirts and badly fitting sweaters, pale and puffy from existing on martinis, teenage girls, and *frites*.

Also: even in Brussels, even when I thought, or knew, my life was over, something else had already been occurring to me. It haunted me. I felt, irrationally, that the others had discovered my secret and that's why they were really kicking me out. They hadn't, of course. They were just assholes. Miguel was barely conscious. Daisy and Vikram were as self-enclosed as ever, psychically curled together, head to toe, in one cockleshell. John gazed at the ceiling. They didn't know anything about my tender ghost: out of the corner of my eye, glimpsed in a window, overheard – that boy in the street in New York before we left, *Never* ever, *never* ever, *bro* – or some sonic bricolage, one or two notes of fork hitting floor in a restaurant, the harmony on a song I heard in Dublin, what was it called? It was late at night, a local band. The woman – young, round, with pockmarked skin – who was singing harmony only came in at entirely unpredictable times, a shadow line. You could barely hear her. The edge of a sound; the place where the sound has mostly rubbed away, leaving just a washed-out stain, like the head of a soldier and nothing else of him that I once saw in a fresco in Arezzo, like Mads's disappearing *r* when he said "wonderland," though I hadn't met Mads yet or lived through the years before him. I kept that harmony to myself for a long time, because I didn't understand it, and because I loved it almost too much.

Daisy and Vikram and The Squares had been all about understatement and 4/4 time; their innovation was pulling the notes back in the millisecond that the listener could anticipate where they were going next. (So like them.) Jouncing from city to city in the van, I decided that understatement in 4/4 time was bullshit, which is probably half-true; instead, I wanted my sound to be a spaceship or a knife, exploratory. I was so raggedy and fucked-up. I felt like hell every minute of the day. I had a rotten tooth that kept me up at night and that felt like my fate in my mouth. When I came off the soul-chilling tour with The Sweet, I walked back into the liberated zone of New York, where it was full-on, rotting midsummer. JFK smelled like an abandoned zoo. Jungle heat, stinking subways. The heat comforted me. The rot, inside and out, was a psychic landmark. Besides the heat and the rot, all I had to my name was a vague ambition, a too-short checkered skirt, about a thousand dollars, and, miracle, my friend Jonah, the sound wizard, who owed me a week of studio time because I had let him live in my tiny, tiny apartment at 19th and First for two months after his girlfriend threw him out. A week is expensive. A week is a long time. In a week you can get to the first stop. I was wounded, exhausted, angry, broke, and past thirty. In other words, I was ready.

It was like going through the eye of a needle. In a week, after hours, Jonah and I, snorting piles of cocaine, roughed out *Whale*. It was a scratchy sort of freedom. Sand in my mouth as I whirled down the dune. The coke, after a while, felt like cold sand, too; my head was filled with sand; my eyes were filled with sand. As if I had walked into a blizzard of sand, but I had to keep going, I couldn't stop, and besides, I had nowhere else to go. Coke-burned, bitter, bereft, empty, untouched literally and figuratively by sunlight, in a state of idiocy. It would be easy to say that I was rotting like my rotten tooth, like the city, but that wouldn't be right, because rot is slow and organic, unavoidable, and everything I did was willed, too fast, airless, like something metal whirling in a vacuum. The studio was cool, low-ceilinged, at the back of a Buddhist meditation center. I never saw any Buddhists that week, maybe they were on vacation in Nirvana. During the day, Jonah raked in a lot of money making people you've heard of sound like they could sing; at night, for free, he returned the one favor I had left to call in. Jonah had a habit of twirling his hair as he worked. We stared at each other through the glass of the studio booth for hours, both of us dogged and sleepless and hopeless, me in socks, him twirling his hair, trichotillomanic. I called up a few people to contribute instrumental tracks and paid them in coke and my good will, promises of future labor, organ donations. I tried to lay down the vocals, but night four, night five went by and I was still hungry, still thirsty for the sound I wanted. My hair seemed to be falling out, squiggly red strands glittering on the floor of the sound booth. My tooth was getting worse, throb-

bing its red warning light, but I needed the money for that cold
sand that was fueling it all.

And then on night six, stinking and exhausted, drowning
in dunes of self-pity, I passed through the eye of the needle to
wonderland – to the broken, the illogical, the roads that double
back on themselves, the weird, the uncanny, the in-between. It
was such a small sonic shift at the time, an awkward half-note,
like a single letter in a familiar word turned backward. And
yet. It changed the entire thing. I saw all at once that my form
would be to be in search of a form, like someone wandering,
tracing an unpredictable path. You can't understate a phrase
you can't predict. Fuck Daisy and Vikram's fucking good taste,
their snowglobe for two, I thought morosely, belligerently.
And I realized something else: the central importance of the
unheard chord, the chord that is never played, the chord that
happens after the music ends. How had I missed it for so long?
It's the sound you don't quite hear, the reverberation coming
off the top or the side or the edges of the note. Not a silence but
a potential sound, a space exactly the shape of what the sound
is about to be. Invisible, inaudible, and yet revelatory, what fin-
ishes and composes the sequence retrospectively: you discover
that it was all going, in the end, toward the chord that isn't
heard but is only anticipated. Which is to say, the last chord
happens in the mind of the listener, as if he is remembering
a sound which in reality he has never heard before. The unheard chord feels like, must feel like, a memory. This was my
ambition.

I followed the awkward half-note, again, again, again. Finally, very late on a Tuesday night, Jonah looked at me from
the other side of the glass of the booth, twirling his hair, nodding. I was saved, not for the last time. In that moment I became the girl of the stumbling half-note, the note that thrilled
the smart people of 2002 and made them feel the heroism of
stumbling. My sound wasn't the propulsive, cathartic shaman-

ism of, you know, fill in the blank with your favorite name. My sound was the sound of the gap, the place where the seams show, where your fate feels like it's quietly rotting inside your head. We used maybe three or four instruments on *Whale,* and Jonah did the percussion himself, wrapping his socks around the drumsticks, twirling his wrist a certain way, and glancing at the beat while seeming also to fall asleep halfway through it and then waking up at the last minute to finish it. The record sounded simultaneously like a dress slipping off a bare shoulder and a girl falling down a well. People liked that sound that year. I stood around on the lip of the half-note, shining my little flashlight up at the night. I wasn't wrong. That half-twisted half-note was the right one, then.

Of course, I was still a wreck. *Very,* as a shrink put it wryly (much) later on, *rock-and-roll.* I felt it was owed me. I barely remember the *Whale* tour, mostly funded by my parents, who still had some money left then (bless their boho optimism) — Pittsburgh, Ann Arbor, Jersey City, San Francisco, and then, as it blew up, New York, Los Angeles, Europe — but everyone else remembers it, it changed their lives, I saw them, I saw through them, they saw themselves in me, prismatically, as through a broken window to a mirror, which makes sense, because I was completely busted to shit, sending bulletins from back behind the back, where even the cardboard boxes are soggy and torn. I didn't let the dentist finish putting the crown on so that I could touch the pointy tooth stump with my tongue, secretly tasting my will. But to everyone else it was the beginning of something, an era, everyone remembers that sound, the sound Jonah and I made in a week of nights out of sand. That was the sound of *then.* From *Whale* forward. Everyone agrees that it started with *Whale,* the new thing that everyone remembers so well. The sound waves spread out from that moment. Around the indie recording studios, I became, for a season, a verb. "Brundaging" meant tearing up the sound, erasing half of it, sending it skittering over the abyss, though no one was able to reproduce the way Jonah twirled his wrist over the drumhead, no one had his socks, so they were never able to copy that exquisitely muffled, glancing beat. In another life, Jonah might have been a tennis champion: he knew the precise, unreturnable angle at which to hit the ball.

By the time we left Los Angeles for Europe, I'd been signed by the adventurous sub-label of a major label. They were even willing to help out with the European tour for *Whale,* add bookings, musicians, upgrade our hotels. This angel manifested in the form of a skinny woman in a red dress with a terrible nose job who appeared in my dressing room on New Year's Eve with a contract. Flattening out the pages on top of my guitar case, I signed. She kissed me on the lips. Her nostrils were enormous. "Congratulations, baby," she said. "Here we go."

Privately, I've always thought that I got famous, in certain circles, because of what the most astute ears could hear: my failure. I broke through, I broke in, but I couldn't entirely break the train. And I knew it. That longing—I longed for so much then, and certainly so much happened—was vast, but the deepest note, the worst part, was my longing to cross that last few inches, to get up, over, or behind the note, topple the train open. The way some people long for the divine, I longed for that. I didn't just want to be famous; I wanted to be something better than famous. I wanted to lie down at last in the heat of the gap. I was stumbling so effortlessly, so perceptively, in my rush to break the train. That's what the smart people heard, whether they were conscious of it or not: my awareness that I was reaching for what I couldn't quite grasp, the space just beyond my fingertips. I imagine pilots feel the same way, flying higher and higher until the sky thins. In fact, I was in wonderland then, but only in some hazy amber of memory. At the time, I wasn't anywhere. I was reaching for the train as it disappeared, flash of silver, around a curve. Now I'm trying to go back to a place I've never been.

• • •

My fans said I was the sound they'd been waiting for. With me, they said, they went to the place, through the eye of the needle. They felt that we went there together, night after night.

I don't remember much about any of that. What I remember is the light on the wall of a hotel room in Budapest. It was the color of piss, it vibrated as trucks passed outside. It was beautiful and I didn't care about it at all. Three hours to showtime. I closed my eyes, indicted.

Göteborg, Later That Day

THE LIGHT IN Göteborg is clear, fine: a transparent light. The boulevards are wide and the trams that run along them are blue. Everyone here, to me, looks like a professor. Poseidon reigns over the top of the main boulevard, naked and muscular in black marble but with a strangely truncated penis; he is staring with some consternation at the massive, compensatory fish he brandishes in one hand. Boone and I are having lunch with Billy Q, shivering at an outside table, because Swedes have a different definition of "summer," it seems. The restaurant, improbably, is called Corazón de la Noche. We are eating tapas, which are actually quite good.

Billy Q looks like a little monk. He is pushing fifty, and he has folded his fame wings around himself like an invisibility cloak, but the magenta heat still comes off him, a mix of extraordinary intelligence, unease, vulnerability, and everything we know and don't know about him, all the places and times we've heard his voice, that burnt vibrato. He is wearing a keffiyeh and several layers of brightly patterned scarves wrapped this way and that, draping down his back and snaking around his shoulders. His gaze is kind but also piercingly curious, restless. His head – his famous head – seems set in the scarves just so, like a precious stone or a crystal ball; his body is incidental, a pedestal, it doesn't interest him.

"I love *Wonderland*," he says. "You're amazing. We've missed you."

Helplessly, I blush. Billy Q missed me? "Thank you. *Quarterlife* was incredible. I can't believe it's been that long–"

"Right? Twenty-five years. Unimaginable." He raises his eyes to the sky. "I feel like I'm a hundred years old."

"No, no."

He runs his finger along the rim of his glass of cava. "Ninety-nine, maybe. I ran into Ezra in Berlin. He was raving about *Wonderland*."

This I hadn't expected. There's only one Ezra in our world, only one in *the* world, full stop. I didn't know that they knew each other, but then again, of course they do. I don't miss a beat. "And how is he doing?"

"You know."

I nod, shrug. I'm not sure what Billy Q means by this, if he means what I mean. "Is he working?"

"Like a demon. He's nearly finished the album, I've heard some of it. Magnum produced – that man is a genius. It's back to basics, very soulful."

"He was always that."

"Will you see him when you guys are there?"

Boone reaches for the salt. I know what I'm supposed to say, which is: *of course*. And *love*. And *brilliant*. And *ever grateful*. But the words stick in my throat.

"He's said he'll come up for a song. Which is amazing, of course. So generous." What is it about the truly famous that creates that zone of instant intimacy? I've never met Billy Q before, and yet I somehow feel compelled to tell the truth. "It's just that what he's become – it's hard to watch."

"And that Ezra knows that," agrees Billy right away, as if we've had this conversation a million times before, in other cities, at dinner, lying on the beach. "Listen, I grew up on that music, he's a legend. He did so much for me when I was starting out, I still don't know why. I adore him. I wouldn't *be* here without him. But we've all tried. Susie's still there, bless her."

"Jesus. I know, I wouldn't be here either. A lot of people wouldn't be here. But I think that makes it worse. How bad is it these days?"

Billy takes my hand. His is dry, soft, warm, surprisingly small, like a little paw. He has, or someone has, drawn a small, wobbly square in black marker, half filled in, on the web of skin between his thumb and forefinger. "Ah." Billy shakes that world-renowned, oddly shaped head of his. "Hard to say. When did you see him last?"

"God. Ages. I gave up, I guess. Maybe that was wrong. Or stupid."

Billy squeezes my hand. "It's not easy for anyone. And, hey, it's not just the drugs—"

"I know. It's the whole thing."

Billy inclines his head. "The whole thing." He smiles. "Right. What the hell is he supposed to do about that? And at his age—it's a little late in the day to expect him to turn it around."

I feel that I have made a gaffe, because Billy knows all about the whole thing, and here he is, intact. Should I be complimenting him? Or would that be another gaffe?

"And those guys," continues Billy. "It was a different time. They were cowboys. They walked on the moon."

Boone crumbles bread into his floridly yellow squash soup. "Ezra's a god. Gods have issues."

Billy Q and I laugh together, as if Boone is our high school friend, standing in a parka outside the 7-Eleven, saying the shit he always says. Billy kisses Boone on the forehead. "When are you in Berlin?"

"Two weeks," I say.

"Oh, I'll be there. I'll come to the show."

"Cool," says Boone. "This soup tastes like limes, isn't that amazing? Do you think there could really be limes in it?"

"No," says Billy Q, winking at me. Boone, I think, actually is some kind of genius. For the first time, I believe that this shadow play might actually work. All the little girls in goggles swing their hammers, exultant.

Standing in the wings (striped stockings), sweating from my set, Tom and Alicia and Zach bunched up in unabashed fandom with me, I see the small, casual form of Billy Q like a piece of yarn standing on end, the packed field, thousands of faces uplifted, eerily serene they look in their rapture, and beyond and above them all the beaten silver of Sweden's summer night sky. I love him, too. We all love him. "Life," Billy sings, as if the word just came to him in a dream, and we feel it, life, its inexorable pulse. Life. Life. The heat: I have always loved this heat. The sound resonates through us, thumping up our legs, our backs, our skulls, almost too loud. Alicia leans close to Zach to murmur in his ear. Tom not very subtly edges in front of me to get a better view. The crowd surges and rolls, like a wave that doesn't quite crest. We all know this song, it was one of his biggest hits, we know all the words. I shiver and sweat and sing with the crowd.

The Order of Things

AS IF IT only happens the second time. Oh, do it again. Tracing the outlines already made, writing over them. The second time is the one we remember, where memory begins. Putting the moments in order is only half the story. What matters is the weight of the moments as they accumulate, which is to say, the place where it catches, where you begin to remember. Time spins backward and forward from that invisible point. Illustration 1: Michelangelo's *Slaves* are massive figures only half carved, caught in the perpetual moment of emerging from the stone. Atlas, for instance, has the body of a man but his head is a solid, squared-off chunk, his forearm disappearing into its weight. That weight, of his own unarticulated head, seems great. No one knows whether Michelangelo ever finished carving the *Slaves,* or if he meant the *Slaves* to remain in that state, a permanent state of becoming. They are slaves to gravity, to history, to earth, to the artist's hand that did or did not intend to finish them, to free them, that possibly intended to leave them there like that, half formed, trapped in rock forever. Where is the moment of choosing, can it be seen as an embodied thing, does it displace air? Was there a choice to begin with? Her weight – in my mind, always a she – that I didn't carry. Dear one, little bird, I think of you.

Illustration 2: There was an enormous clock on the classroom wall of an abandoned schoolhouse in Illinois. My father and his team carefully, apprehensively, took it down; the hands had been still for years. To smash a clock and leave it broken on the ground, to cut a clock, seems like bad luck, the violation of some superstition. No matter that they were going to remove floors and walls from the schoolhouse, divide it from itself, haunt it with the absence of its own removed interiority. Isn't that a violation, might it not carry its own punishment? No one thought so; they thought only of the mechanics, arguing and figuring for months, trying to calculate how to do it. But we take the clock for the thing itself, and we don't want to lose our chance. Not of the first time. Of the second time. My father wrapped the enormous clock in newspaper, tied the bundle of newspaper tight with string, left the clock at the schoolhouse door. "It might be worth something" was his reasoning. He never wore a watch himself, easily lost track of time when he was working. Space was his medium, his angel and devil, not time, not the inevitable progression of one thing after another. He meant that the clock might be worth something as an object, not as a tool. Time is my problem, the problem of music. One, two, three, four. Count me in. Fans don't want to hear the song the first time. They want to hear it again, and to know that they're hearing it again. Maybe that's the motive for the order of things, that knowing.

Göteborg, First Light

ZACH SITS UP in the narrow room in the pale of early morning. "Sorry."

"Did I —"

"No, it's cool. My head gets going." He twirls a finger near his ear. "I get distracted."

"Yeah, okay." I'm thirsty from the drinking, sand-eyed from the light, which is increasing again, after a darkness that couldn't have lasted more than a few hours. In the valley of that darkness there had been a spark; his room is next to mine. Easy.

But now it's grainy.

"I'm going to go try to get a little sleep," he says, kissing me on the cheek. "See ya."

Oh, Jesus. "Right."

Click of my door, and a few seconds later, the click of his. I pull the pillow over my face, trying to convince myself that it's still night and I'm still drunk, neither of which is true.

Letter to Lila

BECAUSE SOMETIMES WE were mermaids and sometimes we were trout. Because Cy Twombly came to lunch and brought us each little posies, making us flower girls for some invisible, possibly devilish wedding. Because of the long afternoons at the Newark house when Mom was in her studio (a.k.a. the shed) in the yard and Dad was at his a few blocks away and we read every day until we got headaches, since no one had remembered to enroll us in school that year. Because we got so good at packing and unpacking that we could pack up, or unpack, in two hours flat. Because Kathy Boudin became obsessed with Dad's work and wrote him long letters from prison about it and its importance to the revolution, and we read them aloud at dinner, standing on chairs. Because the donkey in Spain followed me around like a dog. Because of getting impetigo from scratching relentlessly at our mosquito bites in West Virginia. Because Mom was so beautiful, even her feet were beautiful, and she had been a debutante until she ran away with Dad. Because Dad taught me the names of all the handsaws: crosscut saw, ripsaw, hacksaw, coping saw, keyhole saw, backsaw. Later, the power saws. Because we heard that the FBI kept files on Dad, no one knew why, maybe it was the Kathy Boudin connection, or maybe it was something else altogether that we weren't allowed to know; we hoped so. Because, when we lived in Berlin, you suddenly turned up speaking full sentences in German; you were five, a tiny blond genius. Because of the choreographer who collaborated with Dad, so for a time various Spanish dancers lived with us in Madrid and they worked the donkey into the dance. Because we were on food stamps for a while in Wellfleet and ate amazing orange blocks of government cheese that I can still taste.

It tasted orange. Because when we walked into a restaurant there were always at least eight of us, or ten, or twelve, studio assistants and workers from the current site, speaking various languages, and those odd old-lady friends (often with peculiar disabilities) Mom always made and maybe some other dirty-kneed kids we'd befriended, and maybe somebody's dog and maybe one of Dad's mad sisters, telling everyone's fortune or arguing about the Palestinians. Because one time, in Erice, the mayor came to dinner. Because I lost my virginity at fourteen to one of those dancers, and I couldn't understand, later, why he never answered any of my letters. Because no one else knows what that was like, to be us.

Freedom

IS NOT JUST another word for nothing left to lose. It's rigorous, you can feel like a dog walking along a horizon line – seduced, determined, thirsty.

My father was free. My mother was not. Here are two examples. He had this funny pair of red corduroy pants he wore all the time: they were too big; there was a swath missing from the hem of one of the legs, as if a tiger had taken a bite out of it; he held them up with an old leather belt that belonged to his father, who had been an engineer for a mining company. It was the belt his father had used to beat his kids with. Because of my father's bad foot, you could see him coming a mile away, a listing figure who seemed to be wearing a sagging red sail, happily tilting along the cracked sidewalk in Nyack, or drifting down the beach in Wellfleet, or looking like he'd landed from hippie outer space in Piccadilly Circus, or sitting on the stoop in sandals, face to the sun, on St. Mark's Place. His face was handsome in a delicate way, but his body was crooked. One shoulder was higher than the other. He was never in good health. Always something convalescent about those pants, something therapeutic-looking, like orthopedic shoes. Or like he'd just escaped from the hospital, wearing pants he'd stolen from another patient. But those pants also looked like freedom to me, like sailor's pants. Traveler's pants.

Once my father got famous – the unskilled, oversized photos taken by his drug dealer of the sawed-in-half train caused a sensation at the Tokyo Biennale in 1974 – we went with him wherever he sailed, trailing clothes and books and pets and valentines we'd saved from crushes two schools back. He sailed around the world, cutting things out of structures until they were transformed, made porous, apparently weightless, like paper dolls but also like giants wounded by a giants' war, pock-marked, mutilated. People invited him to come to their countries and cut up their rotting buildings, their abandoned warehouses and barns and hospitals. He preferred to cut up things that were already half ruined, left for dead. He was invited to cut up bigger and bigger things and, ambitious engineer's son that he was, he never refused; he should have stopped before he accepted the commission on the half-built fascist gymnasium in Rome, but it wasn't in him to stop.

Amid the clutter of workmen and machinery, you could always spot my father on top of whatever building or teetering disheveled structure by the divided, billowing, off-kilter red triangle of those pants, like one of those big red arrows on a tourist map: *you are here.* I loved those pants. He still wears them, much patched and unevenly faded, though he hasn't broken anything open in quite a long time. After the gymnasium, or after the aftermath of the gymnasium, the accident, the split from my mother, and the financial meltdown, bit by bit he returned to painting and drawing. His hair is short and gray now; when he paints, he pushes his glasses on top of his head and leans close to the canvas, squinting. I can't help but see his painting as a chastening, though I know I am wrong about this, that it is ungenerous of me to think so.

My mother, by contrast, made curtains. She had a thunkety-thunkety sewing machine, heavier than lead, that she carefully packed in all our pillows and carted from Chicago to Berlin to Wellfleet to London to Madrid. In each place, the first thing she did was haul the machine out and make curtains from local material that she found in a dusty shop on a side street or a flea market or at a church basement sale or at Harrods, splurging: those last were silk, bang-yellow, and they trailed halfway down the floor in a glamorous pool of hypersaturated color. Is stewardship of the house always the consolation prize? I'm sure that's a cliché, but still, I hated all those curtains. I wanted to take a match to them. The hot, cottony smell of the old sewing machine with its worryingly frayed cord was for me the smell of her perpetual defeat. Indeed, once she and my father were divorced, she bought a house in Asbury Park and married a rotund potter named Ed. She hasn't moved in twenty years. She never makes curtains anymore. The most exotic place she travels is Bermuda, in the spring. She is happy.

It all seemed obvious to me then: that my father was continually laboring to open a seam in the world, to split it until it gave up a knowledge it didn't know it had, while my incandescent mother, like a cursed princess in a fairy tale, was continually stitching the winding sheet of her own entrapment. An entrapment in motion, in picturesque places, but an entrapment nonetheless. It all seems less clear to me now, of course, less easy; they did love each other. Was he really so much freer, never turning down a commission, driven to every collapsing roof or unmoored staircase or solid, impenetrable façade, like a knight in a different fairy tale who is condemned to an endless series of nearly undoable tasks, cutting through stone, iron, concrete? He was as quixotic as he was heroic. Over the years of the big work, rotting warehouse by condemned house by roofless armory, he broke his own body down, crumpling a vertebra, a kneecap, a hip, losing the hearing in his right ear. The structures he cut open cut openings in him as well. Metal pins hold significant parts of him together these days. After the collapse of the marble wall at the half-built fascist gymnasium, he was in a coma for two weeks. We were told he might die. My mother, in the hospital in Rome, went and kneeled in the hospital chapel. When he woke up, she left him.

Also, question to self: am I my father or my mother? Think twice before answering.

Prague

HIGH ABOVE THE old town square, the skeleton on the Or-
loj strikes the hour of noon. The air is sweet. Zach and Alicia
and I, along with a throng of tourists, watch the medieval skeleton with his little hammer. We have left the hotel in search of
throat lozenges, socks, and a candle for Alicia's room. All we've
found at the big mall in the center of town are the socks and
bad gelato in supernatural colors. Zach is spooning up neon-
green gelato; Alicia's is bright yellow, in a cone; mine is a swirl
of blue and red that tastes sort of like almonds and sort of like
bubble gum.

"We should go to the Kafka house," I say. "It's not far. I think
there's a bus?"

"When I was on tour with Beck in Russia," says Zach, more
to Alicia than to me, "I went to Stalin's house in Georgia."

"What was it like?" Alicia delicately licks at her bright yellow cone.

"Wooden."

"Huh."

"He was a fascist," offers Zach, eating a spoonful of neon-
green gelato.

I don't bother to correct him. We haven't spoken about the
fumble in Göteborg, and I know that if I acknowledge it in any
way, I will lose. I carefully do not look at him, nor take note of
the proximity of his elbow to Alicia's. Shirtless boys with rats
on their shoulders pass through the crowd in the square. On
one corner, a white, beefy man with short gray hair kneels on
the ground, his forehead touching the cobblestones, before a
cap with coins in it. On the opposite corner, a man who looks
not unlike him does the same thing, except that he is bent over
a dog.

"We're playing with Frogs and Foxes tonight," I say. "And this other big group, some kind of musical collective."

"That Frogs guy is such a douchebag," says Zach.

"I'm thirsty," says Alicia.

A Britney Spears song plays somewhere in the crowd; somewhere else, a pop song in French prances along. Prague is warm at midday, cool by dusk. We arrived yesterday, took a ride on a tourist boat down the Vltava, admired the swans, looked at the sky. Tom drank many beers. A Muslim family at the boat's stern were the only other passengers; like us, they took pictures of the swans with their cell phones. One of the little boys stared quizzically at Boone the entire time. The motion of the boat was slow, oddly restful, like being rocked. I slept for twelve hours last night, woke up unsure for a minute where I was, which city, which year of my life. I looked at my cell phone for the time and remembered: *Czechoslovakia.* It seemed so improbable that I laughed out loud, alone in the vast hotel bed.

Zach says, "I promised my dad I'd go to the Jewish cemetery. Supposedly I've got a great buried there somewhere."

Alicia looks impressed.

"You go ahead," I tell them. "I'll meet up with you in the lobby for dinner." They head off, her face uplifted to his as he gestures, talks, walking in his slightly duck-toed way. I go back to the hotel, where I read the *International Herald Tribune* and then fall asleep again. My dreams are syrupy, heavy afternoon dreams filled with people, with colors. I wake up wanting to call Jim, but manage (just) not to do that. He'd asked me, specifically and respectfully, not to, the one exception being an emergency, like if the plane I was on was plunging out of the sky. I'd said, "I guess I should put you on speed dial, then," but he didn't laugh.

I try to write down the syrupy dreams in *Wonderland,* maybe there's a song there somehow, but the syrup only runs, granulates. I see a text from Boone, sent half an hour ago. *Come on down, we're all going to dinner. Hry.* I put on my shoes, smooth my hair, and rush down to the lobby. Zach, Alicia, Tom, Boone, and a tall black man with short, blond dreads are waiting.

Tom introduces us. "This is my friend Anton. He lives here."

"And what do you do?" I ask Anton as he leads us to dinner, a place he knows where we can sit outside.

"I'm a writer," says Anton, looking down at me.

"What do you write?"

"Novels, mostly. I translate a little."

"You're Czech?"

"My mother was Czech." He smiles. "My father was from Oakland."

We arrive at a restaurant in a square with many tables outside. Set up in the square is a jumbotron on which soccer players, their heads soaked with sweat, mill around tensely. The screen is so big that even at the back of the seating area – the tables in front are full – I can see the hair on the players' legs, the mud on their shoes. Their faces are surreally close. Everyone in the square is watching intently, hushed.

"Who's playing?" I ask Anton.

"Spain versus Germany. Spain is red, Germany is white."

"Like wine."

A player in white on the side of the field picks up the ball to throw it inbounds and the crowd in the square boos and hisses loudly. A few people bang on the wooden tables.

"We're for Spain?"

Anton smiles. "Oh, yes. We're for Spain."

A player in red steals the ball with one quick foot and the crowd cheers. A table nearby waves at us to sit down, get out of the way, so we do.

At another table, two women are smoking, speaking English with British accents. They appear to be the only people here not riveted by the game. "To play that card then," says one of them, in a businesslike blazer and skirt. "To play that." The other, younger, wearing a necklace of large black beads, nods sympathetically.

Anton, in consultation with Tom, does the ordering, which makes me fear what might arrive, but I'm never that hungry before a show anyway. "How do you guys know each other?" I ask.

"From college," says Anton. "We actually – we had a band."

"It was great," says Tom, Purelling his hands, then carefully arranging his napkin in his collar.

"It sucked," says Anton. "But Tom was already really good. We knew he could make it."

Tom shrugs. "Just got lucky."

"Man, when was the last time I saw you?"

Tom pulls at his chin. "I don't know. Was I here when I was out with Carmela?"

"I guess. Time flies."

I wonder about Anton's life here, how long he's been here, as thick brown bread and various big pizzas and terrible wine arrive, as Anton explains that the Czech name for Prague means "threshold," as Spain gets a goal and the restaurant tables nearly fly up in the air with collective joy, as Boone, tapping his watch, reminds us all that we have to get dressed, get ready, be at the venue by nine, we can't be late. Tom folds a last piece of pizza, devours it, and pats his stomach, which I notice is already bigger. Alicia, having eaten nothing but a heel of bread, is smoking and watching the game, shadows in the hollow of her throat. Zach is leaning close to her, talking fervently. Alicia, expertly sending up a smoke ring, nods. Her platinum hair glows in the near-dark. The men on the big screen are clearly exhausted, drenched, but they line up again. They keep watch on the ball as if they are all in love with it.

We go on at midnight. We're playing a basement club tucked way back into a curve of Prague on a cobblestone street. After Frogs and Foxes and the collective, the stage is littered with broken strings, abandoned beers, what looks like a bikini top though I don't remember seeing anyone topless, gum wrappers, a few stubbed-out cigarettes. Tonight is no-stockings, which means I have to remember not to lean over too far, lest I show Prague the world. With no-stockings, I have decided on the braid. My face feels naked. The stage beneath my feet, as I walk onto it, my band behind me, feels uneven, not so much rickety as warped. I need sea legs for this one, and I'm not sure I have them yet. I turn around to smile at my band, all brushed and polished and dressed, and Tom makes devil's horns at me. They all look smart tonight, what my mother would call *spiffy*, and even Tom is in a clean shirt. The light, as it falls on them, makes them look both more and less than mortal. For a moment I don't understand them, why they would come all the way out here with me, wait for me in hotel lobbies in foreign countries, what it is that we think we're doing. Did I ever know what I was doing?

Tom takes his place at the drums, waits for the nod from me. Except for Anton, standing with arms folded at the back of the room, the audience is made up mostly of teenagers, all of whom seem to be on their iPhones, probably texting one another. By my foot, a gangly boy with several nose rings bobs his head up and down, though there is no music playing. He looks up at me beseechingly. I wonder if he thinks he's come to see some other band. The flavor of the crowd is punk, or punkish, which we definitely are not. Standing on the edge of the crowd is the lead singer of Frogs and Foxes, a young British guy with curly brown hair and a crooked nose, his arm around a small, round young woman from the musical collective. He is drinking a beer after his loud set of songs that actually seemed to be about frogs, also zebras. There might have been a giraffe. Zach, arranging himself in his bass, subtly eyes the room, raises an eyebrow at me. Alicia touches her cello gently, leaning forward to it, eyes half closed. I brace my legs on the warp, turn around, nod. Tom raises his drumsticks. I turn back around. 1, 2, 3, 4.

I'm in good voice tonight, we're all in good voice, pacing one another, a team of well-trained horses, well-watered, well-fed. The pizza wasn't bad. Spain won. Prague means threshold. I pace the stage until I get my sea legs – *here* is the dip, and here as well. Here we go. It's our short set, so its mood changes often. The gangly boy bobs his head in the same rhythm no matter what's playing; like a stopped clock that's right twice a day, he's in time with us now and then. The teenagers find beats wherever they can and obligingly dance to them, pretty cheeks pink and damp, hair damp. One young girl sticks her tongue out; I see the little white pill; another girl, quick as a wink, tongues it up. I cue the band for "Orchids" instead of "Waiting for a Sign." "Orchids" is faster, lighter. Alicia spits on her hands, adjusts her grip on the cello bow. Even the bartender in the back is nodding along affably by the middle of "Orchids."

When the crooked nose of the lead singer of Frogs and Foxes rises in the air, my first, irrational thought is that it is his nose alone floating there – are we not in the land of Kafka, after all? But then I see his naked chest (when did he take his shirt off?), the soles of his big shoes, the teenagers staggering under his weight, and I realize he is surfing my crowd. The small, round young woman is dancing ecstatically in his wake, and the teenagers follow suit, forming a loose conga line, slam-dancing to the irregular melody we're playing so beautifully, which can't hold a slam. It is like a fist going through balsa wood. In the split second during which I am trying to decide how to take the ball back – what would Spain do? – Zach picks up an abandoned beer bottle by his feet and lobs it with stunning precision at the douchebag's head. Warm beer rains over me and Alicia. The bottle hits the guy's forehead, a seam in his face opens up, blood falls all over the teenagers, who at first seem to think it's part of the act and laugh hysterically, dropping the douchebag, who hits the floor hard.

Tom stands up behind his drums, mouth open.

We don't finish our set.

Rome, the First Time

HE FELT IT and he didn't feel it at the same time, like a wave crashing over him, except the wave was made of marble. The pain was infinite, and then it was gone, because he was gone. His broken body lay curled and bloody on the ground, one leg bent under him, his fingers curled over his palms, his shirt shredded, but within him there was nothing. One of the assistants told my mother over and over about his watch, miraculously intact and ticking on his wrist, *orologio non rotto non rotto,* as if this were a sign of life, of hope, but in fact he died that day. His spirit left his broken body. It went away on its own. His body, trussed and swaddled and intubated, lay in the hospital bed in Rome, waiting for his spirit to return; the only part of him that could be said to exist was that waiting. He was a space of waiting. Rome – our Rome – whirled around the empty point of his small, slender form in that bed. He looked like an Etruscan statue, a white form without a name. We were not a religious family. We knew he was all but dead – that, in a way, he was dead.

When he woke up, he asked for water. Lila held the glass with both hands, guiding the straw to his lips. He sipped, smiled, slept. The odors of the hospital – bleach, tomato sauce – didn't change. I saw that people could die, people could be born, and nothing about the hospital smell would change. In the weeks that followed, his smile became speech; his arms moved; first one leg moved, then the other. He had surgery. After several weeks more, he was permitted to walk very slowly to the hospital garden and sit in a wooden chair, stubble-faced, with bad breath, pale. Lila and I sat on either side of him, each of us holding one of his hands. His grip was weak. His eyes were dull.

"What was it like?" asked Lila on one of these afternoons, holding his right hand.

"You know how it is when you get the wind knocked out of you?" he said.

"Yeah."

"Like that. Kind of like that."

"But then your breath comes back," I said, holding his left hand, which was smooth and cool.

"I don't know," he said. "Can't say it has."

But I knew that already. It was obvious. He was still waiting. His good leg trembled. Nothing about him looked right. He wasn't a very big man, and without his grand, animating spirit, his slightness showed—his slender wrists, his delicate Adam's apple. You could see when he swallowed, and he seemed to swallow a lot. I don't think it was the physical shattering that put the fear in him. I don't even think it was our mother's leaving him. I think it was the knowledge, hurled into him with such overwhelming force, that the spirit could be separated from the body. From that time forward, he began guarding his spirit closely, but in the way of a man who wasn't entirely sure where his spirit was or who might have stolen it. He became suspicious, prickly. For a while he drank a lot. He has never gone back to Rome.

My Life as a Fan Dancer

I FIRST MET Simon in London. The tail end, as it were, of the European part of the *Whale* tour, the last stop. Closing night. It had all gotten big, bigger than anyone had imagined it could; we didn't understand it; we tilted together giddily through the days and nights. I was so sieved, so ruined, so skinny, that I felt as if all available light could pass through me, a sensation that was as exalting as it was terrifying. A sound made of sand, built on sand. Why did everyone love it so? After the show, a crowd surged into my dressing room and down the corridor. I was in the middle of it all, chilly and dank in the tiny white camisole that was, by then, sweat-stained, road-weary; I'd been wearing it nearly every night for weeks. It had grown loose on me as I thinned. The stitching on the left side was coming undone, but no one could see that from the audience. I was superstitious about the camisole's luck-bringing properties and sometimes slept in it. My fingertips were callused, my hands ached, my shoulders hurt all the time. The bridge on my guitar was coming as loose as the camisole, the strings were shredded. Racing toward some light that kept just eluding me, I had gone up, and up. Someone put a cigarette in my mouth, and though I didn't really smoke, I sucked in its sooty heat, halfway thinking it might warm me up or feed me. When had I last eaten?

A short man pushed through a thicket of pale young bearded men with earrings to shake my hand. "That was incredible. You are extraordinary. I am Simon." I thought he must be from a record company somewhere, with his graying hair, in that bespoke white shirt with the onyx cufflinks, the cream-colored suit jacket.

"Nice to meet you."

"I have to ask you," he said, "I must ask you –"

"Anna!" cried Ingrid, my opener, caught in the arms of the pale young bearded men like a flapping kite in a tree. "Darling, darling. Oh, my darling."

"Do you want to just give me your card? This is insanity right now."

"My card? No, no. I'm a friend of Nils." Nils was our bass player. I could never remember what Nils's original nationality had been – Swedish? Norwegian? International Rich? Something that ovaled his *i*'s. Nils died not long after that tour in a drunken car accident, going through the windshield at a hundred miles an hour. Simon put his warm hand rather firmly on my bare arm. His gaze was restless; his sharp, swarthy face looked as if someone had run a hand over it before it was finished, pushing his nose to one side, tilting his eyes down at the corners. His hair was slicked back off his forehead and curled just below his collar. He looked to me like a jumble of visible aspiration; if a price tag had been dangling from his shirt collar, I wouldn't have been surprised. He didn't belong in that crowd at all. He wore expensive-looking laceless shoes with a thick heel; I wondered why short men think that helps. "Do you know the music of Janáček?" His accent was unplaceable to me, polyglot.

"No," I said. "What?" I dragged on the sooty cigarette. Nils was swanning in his glory across the room, barrel-chested, his broad face flushed, laughing, like Count Himself; the crowd thickened, got louder; we were all exhausted, exhilarated, in love and hate with one another. We knew we would all be together forever. We had found the deep water. We were like one continuous body. Ingrid finally got free of the branches of the pale bearded young men and kissed me, hugged me, spilling the champagne I was trying to guzzle, desperately thirsty, both hot and cold at once. I hadn't slept in three nights, because I knew we were almost there and I didn't want to miss it. I had to stay awake to catch the peak, like the moment of a full eclipse. "Who?" My musical education was as patchy as the rest of my education. Across the room, Nils pointed over people's heads toward the door, eager for the afterparty.

Ignoring Ingrid's many-armed enthusiasm, Simon stepped close enough that I could catch the scent of starch in his shirt. "Let me send you some. It's quite delicate, I think you would like it." Eye to eye as we were, too-tall woman and too-short man, I felt an unnamable sensation envelop us, as if a hood had been thrown over us both at once. That mouth, I wondered, was it pursed selfishly or thoughtfully? Simon's eyes were so dark. He looked like a hawk to me: light, vigilant, a hunter. Something flickered between us, like the flicker of a fan.

"I want *roast pig*," said Ingrid. "Roasted pig!"

"I –" I said, and then the crowd parted us, or maybe it united us. It was one of those nights. The party moved on and on, from bar to flat to club, Simon bobbing on its tide, continually catching my eye with his restless hawk's eye. One for the road, I thought. One more unnamed street, one more, one more, one more time. When we left the last afterparty together, me wearing his cream-colored jacket, which fit me perfectly, I thought that it was all down to the energy of closing night, the knowledge coming in and the knowledge going out, the last hours in the bubble, the mixture of exhausted exhilaration and the faint beginnings, already, of post-tour dread, though I didn't know what that was yet, what darkness was waiting for me after it was all over. Standing in front of the apartment building where I was staying, he kept looking over at me as if trying to gauge something, see something, so I kissed him to let him know that it was all right. I had to bend my head. He made a sound, tugged at my belt loops, seeking something else in the kiss than what I had given, hard. I fumbled for the keys.

The flat – it belonged to an actress someone knew – smelled of cold woodsmoke from the small fireplace. We lay on the bed crosswise, undoing each other's clothes. Without his glasses, Simon looked younger, wide-eyed, and slightly dangerous, smarter than he looked with his glasses on. He pressed his mouth firmly to my bared belly, unlacing the shredding camisole to get at my breast, his wedding ring stiffening my nipple. He looked up into my face. "Anna," he said, as if we had known one another in the past and were now reuniting. "Anna." His sharp face, his tenacity, the keenness of his wide-eyed gaze: a hungry creature, like me. He kicked his laceless shoes to the floor. The unbuttoning, the unzipping, the unlacing, his dick hard in my hand, and then he was inside me, very fast. I almost made him pause, and then I didn't. He was not heavy, not oversized in any way, but dense, as if his molecules were packed more closely together than those of other people. His skin was hot and surprisingly soft. There was a little fat around his waist, the slight fat of a married man who nevertheless goes to the gym. I put my hands on his ass.

"Jesus," he said, closing his eyes. His need was so raw, so unguarded, that it was shocking. "You feel like heaven," he said, "my God." I wrapped myself around him. The fan flickered open involuntarily, called to save him from whatever was hunting him. We outran it, for the moment, together. His skin was so warm. Then we stayed entwined, breathing, his strong hands in my hair, cradling the back of my head, his hawk face in my neck. "Anna," he said. "Anna. Anna."

"Who are you?" I said a bit later. We were lying in that ridiculous cliché of a bed, like something out of Colette, or a bad movie version of Colette, brass with big brass knobs on the bedposts, sheets edged in eyelet lace. I had my feet propped against one of the fat brass rails, my head on his knees, looking at him. I smelled of sweat and sex. My arms were bruised from the way I held the guitar to thump it the particular way I did; my thighs were bruised from where the guitar thumped me back every night. Everything ached; making all that sound, trying to get it to bend right, was manual labor. A long, zigzaggy scratch on my arm was beginning to hurt. How did I get that? I wondered what everyone was doing at the party. I touched my pointy tooth-stump with my tongue.

He stroked my face. "I'm an architect. Strange, why is that the first thing I say, in bed with a beautiful woman? My *credentials*." He smiled. "Lebanese. Forty-one." He paused. "Married. Two children." Simon wound a strand of my dirty, too-long, ragged hair around his fingers. I hadn't had a haircut, also from superstition, since the tour started. "What a beautiful shade of red. Like a fox."

"Are you saying I'm a fox?"

"More like a gazelle. Maybe, onstage, a wild swan –" He had a light, clear lilt in his voice, the rhythm of a different place, several different places at once.

"No. It's an expression. And those cheesy compliments, could you – you're a friend of Nils?"

"Sorry. No compliments." He pulled the covers to my shoulder, tucking me in. "Yes, an old friend from school. Do you think less of me that I'm married?"

"I don't think anything of you. I don't even know you." What time was it? I still felt that inner thrum from fucking him, but I wanted to get up, go back to the party, join everyone I loved and hated so much. Instead, I felt the knots and scars on his knees, they felt like runners' knees, ran my hand up the long muscles of his thigh. I felt on his thigh for the tether I imagined there. Like a falcon, I thought, more like a tethered falcon than a hawk. "Have you always lived in London?"

"I grew up in Lebanon. My parents sent me to school in Wales during the war, because I was . . . getting into trouble. Now I live in Switzerland. But I have a few projects here."

"Switzerland. Wow. Do you feel at home there?"

"I don't know where I would feel at home. Perhaps Beirut, but we can't. We have children. To be exiled in Switzerland . . ." He shrugged. "I don't mind."

"Okay." I was getting sleepy and I didn't want to sleep, not yet. "A few projects, a few . . ."

He turned his head in the dark. "I have never done this. You don't understand."

"Mmmmm."

"And who are you?"

I touched him. He was hard again. "You know who I am. You just saw me."

He turned to kiss me and we began moving together, fast like before, but this time I met his urgency with my own, the last flame of the last night. Exhilarated and exhausted, I wanted to tell this man something, something only a man like him could understand, something the ambitious, snake-hipped drummers and bass players and demi-artists I'd been with before couldn't possibly know, what it was to be alone and out here like this, in a kind of exile. This man — older, tethered, restless, hungry, heavy, warm — was an exile, too, always far from home. We made a mess of the ridiculous soft bed of brass and eyelet lace, like two thieves who had broken into a house and were now fucking in it. I wanted to tell him something about that, exile to exile, hunter to hunter, but at that moment I could show him only with my breasts, my knees, the force of my coming.

I could have said something afterward, but I told myself that I didn't know this man. So instead I glanced around the floor, trying to read the large, sleek watch on top of his pants. "Those are great shoes," I said.

"I bought them just today. To wear tonight. I thought they would be, you know, *hip*."

I had never felt so famous.

"I have to go," I said, sitting up before sleep could catch me.

I found the party, or what was left of it, in a private room in a Soho restaurant. Nils and Boxer, our drummer, were deep in discussion at one end of a long table scattered with champagne and wine bottles, the broken and cut and spilled remains of a feast, uncleared dishes, a stack of *Whale 2003* T-shirts neatly draped over the back of a chair, confetti, glitter, dirty espresso cups. An enormous oil painting of a flamingo ornamented the entire back wall of the room. The pink was hallucinogenic. The flamingo was three times as big as a real one would be. It looked like every album cover I had ever wanted to be. Nils had tied one of the *Whale 2003* T-shirts around his head, and he was explaining what appeared to be some of the finer points of *Das Kapital* to Boxer, who kept shaking his head over and over. "Ah, Jesus," said Boxer in his thick Dublin accent. "Motherfuck."

"Listen," said Nils. "Listen. It's the surplus value. Darling girl, where have you been? They've all gone to see if they can ride on the Eye."

"Fucking that guy, your friend. The short one." I yawned as I sat down with the other two under the hysterical, round-eyed gaze of the huge flamingo. "He was kind of intense."

"Married," said Nils. "Forever. They live in Zurich. Brrrr." He shivered theatrically.

"Quoth the raven. Is he rich?" I ate an olive, then a red grape, then another, fatter olive.

Nils pulled on his ear. "His family is. Before I go completely deaf, I have to stop this, I'm getting too old for it all." He lit a cigarette, winked. "Rust never sleeps."

Boxer was still shaking his head. "I might weep, mate."

Nils and I laughed. Boxer was a fantastic drummer and the opposite of an old soul. It was a brand-new world to him every day. I sometimes wondered if he was a little slow.

I ate a grape that seemed to have been soaked in red wine and cigarette ash. "Me, too. I'm so tired. What happened?" I said to Nils. "What just happened to us?"

Nils eyed me. "Let me give you some advice, Anna. We've stuck our fingers in the socket with this one. Begin drinking on the plane and don't stop until you've been home at least a month. The g-forces will knock you silly." He slapped Boxer on the back. "Let's all weep! Let's weep for the proletariat! Huzzah!"

I left the two of them there, under the eye of the hypertrophied flamingo, and made my way back to the actress's flat. I couldn't get a taxi, but it wasn't far to walk. In the early-morning light, the white stone of London's finer houses was cold and grand as angels standing upright, hands pressed together, eyes closed. The sky was broad and gray. The lorries weren't out yet. All was quiet. My ears rang in the lull. The tips of my fingers, the tip of my nose, were cold as I hurried along, trying to pull my shirtsleeves over my hands. I was exhausted, emptied, yet in that emptiness, supernaturally light, radiant. I had given it all, used it up. I could see myself hurrying along the London street at the drained end of the night, skinny and wrecked and shredded, like a sheaf of bright ribbons, ripped and tangled and trailing down the street. At the same time, I wanted to weep, too, like Boxer, weep until I slept and woke in my own bed, in my tiny tiny apartment on 19th Street, with my own calico cat looking at me from the windowsill, my sky-blue bedroom, my pumpkin-orange living room, my own jewelry hanging from the closet doorknob, my dinged, cobalt-blue teakettle waiting on the small, gassy stove for me to pick it up and fill it. How long had I been on the road? I counted. Six months. Was that possible? I counted again, ticking off the months on my cold fingers. Actually, it was seven. Where had we been? Had we made any money? Was I a star? It had all seemed so slow and random for such a long time, years of secondhand junk, and then it had all gone so fast.

I had no idea. I wasn't even sure I knew what a star was, really. A vertigo uncentered me. I managed the heavy building door, made my way slowly up the steps toward the actress's flat, dizzy. As I put the key in the lock, I realized that I wanted Simon to be there waiting for me. I wanted to untether him, I wanted his face to seek my face, I wanted to feel again the restlessness of his hawk's eye. And what was Janáček? Just before opening the door, my cheek pressed against it, listening for this Simon inside, I remembered the surprising weight and heat of him, and at the center of the motion a deeper, silent motion, the perpetual motion of a man who is never at home anywhere.

I could have wept. Still leaning against the door, I thought, *I'm exhausted,* which I was, and not, *I just got pregnant,* which I also was, as it turned out. I reminded myself that I didn't know this man in real life and doubted I would like him if I did, a too-short, married, fortyish, densely packed, hawk-faced, tethered, Lebanese architect (from Switzerland? from Wales? from Beirut?), with ostentatiously European glasses, bespoke shirts, and expensive laceless shoes. Translation: a married guy with kids. I reminded myself that I had just essentially slept with a fan, and everyone knows that that's the beginning of turning into a crazy hag with breast implants and lipstick drawn way beyond the lips. A little soon, and not very indie, to be there.

I opened the door. The air in the flat was still. The modern appliances gleamed. The mantelpiece was crowded with framed photos, souvenirs, odd and beautiful artsy items. A generous bouquet of dried red roses hung upside down in the fireplace. Frilly, but far from stupid. I could imagine the actress, her rounded laugh. In the bedroom, the bed was neatly made, the pillows fluffed, empty of the impression of Simon's head or mine. The brass bed knobs seemed larger in the morning light, like small suns. No tread of his on the carpet. Folded on the bedside table was a small piece of plain white paper that said *Anna* on the front. Inside he had written, *What a lovely evening, bon voyage,* and his cell phone number.

I put the piece of paper in my filthy pocket, then took all my clothes off and hurled myself into the Colette bed for the second time that long night, buried my skinny, sweaty, aching self in eyelet sheets. Even my kneecaps hurt. I was a single, frayed live wire. I didn't call that number the next day, or the next. I didn't call it when I found out that I was pregnant. (Oh, thirty-three – what I would have given later for such a recklessly easy conception; at the time, I just thought, aggravated, that the energy of the last night had made me reckless, had to look out for that, add it to the list of tour mistakes.) I didn't call when I went for the abortion back in New York. I might have called Nils, the only person I knew who knew Simon, but he was already dead. I didn't call, but I kept the piece of white paper on my dresser top in the 19th Street apartment, next to the two pairs of good earrings, the slender bottle of musky perfume I loved, the dish of various European coins, the bit of rubble from the perforated lighthouse in its vitrine. I went down after that tour, went down hard. The abortion, I'm sorry to put it so coolly, didn't seem to have much to do with Simon at the time. It seemed like part of a larger death. It made me sick, maybe it was the roller coaster of confused hormones, soul fever, I don't know. Even the calico cat got sick, as if my malaise was contagious, and lost big patches of fur. She and I got better, fatter, together, slowly. The crown on my tooth felt like a door closing. Nils had been right, of course, though he neglected to mention that the g-forces get you anyway. It's really just a question of location. It was only later, much later, that the almost-baby mattered.

So I didn't call Simon then, but I did call a year later, from Heathrow. I thought of it as curiosity.

"Anna! Where are you?"

"On my way to Rome. Just for a few days, I'm opening for –"

"Tell me where you'll be."

That was the first time we were in Rome.

Tilting

THE PLACE WHERE it tips. There. You feel it within first, the fulcrum of the seesaw as it shifts. A sliding that isn't falling. If someone says to you, "I want to be in your dreams," what does that mean? Dream of me. Let me in. Write about me, think about me, sing about me. It's the Orpheus problem – once she turned away, she wrote the songs he would sing for the next billion years. But it was he who turned, he turned first, he knew what would happen, so can't it also be said that he decided his own fate in that moment? Maybe he turned into the motion that was already happening within, he had already decided. Turning – in my imagination, he is higher up than she on the dim path as it slopes upward to the surface. He feels it before he sees it, the pull backward. He knew it would happen before it happened, the motion had already begun. You don't know where it begins, not really, but you know where it tips, where the tilt starts. The air seems to grow heavier on one side, lighter on the other. The problem for my father of upending that rotting pier in Trondheim was that, small as it was, it wouldn't stay upended. It kept tilting to one side or the other, it fell, and each time it fell it cracked in a new place, and the question of bracing became massive and, ultimately, insoluble. The Trondheim pier had to express a preference; it had to lean, to tilt, to fall. "I want to be in your dreams," a woman said to me at a party once. As if, once requested, it was a thing that could be done. As if the motion could be inserted. She wasn't in my dreams, not ever, lovely though she was. I don't know where the tilt begins. They didn't either, in Trondheim, so to everyone's vast disappointment they lowered the pier back down. Bent from its recent struggles, it tilted and twisted and sagged into the sea. The Trondheim Arts Council paid the commission in full anyway, but they dismantled the pier, because it had long since rusted; now that it was bent, it was a public-safety hazard. As both art and commerce, it failed. It wouldn't be used. It didn't want to be part of anyone's dreams. Maybe the dismantling is what it wanted all along, who knows?

Trenčín, Slovakia

THE HAY BALES everywhere, why are there hay bales? Don't make this venue feel any less like the airstrip that it is. The festival is enormous, it goes on for acres, guarded at the many gates by big, blond Slovak men who look as if they got out of the secret police yesterday, or might still be in it. I walk the hot tarmac road beside the tents devoted to beer, books, food, Greenpeace, body painting, and hookahs, or simply filled with people lying around on enormous, pouffy, multicolored cushions. I walk out to the edge, to a chainlink fence. A young Asian man with a ring on each thumb is standing there. The noise of the festival is behind us. The afternoon sun has a brute Slovak strength.

I nod hello.

The young man says, "What band are you with?"

"Mine."

"Cool."

"You?"

"I crew for Jason."

I nod as if I know who this is. Together, the young man and I watch a small plane land and taxi in, growing larger, louder, coming to rest fifty yards from us.

"I love that," says the young man. "It looks like a dragonfly, doesn't it?"

The Music in His Head

CLASSICAL, ESPECIALLY CHOPIN. And folk, the kind of songs that are so worn, so ancient, that they no longer have an author, if they ever did. Songs of deaths and drownings, miners lost in the mines, true loves never to be seen again, oceans and rivers and sailing ships. Hymns, though he has never been a religious man. I think he likes their heavy, regular thumping toward Jesus. Ever since he lost the hearing in his right ear, he holds half of a set of big headphones to his left ear, leaning forward, listening, his bad foot twitching. In his studio, he always played the music loud, filling the room with long, melodic loops of sadness. The inevitable next question. No, he didn't. It's true that he never cared how loud or long I slammed away at the guitar, starting at twelve, in Wellfleet and Trondheim and Rome and London and on St. Mark's Place. True that he helped sell T-shirts in the days of The Squares, brought his latest girlfriends to shows, sat in the front, attentive, tapping a finger on the table. He has always liked my voice, that's true, too; he liked the depth and oddness of it, the roughness. That's his line drawing of an anxious little elephant on the front of *Bang Bang*. His drawing skills were extraordinarily fluid; he covered the walls of our rooms, as children, with menageries of creatures real and invented. But the music didn't touch him; he likes a melody. He balked at *Whale*, squinted at *Bang Bang*, was more or less polite about *The Pillars*. When I sent him an early mix of *Wonderland*, he emailed me, "So happy you're working again, Annie. Seems like an awful lot of thought went into this." I mean. The inevitable next question: yes, of course I saw the connection with Simon. No kidding. He translated parts of *Whale* into Arabic, read me his teenage poetry over the phone, laughing at himself, although the poetry was pretty good. Knowing, which happens slowly, takes you only so far. The listening, which happens in an instant, is difficult to refuse.

At the Chateau

THE BARKING OF the deer fucking in the woods outside the chateau was very loud. They were especially active at twilight, which was also the time they usually grazed. When they fucked they made harsh, bellowing sounds that seemed to bear no relation to pleasure. Gigi, who'd heard the males' strangled calls, said their veins stood out on their necks as they craned forward, attenuated, straining, barking hoarsely.

"Such beautiful creatures," she said, "making such a terrible sound in such a terrible way. How can that be?"

"Like us," said Cleo, my backup singer, who was also a painter. She pushed at the soft candle wax that had dripped onto the table, frowning. She had strong, square hands, a strong, square voice; she was expensive, and she knew it.

The others – Ethan, the producer; David, the sound engineer; Jean, the bassist; and Hubert, the all-around rhythm section – made demurring murmurs that hovered soggily in the humid July evening. Gigi, the concierge and major-domo of this domain, maintained a judicious silence, head tilted toward the woods. Condensation beaded on the wine glasses, the water glasses.

The seven of us were at dinner at the long table in the overgrown garden. It was our last week, and we were failing. We had come to the chateau to make *Bang Bang,* my second album, which was going to take me even higher. Ezra, my new friend and patron, had arranged this, shaking the chateau out of the folds of his robes. Legendary records had been made there, legendary things had happened, and more legendary, darker things were rumored to have happened. But so far, for us, nothing was happening.

"They're just looking for some touch," said Ethan, spooning sugar into his tea. Large and bald with faintly pointy ears, Ethan was the genius producer of that moment, the Magnum, the Magus, the Dream, the man who knew your other self, your past lives, your shadow side, and could coax it all onto tape. When he was working, he went off his medication, which meant that sometimes he slept all day and sometimes he didn't sleep at all. At the chateau – he'd been there before, of course, many times – it was his custom not to sleep.

"But are they ever getting it?" said Gigi. "They sound like they're dying."

Cleo molded the soft candle wax into a small, naïve head, rolling it in her palm. "We'd better get it tomorrow," she said. "We'd better get something. I have to be in Munich on Saturday."

Jean, the perfect boy whom everyone wanted and no one could have, said, "Munich!" and drained his wine glass.

Hubert, the sinewy curlicue, glowered at Cleo, whom he could not forgive for wanting him so blatantly. "Don't let us keep you."

"We'll get something," I said. "We've already gotten *something*. A few tracks."

A deer bellowed into the night. Another echoed him. "Poor prick," said Ethan.

I kept the thought to myself that the deer were an embodiment or emanation of Simon, calling to me, barking himself hoarse from some alp. I saved up that thought to tell him later, during the night we had planned in Paris. I also kept the thought to myself that the record was going to blaze up, phoenix-like, at the eleventh hour. I knew that this would happen, but I knew that saying it would seem like the worst sort of whistling in the dark, the witless confidence of the ingénue, the outsider. No one would trust me if I told them how beautiful it was going to be.

Instead, I said, "Ethan and I have been working on some new arrangements," which was a lie, but it wouldn't be by morning.

Ethan winked at me. He knew that meant that I had enough coke to get us through the night. He tugged on his ear, coughed, lit a cigarette. I missed Jonah – his trichotillomania, his socks, his bad breath, which smelled to me like concentration. I missed the missing Buddhists. But Ethan was almost strange enough, something of a eunuch vibe to him, and he was willing to stay up all night, every night, as long as it took, as long as I needed. He brought paper and pencils, nicely sharpened, to our sessions so that I might consider writing down the lyrics. He also brought extra erasers, schoolhouse-red rectangles. He gave me entirely nonseductive neck rubs at three in morning. To myself, I called him the River Boat Captain. I saved that to tell Simon, too.

"I will bring out the cheese," said Gigi, turning gracefully from the table to head toward the chateau, which, when lit up, looked like something out of an Advent calendar.

Ethan leaned back in his chair, cigarette between his teeth, stretching his big arms to take in the night. "Shove your negativity, Cleo. Music is love. And war."

A deer – the same one? – barked, barked again.

You might think from this exchange that we didn't like one another, but in fact the opposite was true: the seven of us had fallen deeply in love, which may have been part of the problem. I hadn't known any of them before, though some of them knew each other. They all knew *Whale;* they had seen me in concert. When we met at lunch in the garden the first day, the air was thick with unvoiced opinions, not all of them bad. The first thing we had agreed on was that we liked the chateau. It was small and gently dilapidated. Wasps lived in the rafters of the music room. Ethan was allergic to wasp stings; every day, he seemed to be risking his life for art, eyeing the rafters warily as we all worked, half expecting death to swoop down from the heavens. The walls were damp, we felt damp in our clothes, the furniture seemed sodden. The small, algae-infested pool, homeopathic, pushed the dampness away for a few hours in the afternoon, if it wasn't raining. Our days ambled around a small, circular track: get up from our damp beds, bread and coffee laid out by Gigi in the big kitchen, quiet midmorning time to stretch and read and smoke, lunch in the echoing dining room, trying to make music into the evening, often into the night, in the music room. Ethan and I, up after everyone else had gone to bed, trying things that didn't work, barking until morning in that vast room with the Persian carpets everywhere, all full of cigarette burns, stained, torn. The long, wavy windows onto the garden.

The magic had come on us slowly. It grew, binding us together, and then, all at once, after a few weeks, it set. The chateau became our submarine; we found one morning that we agreed on everything. Such as: we liked jam. We liked Nutella. We liked the mole-pocked bread man who came every other day. We liked the fireflies that lit the orchard at night. We liked the tan and white dog called La Loup and the cat called Farfalle. We liked to read aloud from a 1965 translation of Cesare Pavese poems that David had found in his room, where the flocked green wallpaper was peeling to reveal moldy, flocked red wallpaper. We liked to walk down the road in a straggling group to the village to get ice cream and cigarettes. We liked a few hits of ecstasy on Sunday afternoons. We didn't like the village church: we felt it had a stingy architecture, narrow and inward-looking. We liked the light on the water of the chateau's pool, because the algae made it thick, uncertain, murky, a primeval light, a dinosaur light. We liked Gigi for her irreverence, liked that she was Ethiopian, because we didn't understand Ethiopia; she was the only one who was local, so she was our link to the world that surrounded the chateau. We liked the way she propped one foot on her knee as she talked. We knew her given name couldn't be Gigi, and it was a point of honor never to ask her about it. We liked Ethan's broad cheekbones, how fat he was, how high his voice was, his faintly pointy ears. We liked David's endless tinkering with anything that had a dial. We liked Hubert's crankiness. We liked the way Cleo sketched us during dinner at the long table in the overgrown garden, reminding us that we existed now, just now, and that time was always passing. We understood that Jean would be ruined if he allowed himself to be taken: he was our unattainable star. We lived in the chateau as if we had always lived there. We were half in love with the terrifying, deathdealing wasps, lying in wait for Ethan and who knew who else, who knew what designs on us the wasps had? We were jealous of the deer, so untuned, so raw, so unabashed. We wished we could sound like the deer. We did lots and lots and lots of cocaine; it was our salt.

We liked to touch each other constantly. We buttoned one another's buttons, held one another's hands. Cleo's rosy complexion; the muscles of David's thighs; the waves and kinks of Gigi's hair; Hubert's prematurely arthritic knuckles; my strange voice that had recently become stranger still, more echoes and odd turnings (Ethan waved his big white hands and sent me down every dark alley of sound, scamper scamper Red Riding Hood); Jean's elegant, aloof cock; the dampness on our hands, our knees, our backs, the wetness of our hair after we'd braved the cloudy pool to touch the penumbra of the moody water spirit we'd named Nakimba; the chemical tang at the back of our throats; the jam on our fingers at breakfast; the smoke of our shared cigarettes – we were composed of that. *Bang Bang* was made of that.

But the one place the magic wasn't showing up was in the music. We couldn't quite seem to get that, us, onto *Bang Bang,* but that only made it more precious to us, the ineffable sound of our union. We pursued it relentlessly, like hunters, but we were getting tired, we found ourselves getting sleepy a lot, even with all the salt. The afternoons were growing warmer as summer thickened. The sound we could hear so well inside all our heads simultaneously – as if together we made up a radio tuned to our small area of the collective unconscious – was refusing to appear on the album. It was happening all the time, and everywhere, except on any known recording device, including a clunky old reel-to-reel that David had dug out of a closet and jury-rigged to the digital system in desperation. We were beginning to wonder if we existed; why couldn't we see ourselves, our gorgeous seven-headed love, in the music's mirror?

Two-thirty a.m. Ethan and I, cross-legged on the Persian carpet in the music room, roughly encircled by a few chairs and sofa cushions. Just outside this circle, several guitars of various sorts, an electronic keyboard, two flutes, a hot-pink electric violin, a drum machine, and Ethan's computer, on which there is a black-and-white picture of his mother taking a large horse over an intimidating jump. Even with the big windows open, it's hot, sticky. The carpet is scratchy. The deer must have gotten some or gone to bed, because they're quiet. I pick out notes on a guitar and Ethan nods, his big damp head down like a flower falling from its stem, his eyes closed. Over the past twenty or so nights, the lyrics, written in pencil, have piled up. The sheaf of paper rests beside us. "Come on," Ethan says softly, "come on come on come on come on, girl," and I try to follow the sound of his voice into the forest, over the jump. I try again. I try again. I try again. If you were, let us say, an angel or a bat hanging upside down in a corner of that vast room, what you would see would be a tall girl, too skinny, huddled over a guitar, nearly knee to knee with a large man who appears to be passing out. You would hear sequences of notes that are interesting, alluring, even beguiling, but, frustratingly, the tall girl keeps stopping the sequence just as it's getting started. She raps on the guitar, raps on her own forehead. The big man nods, eyes closed, smiles – apparently he's still awake. He kisses her on the forehead she just rapped.

"Come on, girl," he says softly. "Come on come on come on."

If you were an angel or a bat hanging upside down in a corner of that vast room, you might distract yourself for a while by listening to the music of the heat, but when you tuned back in, you would find the tall girl still sifting through beguiling sequences of notes. Some of these sequences sound familiar. Is it even the same night?

"It won't break," says the tall girl, putting the guitar down beside her. "How it worked before – it won't go. Goddamnit. Motherfuck. I feel like a retard."

The big man opens his eyes and sits up straight. "Anna, a lot of the folks I've worked with over the years have had a hard time with their second record. They can't go back, they can't go forward, they think they've got some kind of image to protect, they get caught in a loop. A lot of them die right here. Are you planning to die on me?"

"No."

"Then give it to me. Come on, girl."

What a joy it is to be able to rise up on one's wings in the currents neither the tall girl nor the big man can see. The tall girl squints, shakes her head. "Did you hear that?"

"I'm listening."

After another long day of false starts, wrong notes, and bad moods, Ethan, Gigi, and I went into the village for pizza and beer. Gigi drove the cheap little car, coaxing and prodding it over the serpentine, dusty roads. Gravel flew up past the half-open windows. "Shit," said Gigi. "We're going to get a flat, I know it. Fucking France." She downshifted and said something that sounded like "Shusha."

"I think we need some celestes," said Ethan. "I'm going to write my friend Nick."

"That's a fortune," said Gigi.

"What are celestes?" I asked sheepishly from the back seat. Ethan had perfect pitch, an astonishing memory for music, an incredible collection of vinyl, and was known to throw things at his lovers, who either ducked or left. He knew everybody.

Ethan explained, "It's a keyboard instrument with bells inside instead of mallets and strings. Very old. Very expensive." We jolted past a mechanic's garage. Inside, men in jumpsuits hovered over variously opened-up cars.

"I don't think the problem is a lack of celestes," I said, more crankily than I had intended. "The problem is that I suck." I was trying not to panic. I needed a line.

"The celeste tracks can be emailed," said Ethan in his vague, high tone that I always found strangely comforting. "Nick can send them from Iceland."

"Could be worth it, then. The label will pay, Anna. Throw your weight around." Gigi moved the car down another gear. "This fucking road! I'm hungry!"

"We're lost," I said.

"No, the village is right there, look," said Gigi.

"No, I mean the record." The weight of the thing we loved so much, our seven-headed anima, tipping into the murky pool. I grabbed for it once again, Orpheus-like. "We're just so lost, we can't figure it out. We're not going to be able to do it. We're fucked. We're totally fucked." A cold darkness licked the backs of my knees, moving up. The label was going to drop me for sure. I would never see the chateau again.

"Celestes," Ethan said with certainty, driving the darkness back toward my ankles. "Let's get those little olives on the pizza this time."

The village was nothing much – a bakery, the stingy church, a bar-*tabac,* a school, the pizza place. In the pizza place, the families having Friday-night dinner looked at us: fat, bald Ethan in his pointy black boots and his T-shirt with an amoeba drawn on it in felt marker; Gigi with her Modigliani Ethiopian face; and me, far too tall, clearly no one's wife, no one's mother, wearing a short, flowered, girlish cotton shift I'd found in my closet at the chateau – it didn't look right on me, but I knew it was meant for me somehow, it was lucky, and I wore it every-where. I had decided that Kurt Cobain had worn it once. The three of us instinctively drew together as we walked to our ta-ble, then huddled over a single, shared menu.

"Anchovies," said Gigi.

"Onions," I said.

"Those little wrinkled olives," Ethan said, pronouncing the *t*'s, the *k*'s, and the *s*'s with peculiar emphasis and precision; it was almost musical. He passed me the vial under the table, and I charged into the bathroom with it. There was hardly any left. A pinch, a sniff. I returned to the table well salted, but not ex-actly satisfied. I passed Ethan the empty vial.

"Jesus, Anna."

The pizza place smelled of olive oil, coffee, vinegar, and car exhaust from the road outside. The families were scrubbed, weeknight casual, with wine on their tables; already finished eating, the kids, bored, slumped in chairs or hovered itchily around the adults. A muscular teenage boy in a white T-shirt and white apron folded neatly over his jeans came to the table to take our order, which Gigi gave in what sounded to me like bossy French.

"It's getting bad," said Ethan.

"Ride it out," said Gigi, tapping Ethan's knuckles, then holding his hand. He gripped hers in return in his meaty one, tightly, wincing. None of us understood Ethan's weather, but we respected it. We thought the wasps were his familiars, that something had happened there, a history. He denied it, but that buzzing when he was near: we had our suspicions. Only some of us had familiars – Gigi's was La Loup, the tan and white dog; Jean's were the fireflies; Cleo said she had one, but wouldn't say what it was, leaving us to wonder if she was bluff-ing, which would be like her, the minx. I didn't have one, and I yearned for one, or the chutzpah to lie about it. Shouldn't I, as ostensibly the center of this group, have my own familiar? Maybe that was the problem. Maybe that was why we couldn't get the sound to show up on tape. My familiar was missing. I tried to imagine my familiar – fur, fins, feathers? Nothing came through. I sneezed and wondered what I might have lost by sneezing.

A round-faced woman with glasses at a nearby table stared at Gigi and Ethan, still holding hands. They looked as if they were praying together, or as if Ethan was a mental patient and Gigi was his minder, taking him out on a day pass. The woman looked at me, plainly curious. Why wasn't I praying with them? Was Ethan my crazy brother? My husband, hopelessly estranged from me by insanity? I shrugged and smiled at the woman, causing her to drop her gaze to her salad, resume her conversation with a thin-faced man, a Jack Sprat in a black blazer. They sat on the same side of their table and had the innate reserve of French married people. I half hoped they couldn't see the magic on us, half hoped they could. I flexed my fingers, wiggled my toes in my sandals.

We picked at the pizza. There was food around all the time, but we never seemed to gain weight. That was the magic, too. Gigi poured the wine. The other two looked haggard, as if they had spent the past five weeks walking from Paris to here. The darkness rose again, swishing, to my calves. I wanted another line, but there was no more, no more.

"Do you think we need to make another offering to Nakimba?" I asked Gigi.

She shook her head, looking grave. "Won't work."

Ethan harrumphed.

"We barely have three tracks down, and we only have a week left," I said. "Four days, actually. Then Sparrow is coming in."

"He owes money everywhere," said Gigi, who hardly liked anyone, except us. "I'm amazed Elaine is letting him come back." Elaine, was the owner of the chateau; she had been a lover of Jim Morrison's when he recorded there, and was rumored to have some of his come in a little stoppered vial in a safe-deposit box in Paris. Elaine, who was seventy-two, was in Moscow, where she always summered.

"Listen," said Ethan.

We tilted our heads. From far away, the deer were barking.

"It's like they have amplifiers," I said. "How do they do that?"

"They're motivated," Gigi said, eating her pizza with a fork and knife, like all the families in the restaurant.

"Are you saying we're not? Don't we work all the time? Goddamn, Gigi. And why can't we try Nakimba? It worked before. You're being really negative."

Gigi narrowed her eyes. "*Ça suffit,* Anna."

I drummed my fingers on the table. "I might be freaking out. I think I am freaking out. I'm freaking out. This pizza tastes weird. Is it cold in here? Since when does France do air-conditioning? My throat is seizing."

Ethan folded his hands on top of his bald head and closed his eyes. "Shhhh," he said. Jack Sprat's wife frowned in our direction. Gigi and I waited. After several minutes, Ethan opened his eyes and blinked rapidly several times. "I just had a dream," he said. He rubbed his cheekbones. "God, I really need to sleep. Or wake up." He gave me a stern look. "Work tonight?"

"I'm not sure there's a point to that."

Gigi's expression was grave as well. "*L'addition,*" she said brusquely to the teenage boy in the apron, who was pretending not to hover near our table, eavesdropping, trying to figure out what we were. "Let's go," she said, putting down her knife and fork. "We have to go."

She barreled back over the dark, serpentine roads, tight-faced and silent, her hair fastened in a knot at her neck with a rubber band, Ethan bouncing in the seat next to her as if he had taken ill and we were driving him to the hospital. Maybe we *were* driving him to the hospital, or should be, I had no idea, as I ate a bit of bread I'd taken from our bread basket on the way out of the pizza place. I wasn't hungry, but I knew that eating was important. The cheap little car jolted, jounced; towels and paperbacks and random sandals littered the dusty wells behind the front seat. It smelled like wet dog and chlorine and old, baked-in red wine. I lay down, my feet on the window opposite, wondering about Gigi, who her people were. The moon was up, chasing the car as it sped along. I eyed it between my feet, thinking that I really didn't know anyone at the chateau, and how could it be that you could love so deeply without actually knowing who people were? Or was love *more* possible like this, was our love purer, cleaner? Meeting stripped of the familiar. Carrying the clothes we came with, our taste, not much more. I got so lost in the beauty of that thought, lying on my back, admiring the moon in my toes, that I didn't notice when Gigi turned left instead of right, heading away from the chateau.

We came to a stop by the side of the road. "Get out of the car," ordered Gigi, and for a moment I thought she was going to leave us there and speed away, because we had so obviously failed. And not only failed to make the record; we had all failed in some larger, more spiritual sense. I had failed to make the most important, the most beautiful thing in the world appear. If Gigi had pulled out a gun and shot me in the head right then, I wouldn't have blamed her. I scurried out of the car.

Gigi got out, too, slamming the driver's side door. Ethan lumbered up and out, looking like a bear reluctantly extricating himself from a clown car. Marching ahead of us along the side of the road, Gigi flipped open her cell phone and muttered something in a terse tone I couldn't make out.

"Come," she said to us. "I'm taking you somewhere I know. The others are meeting us there."

We followed. Few cars passed. The moon was watching us like a wary white animal. Now I was really hungry, but there was nothing to eat, my pockets were empty. I craved cream, butter, sugar, and milk. Around us, on both sides of the road, were fields with bare stalks. Fallow, nothing to eat there. In the distance were the lights of the little village.

Gigi turned and set off across the uneven surface of the fallow field, her long legs scissoring under her ankle-length skirt. The wavy field was so dark that she looked as if she were walking on a body of water. She kicked off her sandals and scooped them into one hand. Ethan took off his boots, left them in the dirt, and began taking umbrella steps behind Gigi, his meaty arms outstretched, his big broad face gleaming in the moonlight, humming. This was what he must have been like as a child, umbrella-stepping by himself through his family's enormous house; they were rich, violent people. Lagging behind, I slipped off my sandals as well. The dirt under my feet was cool and dry, crumbly soft. I liked it, it felt right. I hiked up my shift, squatted, pushed my underwear aside, and peed in the dirt. My pee smelled strong. Ahead of me, determined Gigi and Ethan, with his looping umbrella steps, looked like gleaners scanning the field for windfalls, using some eccentric system of their own. The night around us was very quiet. I loved Gigi and Ethan so much. I was still terribly hungry.

I ran to catch up with them, grabbed one of Ethan's hands in mine, and then stretched, stretched to reach Gigi, who was weeping. I kissed her wet face, held it in my hands. "What is it?" I asked her. "Oh, what is it? What's wrong?" Her eyes were turned down, her mouth was turned down, like a mask of sadness.

"You will leave me here," she said softly. "You will finish and leave. And I think it's me. I think I'm the one stopping it, so you can never leave, but I have to fix it. I'm ruining everything with my clinging. I'm ruining your record. I am going to fix it."

"No," I said, kissing and kissing her long, brown face. "No, no. It's me, *I'm* ruining it." Ethan stood silently, his hand loose in mine, his head bent; I wondered if he had fallen asleep again, if he was dreaming standing up, like a horse. "It's all my fault," I said. Gigi's tears were salty on my lips. I hugged her tightly until she stopped crying, and then the three of us resumed walking again, slowly, Ethan and I each holding one of Gigi's hands.

She led us into a little wood. From within the wood, half-lit faces emerged, then bodies: Jean, David, Cleo, Hubert. Jean, barefoot and naked from the waist up, tilted out lines of cocaine onto the flat underside of his forearm, held it perfectly still as each of us in turn bent forward. When I bent to it, his forearm smelled of coke and lavender. Last, he tilted out a fat line for himself, bent his head to his own arm, as if inhaling intoxicating fragments of himself mixed with us. Fortified, we walked on, Gigi in the lead. Cleo walked next to me, breathing hard. It occurred to me that she might commit murder one day. David looked serious; he had brought a flashlight and was wearing a sturdy jacket and hiking boots. I wondered if he knew something we didn't. Hubert, bringing up the rear, tripped, swore. Calmness, a greater calm than I had felt in days, enveloped me. It was as if all the darkness was outside now, leaving me light-filled, expectant. I was my own paper lantern. My hands tingled. I knew we could walk together forever like this, that our footsteps would make a music of their own, a songline.

"Stop," said Gigi at the edge of a clearing.

We stopped.

"He is coming," said Gigi. "Shhh."

Hushed, we jostled one another in the shadows, shoulder to shoulder, in an almost imperceptible rhythm. Next to me, Cleo was so distinct, sharp as the smell of lemon. David, standing next to her on the other side, turned off his flashlight. Jean crouched in the dirt, the glorious wings of his back muscles expanding. Gigi, gatekeeper and prisoner of the chateau, stood very still. I felt, with a kind of ecstasy, the weight of the seven of us, a weight that simultaneously, paradoxically, pulled me under and buoyed me up.

"What are we doing?" said Cleo, not really whispering.

"We are waiting for the deer. He will bring his music to us."

"Huh," said Cleo, sitting down in the dirt. She looked like a woman who had turned into a tree stump, a gnarl of skepticism.

And then the deer, some deer, called out. Somewhere nearby, a deer let out his extraordinarily loud, unearthly, desperate sound – we called it barking, but it was nothing like a dog bark, it was more like a guttural, sandpapered lowing – his yodel, his deepest entreaty to . . . whom? Who was listening for him in the night? In agony, he made his noise. Pushing, pulling. *Come to me.* We could imagine the curve of his shoulder blades, strong as sickles. His hooves planted in the dirt as he made his noise of awful yearning. Gigi began to cry. Jean lowered his head. Cleo looked up. Silently, we were calling to the deer as he called aloud to his mate. (We were so high.) He lowed, entreated. I wished that I could get the contours of the deer's emotion onto the album, hooves on the ground, the odor of the night. And blood. Blood, somewhere.

Ethan put his hands up, palms out, to the sound.

The clearing, however, remained empty. We waited. We waited longer.

"Look," said Gigi, wet-faced, her long skirt flat against her legs. "The sky." It was lightening, but the light was new, diffuse, evenly distributed, so that the wood was incandescent, as if the silver luminosity was emanating from within the earth, the trees, the leaves, rather than coming from above. A cool, early-morning wind was picking up. Still, the clearing remained empty.

We sat down in the dirt, one by one, all becoming tree stumps, except for Ethan, who remained standing, his head bent, palms up. Gigi, Cleo, and I sat back to back to back, the crowns of our heads touching. In the thinning dark, we shivered. Jean and David stood up, gathered some loose leaves and twigs, dug a shallow hole in the dirt, and, with a lighter Hubert pulled from his pocket, tried to light the leaves and twigs on fire. The little heap lit, smoldered, went out.

The absent deer called out. And then I knew it, I saw it, I heard it, I knew that we had all heard it: the right notes, the place where *Bang Bang* needed to go. It was so obvious, how had we missed it? That call of the absent deer, some absent deer – that's why we were here, why we had ended up at this place, at this moment, in this way. It was what the deer we couldn't see had gathered us together to show us, what all the deer had been trying to tell us for weeks, calling and calling until we heard them. Gratitude warmed me to my fingertips.

"Oh," I said. "Oh, right. That's it. Ethan, that's it. Isn't it?"

"It is, Anna," he said.

"Cleo, David – that's it. He's not here. You know?"

They nodded.

"Yes," said Gigi. "He's not here."

"I love you," I said. "I love you all so much."

Jean poured more coke on his forearm and snorted it off. Ethan traced a figure eight in the dirt with his fat, bare toe. Cleo had moved to sit on a rock, sketching with a stub of pencil on a small, torn piece of paper. David smiled beatifically. "We love you, too, Anna." The skin on my arms, my chest, goose-pimpled. We remained there for a while, but the deer didn't call out again. The clearing remained empty.

But in that emptiness, it was now obvious, was the answer. We had had it upside down, or inside out. *Bang Bang* wouldn't be the deer, but the *absence* of the mighty deer, the displaced air where the virile, lonely deer hovered just beneath the surface, just out of sight, just beyond the shadow line of the clearing. I grabbed Gigi's hand and squeezed it. I blessed the deer for luring us here to show us the reflection of its absence playing across our exhausted faces, like a half-erased cave paint-

ing. And now that deer was quiet, gone. He had departed when
we weren't listening, leaving us humans, us mortals, alone as
the forest silvered into day. We walked out in single file, our
minds stilled, empty and full at once, infused with desire for
the absent deer who was himself infused with desire for yet
another absent deer. An infinite line of longed-for, absent deer,
receding into the horizon. That was what *Bang Bang* had to be.
Not the awkward half-note of *Whale,* but this echo of desire
that was also a love call, a shout into the night. We needed a
tuba.

"Ethan." Breathless, I caught up to him. "Ethan, can we get
a brass band out here? Today. We need it today."

"Of course," he said.

The chateau's gates closed behind me a few days later. I have
never been back or seen any of them again. The label dropped
me after *Bang Bang* tanked. I sat on my wheeled suitcase with
the precious tape inside, waiting for the car that was going
to take me to the train station. I turned around to look, but I
didn't see much—long windows, stone front steps; it was as
if the chateau were sinking beneath the waves again. Everyone else was inside eating breakfast and smoking, they were
leaving later that day, at different times, but I didn't miss them
yet. Jam kisses streaked my cheek. I hummed the last track,
which we had finished at four that morning. The brass band
from Toulouse was phenomenal. The absent deer had left its
hoofprints all over the tracks. I couldn't wait to play them for
Simon in Paris, although, as it turned out, he couldn't meet me.
Complications. But I didn't know that yet. All I knew was that
the record was good. It was so good.

My Father and I in the Musée de l'Orangerie

"DAMN, I HATE Monet," said my father, bathed in the Orangerie's delicate gray and silver light. "Isn't that terrible? Aren't I a savage?" Inside the museum there are two oval rooms, making it seem as if you've walked into an enormous egg. Wrapped around the curved walls of these rooms is Monet's encompassing *Water Lilies*. The blurry, dimensional layers of green and deep pink and turquoise curve as well, yielding to what seems to be a deeper weight beneath the surface, pulling it backward into time. Skylights, capped by milky-white glass, shed a beneficent, unearthly light. The Louvre rules the Tuileries, but here, tucked into a corner of that pebble-filled garden, is this small reverie of water, flowers, and opaque, luminous sky. If the Louvre is History, this is a far more personal structure – a dream, an elegy, a temple of obsession. The Orangerie has only one, insistent, exquisite thought that never changes.

This is what my father and I did together: we looked at art. I could have written, *My Father and I, in the Prado* or *My Father and I, at the Met* or *My Father and I, in a Gallery off the Highway Near Wellfleet* or *My Father and I, at the Corcoran* or *My Father and I, Reading* The Runaway Bunny. My father and I, looking together, everywhere. Let this one stand for all of them. I was twenty-two, and nothing much had happened to me yet. I was living in Paris for the summer, for no reason, on a small loan from my mother that wouldn't last much past September. I wrote songs constantly, covering page after page of my notebooks with them. They were very wordy songs. I picked out chords on my guitar until my fingers bled, then callused. I listened to everything on my Discman, stopping the CDs every few bars to get the chord, hear the sound. I sang along with my Discman, loudly, on the bus and in the metro and when I was alone at night in my room at the student hostel, until my neighbor pounded on the wall we shared. I smoked cigarettes, though I didn't want to.

By then, I towered over my crooked father; my red hair cascaded in an electrocuted free-for-all nearly to my ass; I was too thin, which made my jaw look larger, my eye sockets prominent. Men looked at me on the street, then looked again, unsure of what they were seeing: babe or freak? I could wear the shortest skirts, because my legs were so long and thin, but my feet were big, my knuckles were big, my eye sockets were pronounced. I was so nervous that I hardly ate, and I was always hungry, hungry for everything: I wanted to put all of it, every person, every city, every sound, every sight, in my mouth. I was avid, unsteady, jumpy. The men, and sometimes the women, who looked at me on the street looked again, squinting. I knew what they saw – that odd knowingness in my expression. I had seen it in the mirror myself. Sometimes it made them want me. Sometimes it did the opposite. I couldn't predict which way it would go, and so I was always curious, always gambling.

"Yes," I said to my father in the Orangerie. "You are a total savage. Come on. Don't you think these are pretty amazing? The depth, the light?"

"I don't know, Annie." He held out his hands to the paintings, palms out. His hands were scarred; the arthritis had started to fold his fingertips. "They feel so . . . they make me itch." He shook his head hard, like a dog shaking water out of his ears. "And this room. I feel like I'm in a tomb. Or a department store." He smiled his bright smile, showing his crooked teeth. He glanced up at the skylight. "Maybe if we could pop that off."

I sat down on a bench, sliding my sandal half off one foot. "No," I said. "You're wrong. You just don't like nature. You don't like nature poetry, nature writing, nature painting. You think it's all sentimental."

My father had inadvertently – I think it was inadvertently—centered himself amid the *Water Lilies*. It was funny, as if someone had pasted a cutout figure, a Polaroid, on top of the famous murals. I smiled. His hair was already gray, but trimmed short. He was wearing jeans, a black T-shirt, and black canvas high-tops. A battered brown leather jacket, his fists balled in the pockets. His always fragile beauty was turning into something different: a well-proportioned plainness, a visual decency, a rectilinearity. As if, having once been a soaring, bright-plumaged bird, or a flock of them, perched on the tops and ledges of buildings, he was now resolving into a simple box. His eyes were still that saturated blue, his gaze still restless. I could feel his keen disappointment in Monet, his sense that Monet wasn't giving him what he came for, what he needed. He didn't look at art so much as ransack it, turn it upside down and inside out, study its seams to see how it was made. Art never bored him, it only failed him. The *Water Lilies,* curving before and behind him, hovered in their pinks and endless shades of green, exuding so many notes of light that I wanted to put my hands over my ears. I wondered if I could write that, a set of songs inspired by the *Water Lilies*. Later on, when my father had limped off to meet his old Paris friends, the ones he'd been with in the collective, I would start. I didn't care what he thought.

His expression turned stern. "You are totally wrong, Annie. I came up in nature. I know what it is. It's wrong to take all the weight out of it like this, it's like pornography. I feel like I'm looking at a huge pair of fake sugared tits." He cupped his arms out in front of him, fingers spread. A woman with headphones standing nearby frowned, shook her head, raised a finger to her lips.

My father leaned forward, stage-whispering. "He made it too easy on people. It's pandering. If I ever do that, shoot me."

I laughed in spite of myself. "You were the one who wanted to come here. We could have gone to the Louvre."

He straightened up, sober. "No, not today."

"Why not?" I was admiring my own bare foot, flexing and pointing it. There was a Portuguese boy at the youth hostel who said he'd take me to a party in Montmartre. He had long arms, a tough and sensual mouth. We were going to meet at ten. I imagined singing my first *Water Lilies* song for him, the pleasure in his face. He would be amazed.

Now it was my father's turn to turn a small smile at me, though I didn't know why. He seemed to be smiling from very far away. "I couldn't stand it," he said.

"God, you're so egotistical." Cold-hearted girl I was, twirling my long, bare foot in the diffuse light of the Orangerie. I had painted the nail of my left big toe hot pink. "What, do you have to be Leonardo da Vinci?"

He passed a hand over his face. "I'm thirsty. Let's go outside."

"You go ahead. I want to stay a little longer." I was annoyed with him, but I also truly did want to stay. There was a sound in those colors. I wanted to hum it very softly, alone, and especially not in front of him. I knew what he thought of pretty things.

"Okay, Annie. I won't be far. Come when you're ready." He limped out, passing into the next oval, looking, as he receded, shorter and smaller, like a boy walking into a field of flowers. I turned back to the painting and looked for a long time. The notes were sinuous. I wrote them down as best I could, since I didn't read music very well, in my journal.

When I stepped outside the museum and walked down one of the long allées of tawny pebbles, the sky had clouded up. Drops of rain were falling. The park looked nearly deserted. A small black dog, red leash trailing, barked and ran in circles, chased by a man in a white trenchcoat, who finally caught the dog, gathering the animal in his arms and kissing its furry head. The dog wiggled with joy. I felt the wiggle, still half entranced by the water lilies, that milky light, the serenity of the air inside the museum, the beginning of my song, the Portuguese boy who was going to take me to Montmartre.

I couldn't spot my father at first in any of the outdoor café stands that dotted the park. So many aluminum folding chairs triangled open, red umbrellas, low-hanging roofs over the café counters. I crunched over the pebbles, getting rained on; my bare arms were cold. The silver chairs all seemed to be empty. I felt a terrible loneliness, though he would be back at the hotel eventually, I reminded myself. Maybe he was there already. I could take a taxi. I walked across the park toward the Louvre, getting wetter and colder, then turned around and headed back. At last I saw his special shoe, his blue-jeaned leg — he was drawing in his little notebook at a sheltered table close to the Orangerie, his bad leg propped up, chatting to the barman at the same time. The overhang had obscured him. The barman was laughing as I approached, and then that light, the light I liked so much, came into his eyes when he saw me.

"*Ah, oui, c'est ça,*" my father was saying in his Midwest-accented French, half a glass of red wine in front of him on the small table. He turned his head as I crunched damply toward him. "*Ma fille,*" he said proudly to the barman. "*Elle est une chanteuse.*"

"Not yet." I blushed. "*Pas encore.*"

The barman smiled, showing yellow teeth. "But soon, *bien sûr*. Very soon, *mademoiselle.*"

"Maybe." I sat down next to my father and took his hand. "What are you drawing?"

His notebook was thick with pasted-in bits of newspaper and the glossy paper of magazines and postcards, various ticket stubs that must have had some meaning to him, cut-up photographs; the pages were scribbled on, some warped from paint or watercolor. Over his shoulder I could see his crabbed handwriting, a page of closely scrawled numbers. He turned the page. In the center of the next page was a diagram of a five-story building that looked institutional, with five horizontal rows of narrow windows and a flat roof. In front of the building was a fence with coils of barbed wire on top. At the base of the fence, a peaked guardhouse. Rain pattered on the overhang above us.

"Are you planning, like, a prison break?" I said.

"Don't be smart. I've never done a prison—"

"Dad, they're not going to let you cut up a *prison*." The barman, unasked, brought me my own glass of red wine, filled to the top.

"No, not a working prison. But there's an abandoned one in Texas I read about. Way out. I'm thinking of getting a crew together, going out there, seeing what we can do. Just have to find someone to pay for it." He sighed, rubbed his eyes, checked his watch. From his jeans pocket he pulled out two pills, one white, one pink, which he washed down with the rest of his wine. "Hope these don't turn out to give you brain cancer," he said with a laugh.

"But they help, right?"

"Like water wings in the ocean." He winked. "Look at this, Annie, this would be something else."

Sitting close to him at the little table, I could smell the wine on his breath, a hint of garlic from our long lunch earlier in the day. His bent fingers rested on the notebook page, holding it open for me to see and approve, a worn rubber band around his wrist. The nail on his left pinkie was gone, leaving that finger permanently blind. The skin of his neck was ropy, weatherbeaten. He sat up very straight because of the rod in his back that the doctors put there after the accident in Rome. I knew he had at least two girlfriends, one in New York and another in Boston, both younger than him. My mother had already remarried, already settled into her pretty house in Asbury Park with her round-bellied potter. What did the two girlfriends I knew about, not to mention whomever I didn't know about, think when he showed them his prison diagram, the barbed wire coiling in soft charcoal loops across the page? Did he show them at all? Did they understand how long it had been since he did anything like this?

"Can I go with you?"

He closed the notebook, rubber-banded it. "No," he said. Then, "Honey, didn't you and your sister have enough of that, being dragged from pillar to post? If it even happens, which could be years from now, it's going to be long, hot, boring work."

I gulped my wine. "I wouldn't be bored. I was never bored."

"Well." He shook his head. "We'll see. Look at that rain. It's really coming down." It was – rattling the tawny pebbles, splashing in the fountains, silvering the air almost to the shade of the air inside the Orangerie. Above the noise of the rain came a loud, whooshing sound, shouts.

"*Qu'est-ce que c'est?*" I asked the barman.

"*C'est la Tour de France,*" he replied. "*Les cyclistes.*" He turned on the radio. Pop music bounced out.

"Oh, I love this one," I said, singing along.

My father stood up, leaned outside the overhang. "Annie, come look, you can just see all the wheels."

The barman smiled. I inclined my head, letting my hair fall over my face. Was it my hair, my eyes? "Later. I'm listening."

My father turned back to me. "Later? There is no later. It's going past now."

I shrugged. "Next year, then."

The barman held my eye as he turned up the radio. The sound of the rain and the sound of the wheels disappeared into the music. My father held out his hand to me, to come look.

Rome, the First Return

COMING BACK TO Simon, I knew him fully for the first time. The proper order of things; the return. As if it had been one long, continuous night subtending the year since I had met him, and now we were simply waking up together the next day, telling each other our lives. He came to the shows; I was opening for TV on the Radio, enjoying the last ripples of *Whale*'s wake, waiting for the next bit of sonic bricolage to make itself known to me. After the shows, we returned to the room with the long, ornate drapes, the place that had become so important, the place where it tilted. We ordered up a late dinner; he often insisted on champagne, which I found touching – a cliché, and a sign of how little of this there was in his life. He had a lot to say about the music, which was a revelation to him. I brought him my glamorous sweat, my boho childhood, my eccentric education. I showed him my bruised arms, which he kissed. He showed me the seams in himself, the ragged gap between the outward order of his conventional life and the inner chaos, the nightmares, dreams of Israeli soldiers coming to take him, his children, his wife. He was not the cosmopolitan, discerning man he seemed: inside, he was still at war, still a skinny, blade-faced teenager throwing stones at the tanks during the first intifada. He had unpredictable periods of melancholy. He worked like a madman, always had. There were other things he wanted to build, fluid structures for refugees using inexpensive building materials, but he had important commissions, he had a family to support. So. The tether. I loved the irregular lines of his face. His nose that looked as if it had been pushed slightly to one side. His abashed vanity. *This shirt?* He would say to me. *Or this one?* Both shirts, impeccable. Gorgeous cuffs, like wings. His desire to dress well for me, his insecurity about *making a fool of myself at this age. I have fallen in love with a rock-and-roll star, am I ridiculous?* You're the furthest thing from ridiculous, I said, lying in bed watching him scrutinize the shirts, one with the subtlest of stripes, the other with the subtlest of tiny dots. And I'm not a star. I've made exactly one record that a few people liked. And it wasn't really rock-and-roll. And it didn't make any money.

I am wild for you, he said, tossing the shirts to the floor. *I can't explain it.* I crawled on top of him, cradled his face in my hands. Jesus Christ, I said. It's you. The sense of him: harbor, boat, wind. As if my long legs were trailing in the water under the boat as I braced myself on his hands. I woke up on the second night and wasn't sure where I was until I heard a shout in Italian from the street below. In the dark, I felt his hand with the wedding ring on it; I loved it that he didn't bother with the lie of taking it off. And the vulnerability of that, I thought: to be married, who would dare it? It was more foreign to me than Lebanon. His belly against my back, His arm heavy on my waist. He snored. He was an exile, a seeker, but he was also a good Lebanese husband, with a wry, strong-faced Lebanese wife, the two of them marooned in Switzerland. The sheer faith of it, like the impeccable shirts and French cuffs. It made me want to cry for them.

On the third night, late, naked, eating the last of the tiramisù in its silver dish, he said, "Let's tell one another a secret."

"All right. Okay." I tried to think of one. "I'm not sure I have any big secrets. You go first."

"I killed a man," he said. "He was going to kill me, I had to kill him. He was a soldier. But you're never the same after that. That's why they sent me to that horrible boarding school in Wales for the next generation of imperialists, the place where Nils and I met." He set the empty silver dish on the nightstand and lay down with me.

I traced his irregular face in the dark. "Are you telling me the truth?"

"Yes. Anna. It was a war. People die. But tell me – you must have a secret."

"No," I lied. I told myself that it would be wrong, it would be manipulative, to tell him then, there. It would seem like I wanted something. I shook my head.

He kissed my palm. "Then I am your first secret."

"My second, actually," I said, but he didn't ask me to explain.

"They hate us in Switzerland, of course," Simon told me the next evening, our last few hours, as we walked through the Piazza del Popolo. "They're terrible racists. I've always wanted to live in New York, you know?" Shy glance at me, abashed again. "Well." He shrugged. "I have a business, I have children in school. So."

"But you could visit."

"Maybe. Yes. I could visit." Around us, people were launching those funny, whirling, neon-lit toy spaceships into the sky, catching them again. He stopped and kissed me hard, the kiss – though I didn't know it then – of a man who knows he will never visit. We must have looked an odd couple, the older, swarthy, tense-looking man in the impeccable shirt and cream-colored suit jacket, the younger (though not so young, at thirty-four, not really) woman in American jeans and a T-shirt, all elbows and boot heels; we could only have been illicit lovers. Nothing about us matched; we were the wrong height for each other; I looked more like a roadie than the mistress of a man who worked day and night building sprawling, angular, tastefully modernist office buildings in Switzerland and was subject to inexplicable pains in his stomach, his head, his back, a man who dreamed nightly that he was at war. I didn't care. And I didn't think of myself as Simon's mistress; I thought of myself as his opportunity to be free, to be away from the flying bullets, even if only in bursts like this. I was, after all, rich in freedom, it was my dowry and my legacy, I had it to spare. I ran my hand under the collar of that expensive linen suit jacket, the one that did, in fact, make him look ten years older than he was. I cupped his head behind his ears, my fingers in his soft, graying hair. I kissed him back, kissed him again. He was mine. I heard the opening notes of *Bang Bang* in my head, it began right then. It was my record for Simon, to give him back the world in peacetime, its most tender and private spaces. Little neon spaceships whirled upward everywhere. He left on the late train that night.

Berlin

IT'S BOILING HOT in Berlin. Our large, fashionable hotel, which looks a little like a bank, is air-conditioned, with cool marble columns and floors, but everywhere else it is oppressively, apocalyptically hot. The pretty café where we eat lunch is hot inside and out; the boutique next door that sells cute dresses is hot; our hands and feet are hot. At lunch, Zach's head shines, reddens. Boone is flushed. Alicia, pushing salad around on her plate, is even paler than usual. She whispers in my ear, "Do you have a tampon? God, I feel like hell." I dig in my bag, fish one out, pass it to her. Even the plastic wrapping on the tiny object feels hot. A misery: cramps in this heat. Alicia pulls her platinum hair off her neck, puffs out her cheeks. The waiter leans against the bar nearby; the back of his neck is red.

"How's the house?" I ask. The show is tomorrow night.

Boone shakes his head. "About two-thirds sold. I think it's just too fucking hot. Been like this for weeks. Everyone's worn out. People in Russia have died from it, for God's sake." His iPhone tweets, purrs, dings every minute or so, as if trying different, alluring ways to get his attention, but he doesn't answer it. "You're a bad influence," he says to me. "Next thing you know I'll be turning it off. Suicide by iPhone power button."

Tom raises a finger to the waiter, who nods and brings over another beer. Purelling his hands, his wrists, Tom says, "Boone, did the runner bring the laundry back yet?" He yawns in the heat, drinks his beer. "Shit."

"I tweeted the show," says Zach. "I commanded the fans to represent."

I smile as if I believe that this will do any good. The last time I was in Berlin, it was early spring; the deep cold still lingered in the air. It was, what? Six years ago. No, five. Jim and I came for a long weekend, a super-cultish band from Serbia he wanted to hear, an extravagance. He was six months clean and sober, skinned, fresh as a baby. We ate a lot of vegetables together, and I didn't think about cocaine anymore, either, which was a good thing. *Bang Bang* had taught me that it wasn't magic after all. Jim was seeing everything again, filled with a gratitude and wonder that bored me a little. We went to a lot of museums and stayed in an expensive hotel. I also felt protective of him, proud of him; he was having trouble with his teeth — we had to call the dentist back home, and this made me feel terribly married. I was proud of that, too, proud of our self-conscious sex in the luscious hotel bed. My old man, down to the bad teeth. Our very bones the obligation of the other. Now, though, I am relieved to be free of him, his frequent, pointed observations about the general bad faith of the entire world.

"Right on," I say to Zach, the scrupulous tweeter.

I order a cookie and the red-necked waiter brings it, enormous and wilting, on a plate, with a napkin and a fork. This makes me stupidly happy, and I eat the whole thing and immediately feel ill, but still happy.

"Tom, you have to do some tweeting, too. Alicia."

Tom laughs. "I'm spending the afternoon sleeping and drinking, man."

Alicia flaps a pale hand at Zach. "My German friends don't go to shows."

Zach looks wounded. "What the fuck?"

Boone nudges me. *Sotto voce,* he says, "Want to go hang out with Billy Q? He's in Mitte with some people. This is bumming me out."

We leave the others and get a taxi; it is hot in the taxi. Boone, flushed, looks even younger, like a college soccer player fresh off the field. "Where did you grow up?" I ask.

"Me? Los Angeles. Hollywood – the cruddy part." He smiles, seems to blush in his flush. "My mom worked on *The Price Is Right*. Still does."

"And your dad?"

"C.P.A. Comb-over." He winks. "But both so sweet. They're the sweetest people ever."

"Do you have siblings?"

"You're funny today. Yeah – twin sisters. Both married, with kids. Turn right," he says to the cab driver. "*Danke*."

"Were you lonely?"

Boone lowers his gaze. "Yes." He flicks his gaze back up at me. "Were you?"

"No. No, I wasn't. Not like that. Strange."

"What?"

"I never thought of it that way before."

"Here!"

The cab jolts to a stop on a smallish street. Boone thrusts some euros at the driver, then waves, but I can't see anyone he's waving to. He leaps out of the cab and I follow; we hurry across the street toward a silver van with its side door open. A face – male, long, lined – leans out of the van. "Yo."

We get into the van; it is hot inside. Boone clambers into the far back seat. There are two women in the front, next to the driver, and two young men and an older woman with a head-set on in the back. In one penumbral corner sits Billy Q, in a bonnet and a long black coat, not unlike the long black coats Hassidic men wear; it might even be one of those coats. White cuffs emerge from the sleeves of the coat. Billy's pants are yellow, with large, iridescent-yellow squares affixed to them. His alligator shoes are pink. "Love," says Billy, kissing me on both cheeks. "Do you want to be in our movie?"

The man with the long, lined face, whose hair is thick and white and reaches to his shoulders, slides the heavy door shut. "Let's go," he says to the driver, a heavyset man with beefy arms. "Jesus, turn on the a/c."

"What's the movie about?"

"It's complicated," says Billy.

"I love your movies," Boone says from the back. "Have you ever seen his movies, Anna?"

"Well, no —"

"They stream on the Internet. Incredible." Boone taps on his iPhone. "Wait, I'll show you one." He hands the phone over the seat. On the small rectangle, a creature flows by that looks something like a gryphon, something like a mermaid, something like a sea serpent; letters, seemingly handwritten in crayon, spell out "Beatrice" over this chimera. There might be music, but I can't hear it over the ambient noise of the van. Something blue, something gold, a shadow on a lawn in black and white. It is beautiful, and though it flashes by quickly, I sense that it's intensely personal, chosen, curated even, from some private storehouse of Billy's memory. What is in Billy's memory?

"Gorgeous," I say.

"They're all I want to do anymore," says Billy. He pulls on his bonnet strings. "I love this thing. An artist in Warsaw made it for me." As my eyes adjust to the gloom, I notice that the bonnet has a pattern pricked out in holes on it, like a constellation, though it isn't any constellation that I know. The bonnet appears to be made out of rubber. "Hey, I'm bringing some friends to your show tomorrow night, is that okay?"

Boone snorts. "No."

The others in the van laugh. The older woman with the headset smiles at the laughing faces, listening to whatever she's listening to inside her head. We are driving through a part of Berlin I have never seen, a scrubby, scrappy, nowhere strip of empty parking lots and Soviet-bloc-style apartment buildings that appear uninhabited. The neighborhood looks like Late Urban Anywhere, not dangerous, just deflated, forgotten. Billy's profile, framed by the rim of the bonnet, passes across the landscape. Perhaps he is blessing it.

The van stops in a parking lot indistinguishable from any of the others we've passed. We all pile out, back into the heat. Billy exits last, squinting. The iridescent-yellow squares glow in the sun; his pink shoes are pinker still, and come to pointy pink tips, like otherworldly nipples. He is simultaneously foolish and grand, and a ripple passes through the little crowd of us in the parking lot, a palpable delight.

"Look at you," I say. He smiles shyly.

Boone walks off a ways, to the next parking lot, talking softly on his phone. The others take up their positions – the man with the long, lined face holds a camera, the headset woman bears a small, portable mic not much bigger than the kind you can get in a toy store for kids to play rock star, the two young men hold still cameras and coils of electrical cord that feed back into the van. The other woman sits in the open van eating a sandwich. I don't know how she can stand it in there; it's shady, but it must be very hot indeed. Billy walks to the center of the parking lot, sighs, shifts his shoulders back and forth, does a few deep knee bends. Sweat is already beading his forehead just beneath the edge of the rubber bonnet. The man with the long, lined face nods, flaps his hand.

Billy, black-coated, yellow-legged, pink-footed, rubber-bonneted, walks in a large circle. He walks casually but deliberately, tracing a line of which he seems to be sure with an open, unmarked expression. His expression isn't blank; on the contrary, it is an expression of willed and somehow urgent receptivity, as if he wants this moment in Berlin to be inscribed on his face but has only the amount of time it will take him to walk around the circle to accomplish this. I wonder if his outlandish outfit is some kind of technology to catch the moment off-guard, a spiritual tuning fork. He holds his hands ever so slightly away from his body. The bright white cuffs fall nearly to his knuckles – one might almost imagine that he is shrinking as he walks, that by the end he will emerge, tiny, naked, from a puddle of strong, clashing color and material. A hot wind blows over us all, brightening our faces. He comes to a halt at the spot where he started.

The man with the long, lined face shakes his head.

"Fuck," says Billy. One of the young men brings him a bottle of water, and he drinks it down at once.

"It's just . . . ," says the lined-face man.

"I know," replies Billy. "It's not like we can go back to Bang-kok."

"Not this week," says the lined-face man.

Billy looks up at the sky, gazes thoughtfully at Boone on the phone in the next lot, and points a pink alligator toe straight down, as if he might go up en pointe, tapping the empty water bottle against his thigh. "All right." He turns to me, holds out his hand. The young man takes the water bottle away. "Can you try? We'll go together."

I take his hand, which is as soft and warm as it was in Swe-den, though damp now between the fingers, damp on the palm. The sun is heavy on my head; it's hard to breathe; I'm also starving. Boone waves from across the way, gives me a thumbs-up. I am a little taller than Billy. Although he is older than me, I feel like a mother taking her adolescent son's hand for a rare walk. I want to kiss him on the crown of his bonnet, tell him that everything is all right, because he feels nervous, sweaty, impatient for something that I don't know if I can pro-vide. What does he want from me? What is the meaning of the circle?

Holding Billy's soft, warm hand, I take a step, and he steps with me. I take another step – I hope I am tracing this invisible arc, I'm not sure where it is or what the point of this is – and he steps with me. The bonnet smells of hot rubber and sweat. Our shoulders brush against each other. We take a step. It feels like we're ice-skating together, and I am bad at ice-skating, but so is he, it turns out. We tilt, stumble. We stop. Billy looks up at me; his eyelashes are strangely long in his sorrowful, monk-ish face. His gaze is very strong, he is counting on me. I grip his hand more tightly, lean into where I think the circle is. We take a step. I feel the arc. His shirt-cuff tickles my hot wrist. My face is hot, too, but the arc is so pleasing. I want to follow it. The arc is seducing me. We take a step, we take a step, we take a step. Out of the corner of my eye, I see that the camera is moving ever so slightly. The flow comes up through my heels, the soles of my feet, travels up the backs of my legs, the way the famous song did at the festival in Göteborg, although it is utterly quiet in this parking lot in Berlin. Billy smiles, we lean into the turn. What is the lined-face man filming—both of us, my arm, my hand, our contiguous shoulders, the edge of the rubber bonnet? Vertiginously, I don't know. We enter a dangerous part of the circle, holding both hands across our bodies, this is the downward slope, the belly, we are crossing some equator. I feel faint. Billy pulls. Up we go. His pointy pink shoes find the invisible line; I cross my leg in front of his and we both laugh. It is as if we are running, but we aren't running, we are walking at an even pace. The inside of the circle is like the sea, and we are walking on the edge of the sea, all around the world. Joy.

We take a step, we take a step. At the top of the circle, now in the spot where we began, we stop. We touch forehead to forehead, breathing hot breath together, winded, our foreheads wet with sweat, still holding both hands, as something passes between us. It is like a kiss. "Thank you," whispers Billy, breaking the hold of our joined hands at last, stepping back, pulling off the bonnet and wiping his face, his head, with a white cuff, which comes away gray. Everybody claps.

Boone, dashing toward us across the parking lot, says, "I got it all on my cell. That was *amazing!*"

"Lunch," says the lined-face man, but he's smiling. We have completed the circle, built the pyramid. I pull my damp shirt away from my body, blow down into the sweat between my breasts, lift my face to the sun.

· · ·

Ezra. Moon man, wing walker, the one and only. Everyone, or nearly everyone, knows his skinny arms, his rings, his heavy, nearly Neanderthal brow. The high scrape of his Australian accent. He's what, sixty-five? sixty-six? The image of him leaping, shirtless and barefoot, off a roof on the cover of 1978's *Here and Now* is inscribed on the retina. We who were helpless before that flight. I listened to his eighth record, *Twist & Rain*, over and over in Paris. That drum solo, which no one can hear without thinking of how the drummer hanged himself three nights after he laid down the track. Ezra has been a superstar for such a long time that I almost can't remember the world without his fame in it. Fame was different for Ezra and his kind; it turned slowly and heavily. It was Ezra who heard *Whale* and got excited by it, Ezra who brought me into the label for *Bang Bang,* who sent me to the chateau, connected me to Ethan. It was Ezra whom I failed. But tonight he hugged me close, as if I were still a rising star. And then he quickly turned away to murmur to Billy, who shook his head. In the courtyard, before the show, no one notices Ezra because he has pulled in his aura. He wears jeans and Keds. He leans against the wall, cap pulled low, it's dark except for the light of the bar on the other side of the gravel-filled square. I can't see his face. It may be for this reason that no one notices any of us: the show they came to see, and then some. Me, Zach, Alicia, Billy, and the three *zaftig* redheaded women who sing backup for the opening act, one more luscious than the next. Alicia, sheathed in a black bodysuit like Catwoman, has been handing out tabs of MDMA as if they were communion wafers, blessing every tongue. I politely decline.

Also within our circle is William, the proprietor of this venue. He is perhaps fifty-five. He wears glasses. His lined face is handsome. He is wearing an elegant white button-down shirt with the sleeves carefully rolled up to the elbow. His pale blue eyes behind his glasses are shy, with surprisingly long lashes. We've been in the courtyard for only forty-five minutes or so, but already I know that he travels often to Amsterdam, because he shares custody of his children with his ex-wife, who is Dutch. He misses them very much when they aren't with him. I like William, and he seems to like me, too, leaning in to listen, gazing steadily into my eyes. For Berlin I wear black stockings, and my hair has been done up by a tiny man with muttonchops: it is pomaded into a 1940s twist. Thick, shiny red lipstick. The overall effect is of a theatrical decadence that isn't really sexy; it only references sex, references decadence. Real sex is curled up, dusty, within its citations, like a figure from Pompeii.

"Where have you been so far?" asks William.

"North – Denmark, a festival in Sweden."

"Ah, near Göteborg, yes?"

"Yes. Billy killed, he was amazing."

"This, tonight, will be amazing," says William. He leaned in, softly touching my arm. "I can't believe Ezra is here. You know, we all thought he had died."

I laugh. "What?"

William doesn't laugh. "Maybe the story didn't make it to the U.S. He was in the hospital, some sort of overdose, the early reports here were that he had died."

"When was this?"

"Maybe a month ago? They said he was in rehab, but I don't know, here he is."

I thought that Boone had arranged for Ezra to sit in with us as a favor to me, but now I see that it might have been a hand extended to Ezra, a reminder of the old days, when he had such an incredible ear. Before it all got the way it did.

"Is that why his wife – ?"

William inclines his chin in something less than a nod. "Well, one can't know, but my God, thirty years of this. Perhaps the poor woman got tired."

"The last time I saw Susie, she was keeping right up with him."

William touches my arm again. "I think that was some years ago. She cleaned up after his stroke."

"His *stroke?* His stroke?"

"Shhh." William puts a finger to his lips, half stagily, making a joke of gossiping the way we are; we stand closer so as not to be overheard. He smells of soap, not yet of cigarette smoke. "Yes. Last year. Don't you get the news?"

The hundred little girls holding hammers study their nails, smirking. "I guess I missed it."

Ezra, chatting, laughs his famously peculiar laugh, a kind of Aussie Woody Woodpecker sound. I can't see the stroke on him, the overdose. He looks to me so unmarked, or, more accurately, he is already so marked that I doubt I could tell the recent marks from the older ones. He is not a handsome man, never has been. His face, in the half-light, has an ursine, lumpy quality. What can be seen of his hairline plunges, Ben Franklin style, nearly to his ears; his fringe of hair is wispy, of indeterminate color, and coarse. His face is pitted with acne scars. His eyes are small, tend toward the red. His magic emanates in part from that, from his unregenerate ugliness. He looks like a creature of the night who can hold his own with creatures of the night. Alicia, in her Catwoman bodysuit, glides up, and he opens his mouth and extends his famously long tongue.

"Jesus."

"Berlin," says William, "is not such a good place for him. You can get everything here so easily. He barely has to ask. Like now, look at him. And you?" He looks into my eyes, thickly ringed by false eyelashes, applied one by one by the mutton-chop man.

"Oh, that? No." I return William's touch, lightly. "I have cheaper ways of self-destructing."

William nods. "As do we all. Excuse me, I need to prepare a few things." He crunches across the gravel and goes inside, walking at a slight angle, like a man in a strong wind.

I lean against the wall near Ezra, resting my feet, trying to take in what William has just told me. Jim and I didn't see Ezra when we were here last. The last time I saw Ezra was in New York, just after *The Pillars*. A party somewhere in Tribeca. Ezra, in a black suit, like a preacher, surrounded. Tiny, skinny girls in towering shoes on the arms of men with tight faces: one of those parties, an industry thing. He invited me to help me out, not that anyone really could by then. Fame had long since evolved from the monument to the glimpse, and I had been glimpsed already, glimpsed as the maker of glimpses that I was. I shouldn't have minded; I knew better. And wasn't I my father's daughter? Didn't I have better taste, better politics than that? Oh, but still. Ezra, in Tribeca, waved me over to join him and Slash, and I didn't hesitate for a second.

I look over at Ezra, singed, always burning. Still burning now, burning down. He is licking Alicia's palm up to the wrist. He has never had any eyebrows to speak of, and where they went is one of the vast array of facts that aren't known about Ezra, if that is even the name on his birth certificate. He says he's from Australia but was really born in New Zealand; his entire family died in a fire, goes the story, and perhaps the fire took his eyebrows to mark him as its own. Fire and flame are recurrent images in his songs, but then again, no one has ever found the graves or the ashes of the outstation. And many have looked. The orphanage appears to be real, and to have raised him. The school records show that he was often disciplined. His cigarette glows in the dark. Alicia glides away on her little cat feet.

"Anna." Ezra squints under the cap. "It's great to see you. You look great."

"Thanks," I say. "You, too."

Ezra taps out a cigarette, lights it. "You should stay awhile. You'd love it. There are amazing people here now." He leans over, kisses one of the three luscious redheads: Beauty and the Beast.

She licks her lips. "Like me." She fairly glows in the dark, her freckles backlit by her skin.

Ezra pulls back in mock surprise, one sparse eyebrow raised. "Jesus. Give an old dag a break."

She shrugs. "I worship you. I mean it. I used to dress up like I was you, the thing with the torn jacket? In kindergarten. My mom has pictures. She was a huge fan of yours, too."

Ezra adjusts his cap. "Well, thank you, ma'am. I'm honored." He says this with utter sincerity. I wonder if the liposuction rumors are true; his gut protrudes anyway, defiant, unregenerate, like a thickly knotted root. He still wears his jeans so low that a wisp of grayish pubic hair is visible.

She hands him a card. "This is us, see? This is our site."

I smile at him in the near-dark, but he doesn't see me because he is earnestly studying the card. Billy and I exchange a glance.

"Your new record is incredible," says Billy to Ezra. "It killed me."

"Nearly killed me, too," says Ezra, flicking his dead cigarette onto the gravel and lighting up another. "I had hair when we started."

"I can't stay," I say. "Wish I could."

Ezra regards me. "Why not?"

"We leave in the morning." All the little girls with hammers look at me gravely, their hammers by their sides. I am sweating in the black stockings, the pomade. I am queasy, breathless, ready to go onstage. "Maybe I'll come back after the tour. It's not a very long one."

Boone, clicking on his phone, glances up, grins. "I love this venue," he says. "It used to be a police station." He returns to his phone.

Ezra says, "I'm serious, Anna."

And now I hear it, the note of urgency. "How's Susie?"

"She's back in the States. She felt like she needed to go home for a while, check in with the kids." Ezra hitches up his pants. "She doesn't like these winters."

"But now it's —"

"I'll be here most of the winter," says Billy in his soft voice. "Let's work on something. I know some incredible artists who would love to hang out."

Ezra's small, reddish gaze, however, is fixed on me. He squints. "You got married, right? To that guy — the one from Stonecreek?"

"Jim. It didn't work out."

"Why?"

"Oh, I don't know. We just fell apart. We're not like you and Susie." I offer up this disingenuous flattery, then, ashamed, reel it back in. "He got sober." I shrug, as if that weren't a dig. "We didn't know each other well enough, maybe. But he's a great guy, he helped me out a lot on *Wonderland*. His own stuff is amazing. He's a fiddle virtuoso — brilliant."

Ezra nods rabbinically. "I've heard that."

"I did try," I say, embarrassed to find myself tearing up.

"I'm divorced," Alicia offers sympathetically. "I got married too young."

"Me, too," says one of the luscious redheads. "He kept the dog. I loved that dog. I tried to steal her, but it didn't work. I spent a night in jail." One of the other luscious redheads squeezes her hand.

Billy Q smiles radiantly. "Your set is going to be awesome," he says.

Upstairs, a corridor lined with large rooms constitutes the backstage, the green room, the dressing rooms, and the kitchen, where two massive bald men stand guard over melting cakes and steam trays of dubious, lumpy concoctions, neatly labeled *Pepperballs with Meatballs* and *Catfish on Cucumbers and Tomatoes*. It is as hot as hell, post-apocalyptically deserted, as if nearly everyone has just run out into the street, leaving everything behind. Empty water bottles are scattered everywhere. In the men's dressing room, the bespectacled lead singer of the opening act is sleeping on a sofa, his bare feet propped on the sofa arm. Picking my way carefully down the corridor in my outfit, I turn into the putative women's dressing room, which is filled with racks of clothes, open makeup cases, and a curling iron – the one used on me? – which has been left on, the better, I suppose, to burn the place down and cause a fatal stampede, perhaps in the middle of my set. I turn it off, sit down gingerly on the edge of a chair. I open my tiny black mesh bag, barely big enough for my phone and a hotel key card, which is blank, a plain white rectangle. I hold up the key card, but no fissure opens up in the space-time continuum. There isn't even a breeze. I take out my phone and turn it on for the first time today. It is bristling with texts from Boone, as always.

My mother picks up right away. "Honey? Where are you?"

"Berlin. It's insanely hot."

"You have to stay hydrated. Are you performing tonight?"

"Yeah. In a few hours. How are the cats?"

"Oh, you know." She laughs. "Still fat. I give up. I think it's because the mice are fat here. And then we feed them on top of it."

"Do you think I should have stayed with Jim? Did I make a mistake?"

One of the things I love about my mother is that she doesn't ask why I'm calling her from backstage before a show in Berlin to ask such a question. Instead, she says, "It always seemed to me – don't take this the wrong way – kind of like an arranged marriage somehow. I don't know." I hear the patter of kibble being poured into the cats' bowls.

"What?" I spot a Bounty bar under a chair and grab it. Melted bad chocolate and syrupy coconut: I hold it carefully in my fingers, eat it in two bites. It is delicious.

"I just mean – what do I mean?"

One of the massive bald men shuffles into the room to drink

a beer by the breezeless open window, next to a nearly de-
nuded ficus tree that barely covers its corner. "*Ist okay?*" he
asks. I nod. He sits down and wipes his brow.

My mother continues, "Consider the source, Anna. What
do I know? He was a good guy, obviously very talented. And
I know you had been struggling. We liked him – Ed and I both
liked him. Very much."

"But?"

"You know, honey, it was the first time I ever knew you to
make such an *organized* choice – you and Lila were always so
different that way – and I guess Ed and I wondered . . . you
know. Oh, I don't know."

"Now I'm freaking out. What are you saying?" The massive
bald man holds the cold beer to his forehead, closes his heavy-
lidded eyes. He looks like the man in the moon.

My mother sighs. "Remember, your father and I never got
married –"

"I know, but –"

"Anyway, all I'm saying is that I felt you were trying to arrange things for yourself and he *was* a good guy, maybe a little
gloomy. But very committed to his music. It wasn't hard to understand why you thought he might be a solution, and maybe,
you know – he got you back out there. You helped him with his
drug problems. It made a certain kind of sense, I guess."

"Don't people go through bad patches? Haven't you and Ed
had bad patches?"

"Sure."

"So –"

"Do you want to go back to him?"

"No."

"Well."

"But I don't know why not." I hope the bald man, medita-
tively drinking his beer, doesn't speak English. He looks as if
he might be falling asleep, cheeks flushed, the moon setting.

"That's a different question. When you're done with the

tour, why don't you come down for a while? You're always so exhausted after those things. The swimming will be great then. I can show you what I've been working on for that show in Philadelphia. It's been incredibly complicated, I'm half blind from it."

"Okay." I shift on the chair, rest my chin in my hand, taking care not to smear my makeup, which was also done, in expert layers, by the tiny German man with thick muttonchops. "Are you guys all right?"

"We're fine. Have a great show."

"Okay. Thanks, Mom."

"Love you, honey."

Onstage, Ezra and I are standing about three feet from each other as the slow opening chords of "Burning Horse" sound. The band — there's a lot of it, mine and pieces of his, plus bits from the opening act, mixed together — is piled up behind us, double-stuffed onto risers, sharing microphones. A young man in a spangly minidress is dancing like a snake, or an imp, darting from crevice to crevice, popping up unexpectedly. He is left over from the opening act, apparently unwilling or unable to stop. The smell of collective sweat mixes with the smell of old beer, overpiney floor cleaner, and, when he wiggles up close behind me, a light perfume on the dance-dress-snake man. We drop with uncanny quiet into the first verse. Singing with Ezra is weightless. This is how it all starts to happen, of course. This is why he's been such an enormous star, and such a legendary addict. They go together; you're not supposed to say that, but it's true, though in a specific way, not the way you might assume: Ezra is like a ghost, he can walk through walls, especially when he's as high as he is now. When you're with him, you can walk through walls, too. This is what we do so well, what we did from the beginning. Together, we exist as ghosts, hand in hand against the wallpaper, semi-transparent, perfectly orthogonal to every known note.

I take the first notes of the chorus and, after a time, he turns and follows. He acts as if he is following my lead, and maybe he is. I've never wanted him, but I've always wanted to be the one who encircles his wrist with my fingers and takes him somewhere else. He's always let me do it, from the very first time we caused a sensation with this song. (This is also how a man as ugly as he is enchants so many women: the unicorn, the Beast, kneeling in the garden at her skirt. He knows the power of his submission.) His line is the melody, mine is the unpredictable shred. Even as I tear up the notes, I know that this is why, even in an earlier era, I would never have been a star the way he is, and every note I tear only confirms it: torn tickets. To be a star like Ezra, you have to leave a blank space, like my hotel key, where people can make of you what they will, and much of what they make is dross. Ezra doesn't mind the dross the way he doesn't mind his acne scars. And, cynically, he invites it: the dross is where you make your money, and Ezra has an extraordinary amount of it.

The band joins harder, we go harder, melancholy-cacophonous. "Burning Horse" is the song we did, the song I changed forever, that first time at Glastonbury over a decade ago, the song we've done so many times since, that I've done without him, that he's done without me. "Burning Horse" was a classic even before I reinvented it. I first heard it when I was fifteen, in Buenos Aires. I heard it in a car commercial in the States two months ago. I almost don't mind that he copied our duet a few years later, note for note, with Kylie Minogue; it's a business, after all, and the song is so famous it's almost public property. I hear all these versions, and more, on the radio in my head, even now, as we sing it. I plant my feet apart to get a grip on the stage; my skirt and top hold me tight, upright. My hair stays shellacked into place. Ezra, in his jeans and Keds and faded Pink Floyd T-shirt, holds the microphone close, as if he's never held one before. It is like running downhill: I remember this. He eyes me, smiling. The crowd is red in the red light, the front row reaches toward us, red hands, red fingers, upturned red faces. Shouts of "Ez!" "Anna!" "Z-man!" "Berlin loves you!" I am sweating so profusely I'm afraid I'm going to drop the mic. I can make out Billy Q at the back of the house, swathed in keffiyehs, deeply embedded in a thicket of people; Boone is murmuring in his ear. His circle, caught on film today: it doesn't do this. Nothing can do this anymore. The horse on fire runs through us. The meridians blaze, the audience burns and begs to burn, fingers red, alight. We know the story, the whole thing. All is forgiven, and, after all, am I not a sinner, too? My hands are no cleaner than anyone else's, when it comes down to it. I want this. I always have. The hundred little girls hold their hammers high and swing them.

When I turn around to dance a little ("Anna!"), I see that Zach is exhilarated, eyes closed, shoulder to shoulder with one of his idols, John Strong, Ezra's bassist from the beginning. John has never changed one iota of his casually ratty look; his gentle eyes peer out of an increasingly fallen, still quite handsome face. Zach is sweating madly, muscles flexing; his bald head is drenched. As I shake my ass, I think, Well, at least I gave him this. Alicia, marooned at the tiptop of the musical pantheon like a cat stuck in a tree, looks as if she is about to faint, sweat-soaked, diligently plying her cello bow. Ezra glances up at her, winks.

I turn back around for the last chorus. Ezra and I roll up together. We go all the way down, fast, loud, and hard. The band piled up behind us avalanches sound. I'm singing so hard that I know I'm singing badly, ruining my voice, and I never, ever want to stop. Out of the corner of my eye, I spot the two massive bald men from the kitchen in the wings. The sun and the moon are smiling. Ezra leaves the stage with a wave and the rest of the set flies straight toward morning.

Upstairs after the show, I find Ezra in the kitchen, standing by a tray, holding up something with a plastic fork that must, I guess, be a pepperball, unless it's a meatball. He is staring so intently at it that I wonder if it's staring back. His stringy fringe of hair is still dark with sweat. He has taken off his T-shirt and stuffed it into his back pocket. He is as skinny as a spider, all knots and tendons, with the famous tattoo of the eye gazing out from between his smooth, almost boyish shoulder blades. Even now he is a creature from another world. No amount of money or fame can disguise that. He looks at the red ball of meat quizzically, then puts it back in the tray. The eye on his back shudders, damp, ever open. The veins in the eye always seemed a little juvie to me – we *got* the point – but now they look oddly sweet, almost optimistic, poignant.

"Thank you," I say. My own sweat veils me, head to toe. My feet, wet, slide in my shoes. My toes are wet. My ears are wet. "That was incredible."

"It was fun, yeah. Have you seen Alicia?"

Down the corridor, people are laughing, talking. Just here, just now, Ezra and I are suspended in the heat together. He looks straight at me, his unpainted eyes wide, unfocused. I wonder if he knows where he is. He seems like a man sending a hologram of himself from a distant planet, silently desperate that you agree that this is the real thing. "Ezra," I begin, but my nerve fails me, for which, one day, there is sure to be a reckoning.

"Anna, come back. You and your band could stay here with me this winter – there are amazing people here. You'd love it. Bring that guy from Stonecreek – didn't you get married?"

I wonder that he doesn't remember, then I don't wonder. "Jim. It didn't work out."

"Ah, fuck. Fucking musicians, right? Never quit while they're ahead. What did he play?"

"The fiddle. Like an angel."

William is waiting for me at the bar when I come down, shucked of my glamour, returned to the blouse and jeans I came in wearing. I feel satisfied, as if I have gone to outer space and am now splashing down, wallowing in gravity. My hair remains extravagantly sculpted because of all the products the tiny muttonchop man used to invent it. The armature of my hair is strangely elevating; I have the fantasy that it is making me stand up straighter. I kept the false eyelashes on, partly because I'm not sure how to take them off. Billy Q, Boone, the three luscious redheads, the dance-dress-snake man (now meek, unremarkable, with a caterpillar's face), Zach, the bespectacled lead singer of the opening act, and various roadies and crew members are spread out around the bar, giving off a glow, congratulating one another, collecting compliments from fans. Tom, in his fisherman's hat, is standing with the sun and the moon, drinking beer. I turn and glimpse the back of Ezra's faded T-shirt and the sole of one sneaker as he ducks out a side door. Just in front of him, the long black curve of Alicia's bodysuit, his hand in the ebony small of her back. The side door closes. A plump man in a vest, wearing yellow-rimmed glasses, face shining with sweat, takes my hands in both of his and says, "There are no words. No words. You are an artist. Please come back to Berlin."

I assure him that I will, of course. Over the plump man's shoulder, I smile at William, he smiles at me, hands me a whiskey, kisses my hand without irony. I kiss his hand back. "You are lucky for us," I tell him. "Thank you."

Boone's pale face swirls close. "We're all going to Zoo."

"All right." I am returning William's gaze. "In a while."

Boone swirls away, one white thumb turned up. He gathers people as he goes, a moving, agglutinating ball of the luscious and the ugly and the famous and Zach, glancing around at the emptying bar. I drink my whiskey slowly, returning to earth.

William says, "I live not too far from here. Would you like to come over for a drink?"

"Yes."

William says something in German to the woman behind the bar, and she nods.

"*Kein problem*," she says.

We leave the former police station. I wonder who left it in previous years, in what states. The heat hasn't changed intensity, only color. Where it was bright and bleached during the day, now it is full of high contrasts, neon and shadow, streetlight yellows, taxicab whites. We soon turn off the main avenue and head into what seems to be a business district, quiet at this late hour. There are few people on the dark street. William takes my hand; we intertwine fingers as if we are lovers. Berlin, everywhere, seems to be under construction. Plastic tarps scrim the fronts of buildings, rendering the insides watery and indistinct. An orange crane is stilled in an empty lot. One half of a building, vertically, is still nondescript gray stone, while the other half is modern glass and steel, like half a face stripped to the bone. I'm not sure which I prefer. Outside a synagogue, armed guards lean on a wooden barricade. I'd forgotten this about Europe — the casual presence of soldiers. A tall, dark-haired one with long sideburns winks at me. I smile as we pass.

The hot night air gets under the line of my blouse, dampens my sleeves. I taste licorice in the back of my throat. William guides us to the left. This small street is quieter still, quite graceful, with one spare building that's fronted by a peculiar sort of frosted green glass that changes subtly as I walk past it, becoming momentarily transparent in the street light. Through a ground-floor window in an empty, lighted room, I see a desk, papers, a dark computer monitor, a closed office door, an empty coat hook on the wall, before the glass goes green, then dark again, reseams itself. All of the buildings on this small street are closed, silent; these must be businesses, though it also looks as if they could be part of a single university or set of government offices.

"We are almost there," he says. "Are you tired from the show?"

"No. I'm pumped."

"What?"

"Energetic."

"Ah."

We turn left. I realize that I am not just pumped, I am happy. I will write that in the composition book later: *I am happy*. It is a happiness that, if it had a color, would be an almost electric light blue, like the eye of a peacock's tail. An improbable, excessive, supersaturated blue. The blue floods me with surprising force, pure oxygen, the heat of this night, slight pressure of William's fingers, the green and white sign of a cheap kebab place, the scent of lamb cooking, we pass through a little group of German teenagers singing raggedly, drunkenly. The electric light blue prickles the skin on the back of my neck, widens my eyes, lightens my bones. I feel that I must be getting taller. William takes us into a smaller street, a cul-de-sac.

His apartment is above a restaurant and looks out over a square behind the cul-de-sac. He opens a few windows. Some of the furniture looks as if it must have been his parents', being large and dark and old, but there are modern photographs on the thick, uneven walls that tell me he is curious, melancholy, carnal, with a biting sense of humor. Three vintage electric guitars – good ones – hang on the wall as well. We embrace, we kiss. I stroke the shoulders of his white shirt, feeling his arms beneath the good cotton. He is hard almost immediately and I am wet, taking his cock in my mouth, unbuttoning my blouse, unfastening my bra, with one awkward hand to get my skin closer to his. It is very warm up here; we sweat. He takes off his glasses. When I rise to kiss him, his tongue is hard, too, his lips are hard. I like the fervor of it even as I wonder, stepping out of my pants, how he could have gotten through life like this, with these hard kisses. I wonder what his ex-wife is like. He bends to suck at my nipples, the part in his salt-and-pepper hair exposed, and then, kneeling, he folds that hard tongue inside my cunt, his damp, warm hands on my knees. I hear him breathe. I lie down on his bed and spread my legs, stroke his head as he licks until I beg him to fuck me.

He stands, looks down at me as he unwraps the condom, a look on his face of wonder and excitement but also some other, darker emotion, a premonition of doubt, not sexually, but in some other, larger way. Some way I won't be here, later, to see. The lines in his face are more prominent as he gazes down, his eyes bare. I lick my forefinger and touch it to my clit, looking back at him. We fuck and it is only, sheerly, ridiculously good. Our bodies fit, our rhythms match, as if we've been fucking our entire lives, as if I came across the world just to be here at this moment, in this room, with this man, in exactly this way. It is all electric light blue.

I don't know this man, this William, at all, and yet I feel I know him very well. Just like with Simon, how it started. His small nipples, the delicate scattering of salt-and-pepper hair on his chest, the interconnected freckles on his shoulders. He murmurs, "My God, this is such a good fuck, I'm barely moving." And it's true. He is far in me, rocking in a movement so small, intense, and precise that it's like a sound only the two of us can hear. This is who he is, a man for whom a good fuck, the best fuck, is one that almost can't be seen, only felt deep within. He is a shy man. I am nearly coming, desperate to come, but also enjoying the tug of waiting, because in this bed, in this room, on this street of which I don't even remember the name, in Berlin, I trust this man completely for these few minutes. I have no idea where I am, and I know exactly where I am. I am here with him, in the near silence, now, in the inner room. We fuck, we fuck, and the waves come over me, then over him as he lets go with a low sound.

We move apart, lie side by side, sweating, breathing. The waves spread out, growing fainter, becoming the past. He takes the condom off carefully, ties a knot at the top, discreetly drops it over the side of the bed. When I leave, he'll throw it in the trash, wash up. His mattress is lumpy and soft, the sheets are soft as well, clean and worn.

"Do you do this a lot?"

He smiles. "Sometimes. I meet so many interesting people, you know." He turns on his side. "And you?"

"It comes easily to me. I don't know why."

"People on the road," he says, palming my belly, damp with sweat. "I used to be in a band, I know how it is."

"I guess."

His belly is taut on the surface, but it bows out on the sides. There is gray in his pubic hair, gray on his thighs. His dick is soft, but I want him again; I put his hand between my legs and he circles his thumb slowly over my clit. I touch my tongue to his chest. He tastes of sweat and soap. His chest is barely sagging, surprisingly strong. The muscles in his pale arms are solid. He looks almost dreamy, concentrating. His thumb circles firmly, precisely, sure. I think about how much physical labor club work is, how many boxes of liquor he must have carried over the years, how long he must be on his feet every day, how he will run the club until he is an old man, how his grown children will come to see him in this apartment, talk about his health and his misconceptions on the stair. There is an oval burn scar, raised flesh, on the inside of one of his forearms. He watches me come, I close my eyes.

I rest my head against his chest, sighing, he touches my hair, my back. A weak breeze finds us, tickles us. Why do I like this sort of encounter so much, why has it always come so easily, beyond the plain pleasures of it? Because it feels pure, though I know that's an illusion? Because it feels like only the touch of a stranger is this clean? No: because it feels like the way in. I believe that it is the way in, that I'm going somewhere at the moment, at every moment like this. I open my eyes. The room has gone dark since we've come up here. I can't make out the details in the photographs on the walls anymore; the shapes are softening, draining of color, turning to blank squares of glass. Downstairs, cutlery dings. Laughter, doors opening and shutting, the sound of an iron pan or pot crashing to the floor. People speaking French outside the restaurant. Music of an ordinary night. It's as if the dimming of the visual field inside this room has increased our ability to hear the sounds outside it. They seem near and far simultaneously, so different are they in quality from the silence, the small sounds, here. Somewhere else in the building, a door closes.

He turns on the lamp next to the bed, puts on his glasses. "Do you want some coffee? I am about to make some," he says. "I will have to go back to the club to close up. You can stay? It won't take long." His face in the light is sober, angular. His body, in the light, looks different from the body I touched – ropier, longer. Even his voice in the light, a foot away rather than right in my ear, is different – higher and kinder. I half expect to see *AMOR* written over his belly button, but the flesh is unmarked.

"No, I have to go." I begin fishing around for my underwear, my clothes, bending over at what is probably an unattractive angle. I stop. "What is the German word for 'beautiful'?"

"*Schön.*"

"*Schön.*" I lean back to the bed to kiss him. "*Schön. Schön.*" I'm not sure which I mean – the man in the dark, the man in the light, both, neither.

Back at the hotel, the sky just beginning to lighten outside my tall windows overlooking Berlin, I find a note from Boone slipped under my door: *Call as soon as you get in.* When I call, Boone doesn't ask why I haven't turned my phone on all night. He just tells me, very gently and straightforwardly, that my father has died, of a heart attack.

THE BRIDGE

West Vernon, Vermont

MY FATHER'S STUDIO, a red box, stands in a field of wild-flowers. Outside, birds chirp. It's quite cool inside the studio, because summer proper hasn't arrived in Vermont yet. In any patch of shade, it's still early spring. Lila touches a large, unfinished canvas of my father's resting on the main easel; it seems to depict the field outside his window, rendered brushily, lyrically, even.

"I just had a vision of that color in Berlin," I say to Lila, pointing. "That blue."

"You think it was Dad?"

"Maybe."

"I don't know." Lila stands awkwardly before the canvas. "Why was he doing this? It looks like a postcard."

The studio looks like a postcard, too, perhaps from a better store. The floor is made of wide, aged planks, paint-splattered. Long windows open the walls to the field of wildflowers, transparently frame the start of forest at the north end of the building. Shadows delicately dapple the old, marked-up floor. The room smells of paint, turpentine, plaster, and yellow soap. A pair of my father's glasses lies open on a worktable, clearly tossed down as he rubbed his forehead, or picked up a different pair, or went to pee outside. There are three worktables in the room, each one scattered with stuff: the skulls of several small animals; colors he was mixing—a complicated reddish brown, a white, four different blues—crusting in their cracked plastic dishes; a jigsaw blade; a sheaf of enormous, deep green ferns; an old white enameled bedpan with a voluptuous white curve; a ragged block of veined marble, perhaps four by four uneven inches; a hand-tinted picture of his mother; the browning core of an apple with his teeth marks in it. A taxidermied, surprisingly lifelike raccoon with a button in place of one of its eyes. A hurricane lamp. Two broken bricks. A few of my father's many orthotics are scattered over one table; the impression of his bad foot rests, like a series of prints, in each one: shadows of big toe, arch, rind of heel. An invitation to a show of someone else's work at the Miami Biennale two years ago. A half-empty pack of Gitanes. A dirty glass ashtray. A battered sketchpad with ruffled pages, as if they fell in water.

It's perfect, really. A well-composed still life of an artist's workspace. Lila and I, our cups of coffee clutched like life preservers, eye the studio, and each other, uneasily. Lila is right about the big field painting. It's bad. It's just a patch of pleasantly colored paint with a little motion in it, suitable for framing. Resting against the exquisitely rough-hewn walls are stacks of other canvases. Lila and I clack through them: one after another, we discover, they depict the field, the field, the field. It's difficult to tell which are older and which are more recent. He seemed to go through a phase where he included the window frame around the view of the field; then another where the field is so smudged, so abstract, that it might be a cloud; then yet another that was close to botanical illustration; another that might be described as angry, with slashing brushstrokes. Lila, squatting on her heels, says, "Jesus Christ. I feel like I don't even know the man who painted these."

"They're so weird." I let fall my stack, the light canvases exhaling their weight against the wall, glad to lean again. I look at the one that's in front: a billowing, even blowsy field, Watteau-esque. One could almost imagine a girl in dishabille running barefoot through it, laughing over her shoulder at an unseen suitor in pursuit. "They're pretty, I guess."

Lila stands up, dusting her hands on her pants. "There's nothing going on in them. They're totally empty."

"Harsh," I murmur, but she's right. Every painting, every single one, fails. In none of them did he apprehend what he saw outside his window every day. All he did was paint a picture of it. I can't decide which is worse, to imagine that he knew it, or that he didn't.

Lila and I turn our backs to the walls with their feather-light cadavers and hover awkwardly in the center of the room, as if some sort of warmth is concentrated there, though it isn't. In fact, it's colder away from the windows and the light that pools in glowing, graceful trapezoids beneath them. I hold the coffee cup against my cheek to get its fading heat. It is supposed to be my and Lila's job to inventory what is in our father's studio, arrange for the distribution of whatever is valuable in it with his dealer in New York, and then decide what to do with the rest. Jenny, our father's second wife, has sent us out here to "get a start" on it. She is making phone calls in the kitchen, one eye on the six-year-old twins – our half-brothers. Everything about Jenny, a forty-two-year-old lawyer who works with disadvantaged children, is practical and fair and sensible; assigning us this task is her concession to our mother, to the more glamorous and slightly suspect life our father once led, to the Brundage myth. When we fled the kitchen, she was up to flowers, lots of flowers. The twins were eating gingerbread men.

Lila picks up our father's cane, a metal contraption with a flesh-colored plastic bulb on the end, duct tape wrapped around the handle, and puts it down again. "Lord," she says. "What are we going to do with all this? What are we going to say to Jenny?"

"I have no idea."

"I blame that stupid prison in Texas. He couldn't do anything after that mess."

"Well. Don't you think it started before that? Since Rome –"

Lila shrugs. "Rome, I don't know." Her eyes are red from crying on the several connecting flights from Wyoming, but she isn't crying now, nor am I. We look like sisters around the eyes, the shape of our mouths. We both still wear our hair long. But whereas I am tall, long-armed, bony-kneed, Lila's face and body are even, classic, firm. She wears a tiny diamond stud in her nose; that and the cascade of blond hair are her only visible rebellions against the norm. Otherwise, she could be any suburban wife and mom anywhere, though an especially beautiful one, in sneakers and sweatpants, a long-sleeved jersey. A single golden wedding band. Her physical perfection, now that she is slightly older, has the effect of making her seem more vulnerable, like a precious vase. I wonder if her husband sees that, if he treasures her more because of it, or if it frightens him. She suspects him of having affairs, and her reasons always sound uncomfortably plausible. Lila, as far as I know, has never had an affair. Emotionally as well as physically, she is terrifyingly true.

"How's the tour going?" she asks, but her voice is flat.

I nod. "It's all right. We were just getting started, really, when –" I nearly begin to cry again, then abruptly stop. The grief moves like this, I've learned in the past two days, expanding and contracting unpredictably. I feel simultaneously transparent and weighed-down; my skin hurts as if I have a fever. My bones hurt. I can't remember the last time I washed my hair. I put a hand to it – too long ago, apparently. I have a sudden urge to call Billy Q; I'm sure he would listen attentively. Unfortunately, or fortunately, I don't have his number.

"Do you think it will be a success?" she asks, rummaging around a worktable. She finds a faded Polaroid. "Look at this. It's Mom and Dad in Disneyland, of all places."

"What kind of question is that?"

Her blond hair falls across her face, veiling it. "Don't be so paranoid, Anna. It's just a question."

"No, it isn't."

Lila shrugs.

Don't take the bait, don't take the bait, don't take the bait. "I can't believe this. I can't believe he's dead. It feels surreal."

Lila says, "Not to me."

"What?"

She puts the picture down. "Look at it in here." Her voice is sharp. "It's a sarcophagus. Do you remember the old studio?"

I know the one she means, the only one of the many that we call "the old studio"– it was in Newark, at the back of a defunct tannery; it looked like a mélange of woodworking shop, butcher shop, junkyard, and cabinet of curiosities. The fluorescent lighting, when it had to be on, made everyone look like the undead. There were tools everywhere, a winch hanging from the ceiling, vises and blowtorches, architects' blueprints, the front fender of a car. It smelled, for some reason we could never figure out, like rotting fish. The windows were cracked, some mended with cardboard and electrical tape. The stray cats my father fed, too generously, milled around outside the windows, yowling.

"You broke your arm in there," I say.

Lila holds her right arm out, smiling. "It's still not entirely straight. Never will be." I can't see the curve, but I know it's there, a very subtle warp in her forearm.

"Okay, I know," I say. "We both know. But what else was he going to do? The big commissions weren't coming his way anymore. Things changed, he changed . . ."

"That's one word for it. And Jenny. It's like he married his nurse." She shakes her head. "He never should have moved to Vermont. Those kids, Jesus. What is she going to do?"

"Well, it's cheaper here. Jenny's from here, she knows people." I'm not sure why I'm being so placating. I hate it, too, all the empty prettiness, the easy, lazy appeal to the viewer. Where is the man who broke the train in half? Why did he lose heart? And that field, was it a field of poppies? Was he vapidly happy painting it? Or did it, not the prison, defeat him? Was he trying to paint his way out? Or farther under, already burying himself? The repetition says the former, but the picturesque studio says the latter. Hard to tell if he was killed by the field, or if he suffocated himself with it, mouth stuffed with wild-flowers.

Lila picks up the sheaf of green ferns and hurls it ineptly to the floor. She begins crying in jagged, choking sobs, her fingers to her face, like a cage. "I *hate* it here," she sobs. "This place is awful."

"Isn't Wyoming sort of like this?" I ask, almost innocently. "It was quiet, I don't know —"

"Wyoming is *nothing* like this. Wyoming is real. Everything here is fake." She glares at me, her face red and damp. "If you ever came to visit, you'd know that."

"I have come, that's not fair."

"Not since the kids were in diapers. Jake is in junior high now."

"Well," I say, "I —" There is no answer to this. "I was a mess, Lila. Did you want them to see me like that?" This is only half the truth, of course. "I was going through a bad time."

Lila glares, wrapping her arms around herself. "You're so full of shit, Anna. You don't know anything."

I stoop to pick up the ferns, set them on a worktable. The pliancy of the green fronds reminds me of his hands: square, scarred, a worker's hands, but so dexterous. Pearly ovals of sturdy fingernails. When he drew, he held the pencil or charcoal poised with great delicacy, nearly seeming to float between his index and second finger. You couldn't see where the pressure was being exerted as the shapes formed rapidly on the page. He always drew in a hurry, squinting and frowning, looking like he was in pain. He banged at the paper percussively with the charcoal. "What happened to all those drawings of you? Those were so much better than any of this stuff."

Lila shakes her head. "God, I don't know. Maybe Mom has them. I hope she burned them."

A small silence falls between us. "Lila," I say, and say it firmly.

"So when are you leaving?" she says with unmistakable bitterness. Her cheeks are flushed, lineless.

"I'll go back in a few days. We can't sort all of this out now anyway." Lila's face is turned away from me, hidden by the fall of golden hair. "Aren't you going back to your family?"

"Dave and the boys are coming tomorrow," she murmurs.

Silence. I think Lila is crying, but she won't let me see her face.

I try again. "Lila."

"He's dead."

"Lila—"

"It's nothing that simple. Nothing that grotesque. I can't explain it, I've never been able to explain it." She looks directly at me, tear-streaked, red-faced. "I don't understand anything, either."

"I sold the lighthouse rock," I offer. "For the tour."

She rears back. "You did what? You had no right to do that. Anna, that was a *gift*—you squandered that, and for what? Some desperate fantasy?"

I walk outside the studio so that I don't hit her, or, more likely, say something so completely unsayable—*he didn't draw me*—that it can never be repaired. I slam the studio door and sit down on the sagging wooden step. I am shaking. I mop my runny nose with my hand. I think of the *schön* man, William, and cry harder. I don't know his last name, or what the name of the street or the restaurant was; I caught a taxi back to the hotel that night. I wouldn't know how to find my way back. Would William know, could he tell me, what happened to the four of us? Could he tell me, for instance, what wounded my father so deeply he couldn't ever really recover? What was that look that crossed William's face? He wouldn't want me to know, and it's not my business. Anyway, we're not going back to Berlin.

I want to tell someone, maybe William, that I can't bear it that we're going to box up our father's studio. It feels like we're dismembering him, like we're surrendering, too. But I already betrayed him. I should have been here when it happened, I should have held his hand as he was dying. Lila is

right about all my failures. The tears come again, uncontrolla-
ble. What I should do is call Jim, that would be the right thing
to do, but I can't bring myself to do it. He can say the sober,
appropriate thing to me tomorrow. I look at the field of Vermont wildflowers with the sun playing over it and think of the
field out the window of the train to Göteborg. Is there a rhyme
there, a synchrony? Only the easy answer is yes. Someone else,
not me, Jim maybe (why am I being so mean?), would make
a lyric out of that. The butterflies hover over the field's surface, their Technicolor wings fluttering. It is impossible, this
place, Lila is right about that, too. No one could paint anything
here. The field defeated him and he knew it, and his heart just
stopped.

The studio door opens and Lila comes out with the crum-
pled pack of Gitanes and a match. She takes a cigarette, hands
the pack to me, and I take one. Lila and I sit on the front step,
ass to ass, in silence. I slowly draw on the Gitane, which is stale
and tastes like smoldering asphalt. I don't like it but smoke it
anyway. I want to feel the edge of something irrefutable and
real and toxic. The smoke rises and disperses around us, above
us. Lila hums a tune I don't recognize. I look at my sister, at her
angry, perfect profile. Her eyes are red-rimmed but still beautiful, expressive, tilting down at the corners in the way I have
always thought of as Russian. *Where have you been?* I want to
say to her. *The north?*

Instead, willingly laying my head on the chopping block
again, I ask, "When is Mom coming? I didn't have time to call,
I just got on the first plane out, it was midnight in the States —"

"She might not be. She said she might be too upset, she
doesn't want to make a scene. She's really torn up about this."
Lila says this with perfect evenness, clearly making an effort,
in our fragile truce, not to indicate that she, Lila, is superior
for having called our mother and gathered this emotional information that I was too lazy/busy/washed up/self-involved
to discover.

"God," I say. "It's awful. What happened."

Lila blows a smoke ring into the sweet Vermont air. It is warmer outside than it was in the studio. "It was what it was."

"Do you remember the house in Trondheim? The one with the octagonal room?"

"Trondheim. Why did we go to Trondheim?"

"Dad was supposed to do that thing with the pier. Which he couldn't do. Mom had the affair with the composer."

"She did?"

"You knew that," I say. "The young one, Erik. Scruffy guy. He was always over." I warm up, too, talking about it – I want to be here, stay here. I want this to be just two sisters, two daughters, the Brundage girls, no one else. Belonging to no one else. "I had a crush on him."

"Yeah," says Lila vaguely. "Me, too. Wow. Mom."

"That raccoon is really the limit," I say. "It's like he wanted everyone to know what a sham this was."

"A cry for help, as it were," says Lila wryly, holding up a hand in a pawlike way.

"I can't stand it," I say, my voice breaking. Lila takes my hand, squeezes it. We fall silent, leaning against the studio door. Jenny comes out of the house, shooing the twins in front of her toward the car. She makes hand gestures that probably mean she'll be back soon. I wave back and force a smile. It's not Jenny's fault. It was before her time. It can't be explained, even if she wanted that, which she doesn't.

"They're all coming in a few hours," Lila says after a while, stubbing out her cigarette. Her face has softened, finally.

"Who?"

"Aunt Laura, Aunt Beth, Aunt Jean. The cousins. The whole thing. Dad's dealer."

"I just want to stay here," I say. "On this step."

"I know," says Lila. "Look at that field. Nature doesn't need our efforts to be beautiful. It isn't composed. It doesn't have to change into anything else." In that long-ago shack, Lila ran naked into the Irish Sea every morning, emerging red, ecstatic, shivering. We sat on the wooden front step of that shack, too, sharing cigarettes and coffee, joints and beers, magic mushrooms and wine, watching the infinite waves. I was always too scared to run into the cold, rough sea, naked or not. Lila was the reckless one, the diver-into-seas, the roller-down-of-dunes, the girl who sent herself away to school, the woman who refuses to compose. How can will take such different forms? One red, one blue. One going north, one going south.

Now the field before us stretches out in all directions under the watery blue of the sky, offering no judgments, no refrains, no consolation. I stub out my cigarette, too, but Lila and I don't move from the step. When my father's sisters trouble the field — Laura plunging in with her long stride, Beth talking a mile a minute, Jean standing at the edge with a hand to her bandannaed head, the sounds from the house getting louder, car doors closing — it creates the illusion that the field is responding, that it has something to say, but by then Lila and I have been watching it for so long that we know that isn't true. It's just a field. An irregular segment of earth. It doesn't know he's dead. Even when we scatter my father's ashes there three days later, the wildflowers wave, the birds chirp, the breeze moves as lightly as ever. The field takes him, effortlessly incorporating the bits of bone and ash. All our fingers are marked with it, smudged gray, as if from some religious ritual. I smoke another horrid stale Gitane, turning that to ash as well, during the singing, the tributes, the stories of his bravery and passion. No one tells the story of when that stopped. Even I can't remember exactly when the tilt turned into falling irreparably behind, falling away. Sometime after Rome.

We populate the field all the way back to the edge near the house, almost everyone who once inhabited my father's consciousness — except our mother, who has taken to her bed in Asbury Park with the cat in her lap. Eddie is bringing her tea. Jenny, pale, stands with a hand on the shoulder of each twin, small boys in dark suits and ties, sober-faced. They look like my father as a child, doubled. Aunt Laura, mammoth in her Wiccan robes, squints resentfully at the sun. "They called for rain," she says. "I knew they were wrong."

In the ample, sun-filled kitchen the next morning, Jenny and Lila and I sit at the round table, coffee mugs in hand, a plate of hyperbolically fat-topped muffins, brought by a neighbor, looming in the middle of the table. Jenny, the lawyer, is neither unkind nor unfair as she explains the situation to us. She doesn't want us to leave Vermont wondering what will happen next. The situation is this: there is nothing but this house we sit in, this house where Jenny and the twins live, and the red box of the studio we can see in the field through the kitchen's French doors. Jenny plans to rent that out, because there is also a fair amount of debt. She has spoken to my father's dealer, and there may be exhibits down the line, museums interested in the documentation of what he did. Everyone expects his reputation to continue to grow, but, as we know, many of those huge structures were demolished after he cut them up, and even those that remain standing can't be collected. No one "collects" a perforated Irish lighthouse, which was, in any case, owned by the Irish government. The fragments and sketches he gave us as birthday gifts, of course, are valuable, even more so now, and how we handle them is entirely up to us. Lila, showing some mercy for once, doesn't look at me. Jenny rubs her temples. Your father was a brilliant man, like no one she had ever known, no one she expects ever to know, but he wasn't a practical one. He made you, she says generously, and that's a lot to give to this world. He and I made our incredible boys. All the rest, his ideas, they're out there forever. I'm sorry, girls, she says. I wish I had better news. I wish I were, well, in a funny way I wish I were older. But I'm not. This is where I live. I work in this town. She looks at her hands. Your dad was a great man.

· · ·

When I wrest from Lila the job of telling our mother the news, it turns out to be a brief conversation. There is a silence, then my mother says, "I wish I could say I was surprised. Give Jenny and the kids my best."

The red pants are still red far down in the veins of the corduroy, but the surface has long since gone past pink to an indeterminate roseate color, the whispered red of a fresco. The safety pins stuck through the spots where the buttons used to be are rusted. The name of the pants' manufacturer on the little tab in the seat is worn away. In one of the pockets I find an irregular slug of metal, maybe an inch and a half long, twisted on one end, pitted. On the plane, I sit with the pants across my lap, touching and touching the bit of metal that he touched, that he saved. I run it around my fingers as if its odd shape will tell me the answer, tell me whom he loved and why. In life, he rarely said. The metal bit is cold. I press it between my palms, giving it the heat of my hands.

My Father Goes Back to the Mountain

MY FATHER IS nine. Because this is just about the middle of the twentieth century, his mother sends him out the back door on an April Saturday morning with a sandwich and an apple and tells him not to come back until suppertime. She has housework, other things to do. His older sisters are going to help her. Laura, for some nefarious reason, has already picked the bathroom. Jean, only a year older than he is, watches wistfully through the window as he goes. She waves.

My father goes up the slight incline of their street, through the little park, across the two-lane highway, and onto the broad path that winds up the mountain. He swings his slender arms, walks with a swing in his step as well, because of his curving foot. He is so happy to be going back to the mountain. He was sick with one thing or another nearly all winter. His father, the engineer who beat them all, taught him to draw, to give him something to do through the long afternoons of coughing and napping. My father drew the things he saw, and a number of things he didn't. He often drew an ocean with an island in the middle of it, though he has never been to the ocean or to an island. Sometimes he drew a hammer or a machine gun. So, in his back pocket he carries a little sketchbook and a pencil. As the road takes him up, it reveals that the mountain is not what it seems from a distance. Walking up the mountain, which he has done many times, sometimes to bring his father his lunch if he's on site that day, he no longer notices that the ground is very dry, with just a few scraggly weeds growing here and there; that a bulldozer sits halfway up the road; that the road itself is pitted, track-marked. A walkie-talkie lies abandoned on the ground. My father picks it up, turns it on. "Hello?" he says. "Ten-four." But there is no answer. My father clips the walkie-talkie onto his belt and feels a slight, satisfying tug. A few yards farther on, there is a length of pipe. My father picks up the pipe and looks at the sun through it; maybe it will burn his eye. It doesn't. He likes the tangy smell of the mountain, the mix of smoke, diesel fumes, earth, and sulfur. He likes the crusty, cracking surface of the mountain, the way it crunches under his feet, like ice. The mountain, he sees, has gotten bigger since the fall. There are more muddy pools of standing water, some of them stained yellow, others brownish black or iridescent green, like a melted lizard. The sky above him is open, blue. The breeze is gentle. He wishes he had a dog to go along with him: the dog would shake himself in the bright treelessness, shake and run off and run back without being called.

The air seems to expand as he ascends, to lift him with it. His chest puffs up. He feels a little sorry for Jean, cooped up at home, but she and Laura and Beth have secrets they don't tell him, either. They don't like the mountain the way he does. They are not the ones who bring their father his lunch. They say the mountain smells, that it's dangerous there. They remind him that the mountain could collapse the way one did in the next town, swallowing five men and all their gear and a bulldozer. The mountain made five widows that day, buried five fathers. His sisters remind him that it is not really a mountain. He understands that it is all ugly and dangerous to them, but the mountain excites him. He would like to live on the mountain; he would like to sleep there and wake up there, and roast animals on sticks and eat them there. He feels the mountain in his heels, as if it is a gigantic magnet that can attract bone.

When I see my father like this, his small towheaded form with its syncopated walk heading determinedly up the road on the mountain that was not really a mountain, I want to gather him in my arms. I see him etched in green, his little green foot arcing blue with each step, the land in black and white, strewn with rubble, earthmovers, broken tools, lengths of wire, scored, crosshatched, incised, toxic, empty inside. In about twenty minutes, he is standing on the flat top of the mountain, looking straight down into the center of the earth.

Being there feels something like flying. He always, just a little bit, would like to jump. It also makes him want to pee. The pit opens about two feet from where he is standing, the gray walls plunging raggedly down to stripped earth. The pit is very, very big, as big as a lake: a lake of air. If my father leans over, he can just see the right side of the pit, or, turning his head, the left side. Cold air and a heady, metallic smell rush up from the vastness, enveloping him in strange. He loves the strange. It feels like a crown under which he is stumbling, drunk. Kicking a stone over the edge, he wants very much to touch the bottom of the pit. The stone, far away, goes *plink*. His father has told him many times, sternly, that if he were to fall into one of these open pits, which can appear unexpectedly as often as they are intentionally dug, it would be very difficult to get him out, that all the men with all their huge equipment might not be able to do it, that he might die down there, all alone. My father imagines, not without a certain amount of pleasure, that he could get lost at the bottom of the pit, that no one would hear his calls for help, and that the men would pile the mountain on top of him and its gargantuan force would crush him and he would become a fossil of smash.

He edges as closely as he dares to the lip of the pit. He leans over almost, almost to the tipping point. The cold, chemical air bathes his face, reddens the tips of his ears. He sees the toes of his sneakers, the gravelly edge of the pit, then the wild nothing. It darkens as a cloud passes overhead. My father holds his breath during the darkness, wondering if he will float up. The wild nothing dims. My father is exalted by it. His heart strains upward from its veins. He tips one finger into the vast air, begins to go over, then quickly clenches his fist, swings his arm out of gravity's reach, and falls backward onto his ass in the dirt. The cloud passes. The wild nothing brightens.

He sits up, eats his sandwich and his apple, then hunches over his sketchbook with his pencil until the afternoon strikes its blue warning note. He is sneaker tips, a short-sleeved plaid shirt, a shock of white-blond hair, alone on the edge of a vast pit.

I think that it was on the way down from one of these expeditions that my father picked up this piece of metal, which probably fell from a truck or was lodged momentarily in a work-boot heel. I think he liked the twist, the pitting, and he put it in his pocket. He was a magpie all his life, endlessly picking up bits of whatever caught his eye, most of it junk, detritus, discards from much larger things.

"And then one morning"–this is how my father told the story, over dinner tables in London, in New York, in Spain, in Wellfleet–"one morning I woke up and the mountain was gone. Totally gone." He'd slap the messy table with his palm, rattling the plates and glasses. "Two weeks later–mountain on the other side. Right?" Everyone always nodded, impressed. The kid from the mining town. The twisted foot, the ambition. The famous sawed-in-half train. "So I went up that one."

And he did. But I think that, at night, as his sisters whispered and giggled in the other room, he could feel the force inside the vanished mountain still, its weird music, his absent deer pulling him close.

Oslo

I COULD FEEL him pulling me close. From across the grimly modernist hotel room in Oslo, Simon's gaze demanded, implored. He sat awkwardly at the Lucite hotel desk, in the casual clothes that never looked casual, the black turtleneck, the corduroy pants, the excellent shoes. He was picking through a gaily striped bag of expensive candy we had bought that day, in lieu of dinner. The others didn't know quite what to make of Simon; in his creased slacks and slicked-back graying hair, he liked to eat candy for dinner, drink late, and pay for everyone, as if we were all on holiday. The guys in the band were polite. On the way to the airport to pick Simon up, however, our drummer, Jorge, at the wheel of the tour van, had muttered, "This wasn't part of the deal."

Simon unwrapped a piece of candy from its gold foil, looking miserable. "Try to understand. I have children."

"You know that's not what I mean." I was angry, again. "I've never asked you to leave your family. I just think it's impossible, and I'm totally frustrated, so let's end it. There's nothing we can be. Let's end it here."

"You want me to leave them. Admit it, Anna. That's what this is about. I am doing everything I can, I have gone so much further than I should." He put the unwrapped candy on the desk. He shook his head, staring into the Lucite desktop as if an answer might write itself across its surface. "Do you want me to leave them?"

I thought his distress was theatrical, hypocritical. His jawline, I could see, was starting to soften, ever so subtly, and I made myself focus on that, and on his stupid perfect shoes made out of ostrich skin. I pitied the ostrich and felt as angry with Simon as if he'd beaten it to death himself.

I said, "You're so fucking self-protective. Has your family's money done this to you, or is it the waiting for it when they die? What did you ever choose, truly choose, yourself? No, I'm not asking you to leave them, because I know you never would. You've said it many times yourself: you can't. What else is there to say?"

"It is a war where I come from," he said. "We did not travel the world making art for rich people. You Americans think everyone has so many choices, but that is an illusion."

He steepled his fingers, leaned back, attempting to appear distant and superior, his hawk eyes very dark, score one for Simon, the existential refugee. But he couldn't maintain it, the steeple he had built just as quickly came undone, the distance between us, between figure and ground, collapsed. I crossed the room.

Sand in my mouth as I whirled down the dunes. Sand in my ears, in my eyes. Wonderland. A riddle: the sea in which we never drown.

He pulled me close to him later, both of us stripped and spent in the cool hotel sheets. His breath smelled of licorice. I wrapped myself around him, inhaled the dear musk of him shamelessly. "Don't go, Anna," he said, his mouth in my hair. "Please don't go."

Between

THE AIRPLANE IS hushed, lights lowered for the night flight, for a few hours of sleep. I put the half-twisted slug of metal back in the pocket of the faded red pants, carefully fold the pants on my lap like a folded flag. I close the black-and-white composition book marked *Wonderland*. Who understands gravity, the pull between people? Not me. I am so tired. I miss him still, my tethered one, my fellow traveler. I have no idea how I am going to do what I have to do next. The plane rocks, flies on over the Atlantic with its heavy cargo of us inside. I wind the green and black scarf around my head – my mourning veil, as it has turned out – and lean back against the headrest. I shift around, trying to find a spot for my legs in the cramped space. I stick them at an angle out into the aisle, daring rudeness. Is this death, then, is this what remains – articles of faded clothing, a twist of metal, broken sleep, lines in a composition book, the muffled sound of an airplane's engines. We salvage what we can, writing letters never sent.

AMOR.

COMING BACK

Hamburg

BY THE TIME we get to "Wonderland," we've lost the audience completely. We're playing a large, soullessly well-appointed club, all beige wood and sconces, that also serves food; long communal tables radiate out from the stage, which is round. It is my job to turn gracefully around and around without falling over while the Hamburgers at the spoke-like tables order, clatter, drink, and talk. The stage lighting is too white; my heels are too high; there are too many instruments and musicians on the small stage. For the Hamburg show we have a guest violin player, a smiley, bald, dark-skinned guy with patches of vitiligo who doesn't speak English and pays no attention to our cues to him to change tempo. I am in constant danger of tripping over the many cables crisscrossing the stage. I try to remember to pick up my feet, like a horse doing dressage, but whenever I do this, I drop a line of the song. I'm having trouble remembering my own lyrics. My perfectly reasonable explanation is that I landed back in Berlin yesterday morning and then took a train, alone, up here. (Why are we going north again? Note to self: ask Boone about all the zigzagging and backtracking.) Technically, I haven't missed any of the tour time, no dates have been canceled, but I've come unstitched from the rhythm somehow and I can't find my way back in. Worse, I'm finding it hard to care. I keep my phone on all the time now, as if my father is going to call from heaven.

Zach, his bass clasped to himself, keeps darting little "get it together" glances my way. He's been in a notably sullen mood since I got back, as if I deserted them rather than went home to bury my father. He and Alicia studiously avoid each other, keeping as far apart as they can on the small, circular stage. Zach plays faster and harder, trying to push me along, but I don't agree to be pushed. His pushing further throws off Tom and Alicia, whose brown roots are coming in. We'll have to get her resilvered, where do we do that? There are faint smudges of fatigue under her eyes, there's a run in her lavender stockings; she's looking thin. She bends to her cello, stumbling over Zach's ever-increasing acceleration, shuttering her large, glittering eyelids, presumably so she can't see the audience drinking, eating, talking, and generally treating us like mood music. They don't care about the reindeer, they refuse to cross the atonal bridge, they are not at all captivated by the questions without answers. They got impatient somewhere around "Five Strings," and now they're in full-on, passive revolt. They prefer their dinners. Ironically, this is the warmest place we've played – my fingers are warm, the tip of my nose is warm, my throat is open and strong. I could sing for hours more, except for the fact that the monitors are making me sound awful, and except for the fact that the audience clearly can't wait for us to finish the last song so that they can go home and have the fuck they've bought and paid for with their rather high minimums, and except for the fact that I'm having a hard time caring. I am an absurdity, if not something worse. The smiley, bald, patchy-skinned violinist bows on, elbow high, oblivious to the rest of us.

Behind me, Tom diligently makes his way down the slalom run of the peculiar, shifting beat of "Wonderland." I can smell his Purell, the alcohol and lemon, from here. I breathe it in, hoping it will help keep me awake. He's more careless on the turns than he used to be. The unexpected shifts have grown all too expected; in fact, he's dropping into them a little too soon. He knows this story. He's heard it many times before, he wants to skip to the end, he wants his own dinner. In this fat city, he and Zach can probably rack up a lot of points in their ongoing eating game. (I don't get it, no one does except them.) His carelessness doesn't matter, since the audience isn't following anyway. I pick up an electric guitar for the small, playful, subtle solo I do in the middle of the song, but something seems off, what is it? I am getting lost, the sound of my guitar is faint, and for a minute I want to get lost entirely. I want to float away. Zach, unsmiling, jabs the amplifier cord into my guitar and stalks two inches off, just in time for an ear-splitting wave of feedback to break over all of us. The sound I make now with the electric guitar is a mess – too loud, covered in sonic trash, like a massive electronic fart. When I take off that guitar and turn around to face another direction, I knock over my two other guitars on stands next to the cello. Alicia's eyes widen. The audience laughs a little, then continues eating. Zach's expression can fairly be described as homicidal. I shrug in a futile attempt to laugh it all off. He won't even look at me, eyes directed to his own hands on his bass. A stagehand scurries up, crouching as he rights the guitars, scurries away again, hopping off the round stage.

I turn around and around, but in every direction the view is the same: well-heeled couples and large groups, looking to be in their mid to late thirties, the women in classic cocktail dresses and smooth, shiny hair worn loose or in artfully disheveled chignons, the men clean-shaven, pink-cheeked, fit. Whose audience is this? What do they think they're listening to? The white light in my eyes is harsh. Dropping yet another line, I try to add it up: if they're these people, then who am I? When did I become so tasteful? From the stage, I watch an exceptionally beautiful, dark-haired woman in a hat with a veil watch me. I don't stare straight at her. I keep her in my sights out of the corner of my eye. Her lips, behind the veil, are a vivid dark red. Her cheekbones are high. Her black dress glitters. She is pretentious, she is playing at being some figure in her imagination, but, in the way of the exceptionally beautiful, her play seems to hint at a larger truth about the illusions of the visible world. Tonight she looks like a torch singer, tomorrow she might be a maid, a soldier, the soldier's widow. She isn't speaking to any of the people seated around her. She may be the only person in the room who is actually listening to us. She taps her glass lightly as I sing, nods. I sing more softly to make her lean in, cock her head; behind the veil, her lips are moving. She is singing with me. I don't turn when I should, bad stagecraft, bad manners, but who cares? The night is a disaster. And I hardly need another look at Zach's scowl.

"By the sea," we sing together, "on the green ship / I will be waiting." To what internal drama of hers am I the soundtrack? Her hand moves, waves. In the corner of my eye, it looks like a small bird fluttering up. "We will go then / only then / only then / we will go then / we will go then / we will go then / wonderland." She lifts the veil to blot her tears with her napkin. She is quite young, I see now, perhaps twenty-two. Is her pain real or is it part of her solitary dress-up? Does it matter? "We will go then / we will go then / we will go then / wonderland." Zach bites off the final chord. When I turn around, he has already left the stage, flash of his white jacket disappearing at the side door.

The rest of us exit to dutiful applause. I gingerly clamber off the stage last, not wanting to trip. The instruments, left behind, look glad to be free of us. The young woman with the veil is clapping madly, smiling, shouting, "Bravo!" What concert is she at? I wish I were there. We go through the side door and hover on the other side, smelling one another's sweat, with shrugs and stiff smiles. There will be no encore tonight, this is a formality. But the woman with the veil keeps clapping so hard that the Hamburgers clap with her, maybe they don't wish for her to be embarrassed, and so we are forced to shuffle back onstage again. Zach, however, is nowhere to be seen. The encore depends on him — we can't do it, or much of anything really, without a bassist. Alicia, Tom, and the smiley bald guy, frozen in position, look from me to the blank space where Zach is supposed to be. At the tables, checks are down, credit cards are slapping on top of them, the sleek women and pink-cheeked men are visibly impatient, squeaking their chairs, putting on their coats.

I mouth "Rush" and we stumble into it, and then we fall and fall. This isn't the encore we've rehearsed. I forget half the words; Alicia, it seems, is playing some other song; Tom's beat is panicky and impossible to follow, the rhythm of someone running away screaming. The bald violinist with vitiligo gamely plucks out a few chords by hand. The woman with the veil is undisappointable, beaming at us from her seat. I turn around, I turn around, I turn around, like a plastic ballerina on top of a music box. In the movie, the heroine who has just lost her father gives the performance of her life, she is tragic and beautiful, she soars. I am not soaring, not transformed by grief. If anything, I feel more stubbornly and irredeemably myself, flattened and contracted, alienated, very much alone, and something like bored. I shouldn't be here. I should be in Vermont, sorting through my father's bad canvases, the overly aestheticized detritus of his later years, the worthless photos and keepsakes I don't want to see. I wish I could forgive him for dying so bewildered and collapsed, but I can't.

I touch my fingertips together in a theatrical gesture. They're callused from playing every night; my left shoulder aches the way it always does by this point on a tour. I feel as if I'm inhabiting someone else's body, hoping that she knows the way. Dropping lines, blowing notes, I long for the strudel with the lobster in it, for ten, twenty wordless minutes with William.

I surrender to the wreck of the evening. I cut the song off, such as it is, a stanza early, bow, and call out, "Good night, Hamburg!" The others stop playing abruptly; I hope the audience thinks it's modern and ragged, but basically I hate them, so I don't really care. Just before I go through the side door, I turn and throw the woman in the veil a kiss. Fuck you, Hamburg.

Boone is waiting alone in the green room (which is, in fact, a tender shade of green, warm, with good, comfortable furniture, a bower for our humiliation), drinking coffee, a pastry in his other hand, his earpiece dangling at his collar, wearing a knit hat with knitted ridges along the top, like the bony plates of a stegosaurus. "Jesus, Anna," he says, "what the hell happened out there? Where's Zach?"

"Isn't he here?"

Boone gestures at the small, empty room.

"Goddamnit," I say, shifting into an irritable rage.

The others tumble in with tense faces. The bald guy begins to put his violin back in its case, still smiling, but not at anyone in the room.

"Shake it off," says Boone. "We have another night, it's almost sold out, don't worry." He closes the green room door. Even on a catastrophic night like this, people will be coming backstage, milling around, wanting to talk, admire, soak up the schadenfreude.

Tom drops onto the sofa. "Motherfuck," he says. "That was excruciating."

"Like being slowly boiled," Alicia says, slumping against the wall, pulling at a split end.

"Or raped in a coma," Tom continues. "In a semi-coma. No one can hear you try to scream. *Hgggghhhlllp. Hgggghhlllp*," he whispers.

"What's up with Zach?" I ask Alicia and Tom. Alicia bites her lip.

"You know," says Alicia. "He's a perfectionist."

"The house sucked," says Tom.

"Give me a break," I say. The rage feels good, orienting. "What was his *fucking* problem out there?"

"Hey, hey," says Boone. "Hey now." He puts his arms around me, hugs me tight. He smells like pastry, like coffee, a sugar dinosaur. He whispers in my ear, "Pull back, sweetheart. It's not their fault."

I sit down next to Alicia on the sofa. She puts her feet in my lap. "I'm sorry," she says.

I take off her golden, complicatedly laced shoes, rub her small feet in their mauve stockings. "We need to get you some new stockings," I say. "These are done in."

"I know," says Alicia, closing her eyes. "I never bring enough of anything."

"Let's get the fuck out of here," says Tom. "Time for the bar."

Boone dunks his pastry, sighs, purses his lips. His woolen stegosaurus ridge remains upright, goofily optimistic. "Rock-and-roll," he says in an airy tone.

The door clicks open and Zach slides in, wraith-like, moves toward the corner of the room. He has intense green eyes, the eyes of a crazy American pioneer, with long lashes. He is light on his feet, but his arm muscles are substantial; the combined effect is that he often seems to be levitating as he walks, hovering disdainfully by his biceps a few inches above the ground. I am a little afraid of him, truth be told. I think he judges me. He does judge me, even now, in my grief.

"Yo," says Tom.

Alicia squints up to see what I am going to do, glances at Zach, blushes. I rub her instep, her pinkie toe. I do this with great concentration, as if it were my job, as if I were the tour masseuse (as if we could afford such a thing) and not the presumptive star. Her mauve feet are warm, like a pair of sweet, furless, mauve animals. Outside, the corridor is buzzing and humming with talk, laughter, exclamations in German. Out of the corner of my eye, that flicker, flicker, quick as a snake's tongue. It lashes me under the ribs.

Zach leans his head against the wall, looking at me from under lowered eyelids. "What happened out there, Anna?" he asks.

I don't answer right away, moving my hand around Alicia's ankle. "You tell me," I say quietly. Alicia tries to slip her foot out of my hand, but I hold it tight. I meet Zach's gaze and do not flinch. "You ever walk off like that again," I say, "and you're fired."

Zach turns his chin up and sideways, like a horse pulling away from the bridle. "The guitars —"

"Fuck the fucking guitars." I push Alicia's feet out of my lap, stand up, right my skirt, settle my feet in my high heels. Flicker, flicker, but I still can't catch it. "You're on the clock. We all are."

The room is silent. Boone dunks his pastry again. His phone is chortling, but he doesn't answer it. Tom and Alicia look at me, then Zach, then back at me. Tom pulls his hat down over his ears. Zach kicks the wall, shrugs. "Sure, boss," he says. "They're your guitars, do what you want."

I cross the room to the door. "Stand up. People are waiting for us." I throw the door open, let in the tide of good and bad will. I expect the woman with the veil to be there, but she isn't. Crazy and young as she is, maybe she understands that there is nothing more to be gained from coming backstage. It is I who wish to see her, to ask her, "What did you see? What did you hear? Who are we to you?"

As the backstage crowd swirls around us, diluting our heat, I text Simon. I tell him that I'm on tour again in Europe, that my father has just died. *My God, Anna,* he writes back with gratifying speed. *Anna. Where are you?*

One Side, and the Other Side

RECORDS USED TO have A sides and B sides – well, there used to *be* records, flat rounds of black vinyl. The sound of the needle bumping against the label. *Skritch, skritch, skritch.* The sound of the end of the evening, end of the party. Turn the record over, holding the disk with your fingertips, if you're still awake. I listened to Talking Heads' *More Songs About Buildings and Food* and The Slits' *Playing with a Different Sex* again and again; *Twist & Rain;* also, endlessly, Prince. I couldn't get enough of Prince. The muscularity of listening, like surfing, like turning into the skid. Like falling, turning over and over; they said my father was lucky, that he turned on his side as the wall began to collapse, immediately knocking him unconscious. His shoulder was shattered, his spine was a mess. They had to put metal inside him to bend him straight again, or straight enough. Straighter, actually, than he'd been before. But if the wall had landed more squarely on his head or his neck, he would have been killed instantly. What is the degree of that arc? One side, and then the other side. They aren't the same; the sides do matter. In this case, one was life and the other death. Flip a coin, feel the weight as it leaves your thumbnail, turns in the air. What law of physics explains how it is that the coin lands this way or that? Can we say that the coin has any control over its fate? Did he know he was turning, and which side was he trying to land on – the wrong one or the right one? I will never be able to ask him now, and in any case he probably didn't remember, given the force of the blow.

The fascist gymnasium project was never finished; it remained as unfinished as the massive, half-built, marble gym itself, intended to build the muscles of the fascist victors of the future. The team had gotten as far as incising partway through an interior wall when the wall collapsed; for various engineering reasons, they needed to work from the inside out, and obviously it still didn't work. Out of respect for what my father was trying to accomplish and the severity of his injuries, the wealthy Italians who had commissioned the project left the wall like that, a circular layer removed from it, leaving a thin, ghostly round of dull, rough stone. I hope it is still there. The one side and the other side, perpetually nearly touching.

The Underground City

THE UNDERGROUND CITY in Perugia is smaller than one might imagine, not at all as big as Perugia itself, which is only a bit bigger than many of the tiny villages tucked into the hills of Tuscany. The underground city is the original city, on top of which a sixteenth-century Pope built a fortress he liked better. Simon and I reached the end of the underground city so fast that we turned around and walked back over its cobblestone streets, away from the day and back into the ancient city's perpetual night. He touched the stone walls, looked up for a long time at the vaulted stone ceilings. "This could still be used," he said. "The construction is beautiful." Above us, endless boutiques selling chocolate, lingerie, bath salts, and myriad varieties of olive oil infused with flowers and spices and fruit. An adulterer's city if ever there was one. In the city beneath the city, sober, unnaturally clean, mottled stone walls; empty streets; iron lamps; empty churches; empty houses; empty squares that were once shops. It was cold and it smelled of earth.

"Arezzo tomorrow," I said. It was the *Bang Bang* tour.

"The last day," Simon said. He sighed. "Anna."

"Should we move here?" I said. "Bring the underground city back to life."

"What would we be?"

"Lamplighters. Work at night, make love and art all day."

He laughed. He tucked his chin in when he laughed, closed his eyes, boyishly gave himself over to it. "I would write poems and you would write music?"

"Yes. In a sooty sort of way."

"Songs about lamps?" He cocked his head, his hawk's eye soft.

"Songs about sparks and shadows."

He came and stood close to me, put his hands on my shoulders, studied my face, held my face in his hands. "You are very beautiful to me. I never thought I would find anyone like you. I wish I had known that you existed."

"I was right, you know"—I tried to point east, although I had no idea where east was—"over there. In the other place. Now I'm here." I heard a bell ring somewhere. East? West?

Simon rested his warm cheek against mine. "I would like to make songs with you about sparks and shadows."

"Okay. We'll start one in Arezzo."

He hummed a melody into my ear, perhaps four or five notes.

Hamburg Redux

ZACH SENDS EVERYONE a text message that says, "Hey, kids, let's have a band meeting." Boone and I, having breakfast in the windowless hotel dining room with the terrifying buffet, receive it at the same time. I think I slept a bit.

"For fuck's sake," I say. "What a baby."

Boone taps his spoon against his cup. "You have to be the one to handle this."

"I know that."

"Look —"

"Just," I say. "Goddamnit. They know better than this, don't they? That this is what happens."

Boone shrugs, strokes the ends of his mustache, which nearly reach his chin. He has begun to look like the wheeler-dealer that he is, someone who might own a white Ducati. He turns his palms up. "This is what you wanted. This is what happens, too."

"Go fuck yourself."

About an hour later, we all crowd into Zach's small room – and that's a tactical error right there, I know that, going to him. Zach perches on the desk. Next to him is a yellow legal pad with bullet points that are legible from across the room, where I take the only armchair. Not much of a move, but it's all I've got at the moment. Tom and Alicia are sitting on the end of the double bed, looking as if it is they who are about to be punished. Boone leans against the wall by the door. I desperately wish to be somewhere else. When I'm awake, I want to be asleep; when I'm asleep, which isn't often, I wake up many times, alarmed. I touch the nubbly chair arm and think, *My father is dead,* but somehow the chairness of the chair refutes this fact. How can my father be dead and the chair still be it-self? How can I be awake if I'm asleep? What time is it? Which life is this? The window blinds are drawn, the bedside lamp is on, further confusing me about the time of day, or night.

"Look, you guys, Anna," Zach says, "I am totally committed to this project, you all know that. This tour was like my dream come true." He palms his head. "But I have to be straight-up here. I think we're in trouble." He picks up the legal pad. "Okay, one: leadership." He doesn't look at me. "No one has to be, like, a dictator, but it seems to me, in my humble opinion, that we've lost some focus. We don't seem to be playing *with* each other out there and it's bumming me out. A lot. Two: re-hearsals. I'm thinking maybe we need to get some rehearsal time in. Boone, I know it's expensive finding space, but—"

"Well—" Boone equivocates, looking at me.

"It's important," Zach interjects, warming to his theme. "See, this is what I'm saying, it's like—"

I stand up. "You don't know what it's like. Don't kid your-self." On my feet, I am at eye level with Zach, sitting on the desk. "You couldn't possibly know what it's *like*. It isn't *like* anything. It's like sometimes shit falls apart, sometimes you fail, sometimes it's just not there. Chances are, I'm over, that's what it's like. I couldn't do it. I thought I could, but I couldn't." Tom and Alicia stare uneasily at me, careful not to break eye contact. Zach licks his lips.

"Anna—" Boone says, holding out his hand.

"I sold the only thing I had to sell. My father just died. We're tanking. I'm going to have to go back to teaching little rich girls how to make birdfeeders for the rest of my life. You want to get off the tour? Go ahead. There's the door. I can't. I've got nowhere else to go. I have to ride this train all the way down whether I like it or not. So I don't give a shit what you do, Zach. We can pick up another bass player."

Zach lowers his head and begins to cry. Tom and Alicia have

obviously left their bodies; their shells are speechless. Boone has put his hand over his eyes.

"Jesus, Anna," says Zach, weeping, "I love you. I love all of you. I'm being such an asshole. Let's rock this thing." He makes a fist in the air. Alicia raises an eyebrow.

What else can I do? I'm out of ideas. I hug him and his absurd biceps, tell him it's all right, apologize for my distraction. Looking at Boone, I tell Zach that we'll find rehearsal space somewhere, this is an amazing band, I'm not myself, I'm sorry, I'm so sorry. Zach takes amazing care of the guitars, they'd be a mess without him. We all troop down to the dark little bar and I buy everyone a drink, even though it's ten-thirty in the morning. And I am sorry. I drink my drink as if what I want is a drink between breakfast and lunch. They all say how awful they feel about my loss, am I okay? On the television screen over the bar, men in yellow dart toward and away from men in black. They look as if they've been choreographed in their seemingly random motion, so balletic are their near-misses.

When I finally get back to my room, exhausted beyond exhausted, I find that the tip of the phone has gone red.

The Distance Between Us

IN AREZZO, A Mylar balloon with the madly smiling face of Mickey Mouse printed on it bumped lightly against the ceiling of the Basilica di San Francesco. The silver of the balloon, the flat black paddles of Mickey's enormous ears, the round, blank, black eyes and oversized grin seemed almost supernaturally present compared to the intricate, faded, demi-erased Piero della Francesca frescoes, *The Legend of the True Cross*, which covered the walls of two adjoining rooms behind the nave of the church. Tourists were crowded into the nave, making that low tourist hum; the line to get in snaked all the way outside, onto the square. Everyone so eager to see the ghosts, the knights, and the martyrs and saints of long ago. I sat down in a pew, unaccountably irritated. The famed church smelled like old wood and dust. I half wanted it to burn down. At times all of Italy seemed like a crypt, or maybe that was just since I had realized that *Bang Bang* was undeniably a disaster. Bang bang, you're dead. I watched the silver balloon bob in the rafters, making grinning Mickey dance. Simon, in a thin overcoat and with his big black glasses on his sharp face, walked up and down the length of the church, peering, considering. His movements were brisk. I knew he was thinking about the relative distribution of stone, air, and arc. I traced a little pattern on my hand, a rhythm maybe. Was it the rhythm of the swifts? One could never tell if they were flying up or down, their movements were so erratic. Or maybe it was the inner sound of *Bang Bang*, the absent deer, which no one but me and my lost tribe from the chateau would ever hear properly. Mickey smiled down at me, or possibly he was smirking. Hard to say. It struck me as funny, a rebuke to all the piety. I laughed, thinking, *Well, Mickey has a point.*

Simon sat down in the pew next to me. His hair had gotten long; it was making small, fanciful graying curls at his collar, lengthening his face. Always, after a lengthy bout of sex, that nearly formal distance between us, the caesura. Not a turning away but a standing apart, face to face, as the waves dispersed. I still longed for his body beneath his clothes, but at the same time didn't want to touch him again, not yet. I loved him so much that I could hardly bear to look at him. I pointed to Mickey above, but my smile was fading.

"It's like that inflatable bat in the club in Perugia on Halloween, remember?" he said.

"That was two days ago. Too soon for nostalgia." I never liked the last day. We had had nearly four days and several cities together, a great luxury. I reminded myself of that, of how lucky I was to have had that, to have such a pure love with Simon, a love so rare.

"He was a very funny bat." He squeezed my hand. I didn't return the squeeze. He would be on a plane home that evening. The band and I would go on to Florence in the morning. That night I would sleep alone, order room service for breakfast, leave the closet doors open, the bed unmade, towels on the floor, empty Limonata cans placed neatly next to the wastebasket, hangers empty, rocking. I would toss out the tourist map with the black circle he had drawn around the Vasari house. Glance out the window at the ceaseless parabolas of the swifts in flight. Click of the door behind me, the hungover faces of my guys in the lobby, luggage piled around them. No one would ask where the older man was, because they didn't like him all that much. At home, because the people there loved that older man, no one would press him to confirm where he'd said he'd been – instead, presents for the kids, a sincere kiss for the wife, a walk after dinner alone, the uncanny privacy and carefully closed doors of marriage. That's the part that astonished me, the part I never understood: that silence between him and his wife, something almost courtly about it, like a bow and curtsy to each other, a deference to one another's inherent unknowability. She knew, without being told, when to become preoccupied with a child's cold, someone's sister's money troubles, redoing the upstairs bathroom. Even after I was married myself, I didn't understand that kind of marriage. Simon called me in Florence, sounding resolved, sorrowful, distant. He made sure to keep the conversation brief. I said, "Please don't do this. Please. Simon, please." And then I went down.

In the pew, we two unmarried, profane lovers, adulterers, looked up together at the Mylar Mickey Mouse balloon smiling down crazily from the ancient rafters. Simon crossed himself with his free hand, caught my eye, laughed.

Hamburg Hauptbahnhof

I WAIT FOR Simon in Hamburg's Hauptbahnhof in the afternoon. I am wearing a black wrap dress, expensive black stockings with tiny diamond shapes embroidered on the ankles,
pointy high-heeled shoes, a belted white coat. I have put my
hair up into a loose chignon, not unlike the ones worn by the
women in the club where we failed so miserably last night. I
sit down on a long wooden bench, cross my legs. I have chosen this look with what I can only describe as a certain reck-
lessness. It has been seven years, and I am sure I look older.
How could I not? He will be older, too. I smooth the lap of the
white coat, tuck a stray strand of hair behind my ear. Europe-
ans come and go around me, hurrying through lives I only half
understand. I flip through *Die Zeit*. A photo of a group of people carrying signs, shouting. What are they protesting? Would
I be for or against? Announcements in German.

Train number 161, from Zurich, pulls in. I stand up, tilt over
one heel, then right myself again. Simon walks toward me
down the platform. I wave a tiny wave. His face looks longer,
sharper, with closely trimmed hair. His glasses are small, rim-
less. He is carrying a briefcase. He nods at me, as if I really am
a business colleague he is meeting here, as if I am carrying my
own briefcase filled with documents to be signed. Then he
smiles, glances down, up again, meeting my eye. I blush and
smile. I walk forward to meet him. When we are within reach,
we stand for a moment, not touching, looking into each other's faces. Simon shrugs, holds his arms out, palms up: *This
is me now.* I laugh – I am so happy to see him, it is absurd, I
know how absurd it is, how ridiculous I am, how I have come
undone in three seconds flat. Even my hair is already coming
loose from the casual, swirling arrangement it took me forty

minutes to construct. We embrace, kiss on both cheeks. As if I have never noticed it before, I am surprised all over again by the strength of him, his density. Weight coils inside him, invisible but heavy in my arms, his warm skin. Just like before. His briefcase rests between us; he touches my face. "Ah, Anna," he says. "What you must have been through. Dear girl, I wish I had known." As if we've been seeing each other all this time, as if the seven years have been seven days.

"It was very unexpected. A heart attack."

He stands back, regarding me. His dark eyes dart over my face. "You look terrific."

"So do you."

"Terrific" is the approximation, the shorthand: he does look strong and healthy, well groomed, but "terrific" is a word for a dessert, a car, and it sounds awkward in his accent. "Terrific"doesn't express what I feel when I see that there is an age spot near his hairline and that his hair is short, precisely combed back; the comb lines are so evenly spaced. I feel thrilled, I feel giddy, as if we have come through something terribly dangerous together and now stand, shaking, alive, shocked, on solid ground. *We almost didn't make it*, I want to say to him. *Jesus Christ, what a miracle.* The skin on his face is looser, but also pinker, smoother. He doesn't look younger, of course, but the seven years that have passed seem to have planed away several surface layers, revealing a smaller, sweeter man. His smile is more open, more naked, or was that always the case? He is past fifty. I am well past forty. What does he see when he looks at me besides terrific?

"Shall we go?" he says, picking up his briefcase. We walk down the platform; no one gives us a second glance, because now we don't look an odd couple at all. The intervening time has shrunk the visual difference between us, though we have been apart for much longer than we were ever together. I am still taller, of course, but otherwise – in my wrap dress, my pointy shoes, and white coat – I could easily be, at the very least, his longtime mistress, if not his younger second wife. Maybe I am his longtime mistress, maybe I have been his mistress since we met, since before we met. I hate the word "mistress." He puts his hand on my back. "I haven't been here in years," he says, looking around at the station. "Terrible city, really."

"I wouldn't know. I've basically seen the hotel and the club. We're bombing, by the way."

"No, no." He shakes his head. "I don't believe that."

"You'll come tonight, you'll see. They hate us here."

"It's Germany. They hate everyone. They hate themselves."

The pressure of his hand on my back. We smile shyly at each other, as complicit as ever. He smells the same. In the plush little taxi he says, "He was a great man, your father. I know how much you admired him."

"Well. Admired, loved, hated, was frustrated by, sought out, lost so long ago, if I'm being honest. The recent paintings." I shake my head. "I don't understand what happened. Never will, maybe."

We glide past a shopping arcade lined with sleek stores. "Time," says Simon, opening his hand, as if to show me its map on his palm. "Perhaps he got tired."

"Simon. Where's your wedding ring?"

"Ah. I am divorced now." He shrugs, coughs.

I am breathless. I just manage to say, "What are you talking about?"

"We got divorced. About two years ago." He glances at me without entirely turning his head, then back toward the busy, prosperous street outside. "It was very . . . it was very difficult. Our daughters were very upset by it. The youngest will never forgive us, it seems. We have only just finished disengaging from the property."

The taxi stops in front of the hotel. Simon pays the driver, says something in German, the taxi driver laughs, nodding. I wonder if Simon said, "I really have no emotional or interper-

sonal skills whatsoever, I'm completely selfish, I'm basically a
total asshole, and I should be on my knees thanking God that
anyone anywhere has ever loved me."

And then maybe the taxi driver, laughing, said, "Me, too!"

But he didn't use enough words for that, so I doubt it. I get
out of the taxi feeling lightheaded. My heart is racing. I am
sweating through the wrap dress. I lose my balance on my heel
again and Simon catches me by the elbow. "Careful," he says
tenderly. The doorman opens the ornate door for us and we go
up in the elevator in silence. I feel as if I am going to be sick.
The corridor has a fusty scent mixed with strong soap and
kitchen smells from downstairs. It reminds me of William's
rooms over the restaurant in Berlin, that earthy mix of food
being cooked and rough cleaning agents. My heels sink into
the pile carpet as I lead us to my room. We have both assumed,
silently, that he will be staying with me; why did I assume
that? More to the point, why did he? His shoulder brushes
mine, our hands touch. When we went down hotel corridors
in the past, our shoulders and hands touched in just this way,
a Morse code of desire, tiny yeses, a sequence of touches that
accelerated as we neared the door to whatever room in whatever hotel in whatever city. A lethargy, an anxiety, overtake
me—I have wanted to see him again for so long, but now I find
myself wondering what I'm going to do with him for the next
five hours. It feels claustrophobic. Madly, I suddenly want to
spend the afternoon alone with my guitar, writing music. The
dress feels absurd, like a costume; I want to put on my baggy-
assed jeans and a T-shirt. I insert the flat, blank plastic key in
the slot. Click-click, green light. The door opens.

His hand on my hip as I open the door. His breath near my
ear. I sway back toward him, pulled, but then move forward
again. A line from a dance song goes through my head, something raunchy and fast about who's giving what to whom
where all night long; it's a path I see that I could take this afternoon, that attitude. One more, one more. A few verses of

erotic nostalgia. But I can't catch my breath. What if I can't catch it by tonight? I unbelt the white coat, kick off the pointy shoes, loosen the dress.

He sets his briefcase down on the floor. "How beautiful you are," he says. "Always so beautiful."

The sun is streaming through the open curtains onto the neatly made bed. Housekeeping has been and gone. Everything is tucked, vacuumed, centered. Chocolates on the square white pillows. The impossible quiet of a hotel room. The lines at his eyes have deepened. Untethered, he holds his arms close to his body, stands very straight, as if trying to look taller. We turn to embrace, he kisses me, his hands on my face; he strokes my hair. My body betrays me without a second's hesitation, folding time; I am his. In the past, this would be when we would begin making love, it was the first thing we always did, beginning at the innermost point and then working our way out to whatever city surrounded us, in spirals.

I turn away, walk slowly in my stockinged feet to the little, uncomfortable armchair, sit down in it, still in my coat. I brace my hands on the chair's arms, put my feet flat on the floor. He remains standing awkwardly at the end of the room's tiny hall, near the television. I pull the pins out of my hair, shake it loose, set the pins on the side table. They make gentle, syncopated clicks. Nothing that is going through my mind seems like the right thing to say, because surely he can imagine all of it himself. *How could you, why didn't you tell me, why did you come here, are you a complete jackass, what if I hadn't written you, why are you standing there as if waiting for permission to approach? You never loved me. Admit it. You always loved me. Admit it. Leave. Stay. Don't make me have to decide, on top of everything else.*

I say, "Simon."

He inclines his head, shakes it. "I thought of calling, of course. But I thought that might be unfair."

"To whom?"

He doesn't answer.

"What happened?"

He sits down on the corner of the enormous, perfectly made bed, looks at his gleaming shoes. Classic loafers. Did he wear them for me this time? "I discovered that she'd been having an affair for some time. With a man we both knew. I confronted her about it and she admitted it at once. I completely fell apart. I thought maybe we could patch it up, but we couldn't – I found that I couldn't forgive her. She is already living with him. I am sure they will marry as soon as they can." He raises his head; tears fill his eyes. "So."

A question is forming in my mind, edged with a vertiginous suspicion. Disingenuously, I ask, "And what did she say when you told her about me?"

"I didn't do that, Anna." In a tone of excessive politeness.

"What do you mean?" Though I know, I know exactly what he means. Haven't I always?

"Why should I give her that?" Less politely. "She betrayed me. She betrayed our marriage, our children. The other man was my *friend,* he had once borrowed money from me –"

"But Simon," and though I try to control it, I can feel my own tone sharpening, "you were hardly faithful to her, we both know what happened, and my God, you and me, what that was –"

"It's not the same thing," he says, much too quickly.

"Not the same thing as *what?* Your marriage?"

He flinches at my intonation of the word "marriage," and though I didn't quite think I intended to say it that way, maybe I did. My stomach heaves. Who could I have possibly convinced myself that I was? I see myself, a slender figure in tattered jeans, on the edge of someone else's five-story, steel-and-glass marriage in Switzerland. A footnote, at best. An adventure. His wonderland. A woman without a key to his house.

"I should not have come here," he says. "I'm sorry. I will go to another hotel." He fumbles in his pocket for his cell phone. His hand shakes.

"Why *did* you come here?" I grip the arms of the chair.

He looks at me, looks at all of me, his hawk's eye as dark and keen as ever in his smaller, more open face. My body, blind to the present moment, alights. "I wanted to see you, Anna."

"Why?"

He presses a button on the cell phone, puts it back in his pocket. "You wrote me, and, I don't know, it had been such a long time, you have lost your father." He pauses. "Perhaps I was curious."

"Curious? You took a ten-hour train ride from Zurich to Hamburg after seven years because you were *curious?* Simon, even for you that's a ridiculous thing to say. You couldn't possibly believe that."

"Eight and a half hours, actually. I took the faster train. I got up very early this morning." He lies back on the bed and gazes at the ceiling. This isn't like him; he was never casual, didn't sprawl and slouch like Americans. I know without seeing it that under his button-down shirt is a bright white undershirt, that his socks are silk, that his feet are smooth and soft, toenails neatly clipped. "I no longer know what I believe. She was my wife and the mother of my children. We were married for twenty-five years. I loved her. After this happened I became very depressed. I take something for it now. I gained weight, I lost weight. I couldn't focus. I felt that I had lost my life, and I still feel that way. I came because I miss you. I have missed you for years. That's the truth. Please come over here."

"I can't be late for sound check." Sound check is three hours from now.

"Please." He reaches a hand out over the bedspread.

I go. I go because I want to, my body is tugging me forward, but I also go because I want to know him, want to know what has happened and where he's been, and only his body can tell me that. I think this might be unfair, a little; I might be taking

advantage of something he can't control. I don't mean the stiff-
ness of his cock. I mean him – his weight, his scent, the way he
moves, the sounds that he makes. He looks straight at me like
a drowning man, as urgent as that first time in London. I climb
on top of him, I can feel the ridge of him, I run my hand inside his pants to his cock, his balls, I unzip him, open his belt
buckle, free him. He runs his hands under the dress, up along
my ass, he pulls at the black stockings, the lacy black panties
underneath. I kick out of them; his thumb, his fingers, part me.
His suit jacket smells of starch; the cufflinks on his light blue
shirt are small bars of brushed steel. I bury my face in his warm
neck as I straddle him, half naked; his cock is hard against my
ass and his hand is inside me, opening me. Our clothes seem to
be everywhere, tangling us, but also nesting us. Silk, linen, cotton, nylon, bunching, dampening, half-exposing skin, pussy,
dick, nipple.

He grips me inside so hard, he pulls against the small,
spongy internal ridge nearly to the point of causing me pain.
"Anna," he says. "Anna. Anna." With his other hand, he pulls
my hair back; I am kissing him, pressed open-legged over his
chest, we are already starting to move together. It is as if he is
making of me a bow, a circuit, or that we complete a circuit together; my length on his weight, my scent on his, my mouth
on his mouth, the force of him pulling at me from within: we
are a chord. Even as I am hearing that chord, I want to hear it
again, to hear it louder. I sit up on him, put my thumbs in his
mouth; he sucks, sucks, his eyes closed, his tongue rolling over
and over my fingers. I make him stand up so that, kneeling on
the bed, I can unbutton his shirt, push it and the suit jacket off
his shoulders, pull and tug him out of his clothes. Naked, he
unwraps me from the wrap dress, un-bras me in one gesture,
buries his face in my breasts. We press together, both naked. I
hold his shoulder blades in my hands. I am shaking.

We lie down. I think of his wife, try not to, but I can't help it.
Even as I pull him in, as I whisper in his ear, as he groans and I

feel him just as I did seven years ago in Arezzo, the swifts darting in their mad arcs in the sky outside, *say it say it say it say it
say it say it,* even as he moves more deeply into me, I wonder
why she left him. I have only the haziest image of her – dark-
haired, short, strong-faced, laughing in a bathing suit, a photo
on his laptop he showed me just once, quickly. He gathers me
closer to him, closer still, but my mind is wandering to this
woman I don't know but who, strangely, is more real to me
at this moment, when I am in bed with the man she left. She
knew his body, this very body, his warm flat feet, she fucked
him in just this way, in all the ways no doubt, for twenty-five
years. And then she left. He knows why, but he doesn't want
to tell me; he isn't going to tell me. Instead, we are going to
fuck. We are fucking. I feel the great weight of it, of their broken marriage, their broken country, his despair, his need, his
breaking again as he comes; the heat and force of it, and that
it has disappeared into time like a train around a curve, into a
past of his that I don't understand and that he can't explain to
me except, perhaps, like this. I don't come, because I am too
busy listening to his body, spying on his heart. He is breathing hard, still inside me. Even with everything, all that I know,
I want him to stay there. He shudders. I remember now – how
did I forget? – that it was his way to stay inside me for a long
time after coming, as long as possible, like a man who wants to
stay at home, to be at home, who feels at home right here, right
now, and who does not, ever, want to be sent out to wander
alone; a man who never wanted to be in exile. He would have
continued to lie about everything, forever, if only she wouldn't
leave him. But she did, and he has come back to me, he is here.
I begin to shake.

"Shhh, Anna," he whispers, stroking my hair. "My darling,
shhhh. I have missed you. I have missed you so much. I am so
glad that we have found one another again."

He turns and curls around me on the bed, holding me. His
legs fit behind mine and his arm is strong, pulling me against

him as he buries his hawk face, softer now, in the back of my neck. I stop shaking very slowly. He holds me to his chest. I pull the bedspread over us. We fall asleep, wake in dim light. I am, in fact, late for sound check. Zach, in the center of the round stage, plucks angrily at the untuned bass strings. My guitars are lined up neatly in their stands. I thank him for setting me up.

The show goes a little better, but just a little. We're not going to woo Hamburg, that's clear. Simon sits with Boone at a small table near the stage sipping a martini, wearing a suit jacket and a crisp white button-down shirt, no tie. Boone, tapping away on his phone, looks like Simon's black-sheep son. As we soldier on through the set, me turning on the circular stage, returning several times to see Simon and Boone, the twelve on my personal clock, I wonder what they could possibly be talking about.

After the show, Simon and I go straight back to the room. In the past, we would have made love again, exhausted but still hungry, just one more, never enough time. Simon hangs up his suit jacket, his shirt. I undo my braid, take off the shoes with the thick black straps and the high white heels. We sit down on the bed. Simon takes my hand. He twines my hair in his fingers, kisses it. "This red — I love this red."

"I dye it now. Simon. You never even told me you got divorced. We wouldn't be here if I hadn't written you — I would never have known."

He bends his head. "I hardly thought I had the right. After everything. I was ashamed. Please forgive me. When you wrote me, I came right away. Thank God you wrote."

I get up. I take a shower with scented hotel soap, washing Hamburg down the drain. When we are settled in bed, my skin damp and cool against his, he says, "I sometimes think about our child, what our child would have been like. Do you?"

"Yes. I think she would have been a girl."

"Ah! So do I. Tall like you, but fiery like me. Very smart. A musician or artist."

"Yes. I'm sorry, Simon."

"That was then," he says.

We don't make love. We sleep curled together, my feet on his flat feet, first setting the alarm on the clock as if there is some reason to do so. In the morning, I wake before him, before the alarm. He is sleeping on his side, facing me. His hand still looks strange to me without the wedding ring, almost unbearably vulnerable. The curtains on the windows are slightly parted, a line of gray between them. I wonder what we will do today. Walk by the water? I have tonight off. I put my hand on one of his. He opens his eyes.

"I love you," he says.

"We leave for Brussels tomorrow."

"And then?"

"Then . . . Luxembourg. Basel. Latvia, some festival. We end in Rome."

"Shall I come to Rome?" He tightens his fingers on mine.

"My ex-husband's name was Jim. He was from Texas. He got clean after ten years of being a pretty serious junkie. You wouldn't know it to look at him, but he had this incredibly hairy chest. We called it the tree of life. He had perfect pitch and tinnitus. He owns fifteen violins, some of them expensive, but he plays on the cheapest one. I teach school for a living."

Simon frowns. "Yes, okay . . ."

"I won't have kids now. That was it."

He shrugs. "My children are grown. I'm free. We're both free."

I put a hand to my eyes. Some kind of light is in them.

"Things have changed, Anna."

I shake my head, keeping my eyes covered.

"Anna? Anna?"

The Backward Force of Water

WHAT RUSHES FORWARD creates a vacuum of equal force behind it. A space filled with nothing but gravity, the pure thing, weight. Air is very heavy. If water rushes forward, consider that it is, in some sense, also pushing backward, donkey-kicking its way into life. We know this in our bones. We have felt it, standing in the ocean, our heels sinking unevenly, always somehow surprisingly, into the wet sand as the waves zoom forward, away from us. We have felt it at the edge of the pit, looking in. We want to know how far, how deep, how wide, standing in the place where one kind of gravity becomes another kind of gravity. I loved you, I loved you, I loved you. When I think of his face, I think of it as a shape in my hands, as the scent of his breath. The visual field scrambles. It is a perversity in me: to have to close my eyes, as it were, to feel him more distinctly as shape, as weight, as air. I don't know why. If I knew why, I wouldn't still be out here. Which is where, exactly? anyone might ask. The same place, but it changes. Time passes. We only really hear the song the second time. The mountain moves to the other side.

Brussels

BOONE AND I take a walk. We leave the hotel and head in a random direction, passing cafés jammed with people watching a soccer game: Uruguay is playing South Korea. Bits of legs, arms, in close-up as we go by. The side of a face, dark hair, a sky-blue jersey. A woman with a long, dark face, perhaps Somali, passes us, looking dreamy. Brussels itself has a dreamy quality, crooked cobblestone streets, signs in both Flemish and French. Flemish admires the vowel, doubling and tripling them up, led by an *h* or a *g*. For some reason I find this quite funny, like the sight of ducks crossing a road. Why didn't I notice how charming this city was when I was here before? All I remember is that cold house, that plexiglass table of my defeat. Today I see that Brussels is inviting, but with a slightly mad quality, like a handsome man with a squirting flower in his lapel.

Boone looks at his phone, then puts it back in his pocket. "So, you've been in love, right?"

"I guess."

"You were married."

"Yes."

Boone scratches at his chin. He sighs. "But now you're not."

"No. Why?"

"There's this guy – his name is Sam – he's exhausting me."

I notice, embarrassed not to have seen it before, that Boone's eyes are dull, his skin is dull. Maybe this is the first time he's been in love. "You know," I say, "yeah, I was married, and he was a good guy, but it felt false, do you know what I mean? I started to feel that there was something false about us, that we looked the part, and we could have gone on that way for a long time. It looked a lot like good love. No one would have noticed that anything was wrong."

"What was wrong?" Boone looks as if he truly wants to know, as if my answer will help him in some way, which of course it won't.

"I don't know how to explain what was missing. Like I said, no one would have noticed if we had continued anyway, probably no one would have noticed our entire lives. We would have died like that."

Boone says, "So it was mutual."

"I didn't say that."

We turn down a crooked little street.

"Do you know what happened to a friend of mine?" says Boone. "He was driving somewhere down south, family business, and he stopped at a lookout to eat lunch. All of a sudden a beautiful boy drops right out of a tree, falls, rolls, looks at my friend for a minute, then jumps up and runs away. Falls out of a tree."

"Falls out of a tree?"

"Falls out of a tree."

Boone stops in front of a shop window. The shop is closed, as they all seem to be, inexplicably, on this Tuesday afternoon. Are they closed for the soccer match? "Look here. What is this?" In the window are a picture book open to a page of fluffy white dogs, an old portable record player (pink), a toy car (also pink), a grinning Sambo figure in a green jacket, and a stereo set that looks to be from about 1995. In the window glass, pinkening as well from the setting sun, I see myself and Boone from the waist up, haunting these odds and ends, placed among them like two more items to be sold: a tall lady and a man with a chipped-plate face. Somewhere nearby, a shout goes up. Do the Belgians root for Uruguay or South Korea?

"I guess it's just stuff someone likes," I say. "Do you have any pets?"

"Can't. I'm gone too much." He laughs. "God, I'm so doomed . . ."

I take his hand. In the window, the tall lady holds the hand of the man with the chipped-plate face. He turns his head and she sees him in ten years, fifteen years. He won't have the ambivalent beard then; his face will be tight. "But if you had a dog, what would you name it?"

"Wellbutrin."

"Do you think this could be someone's house?"

"No. But it is someone's fantasy."

The tall lady and the man with the chipped-plate face regard the contents of the shop window for a minute or two more, then depart without disturbing the fluffy dogs, the car, the hideous grinning figure in the green jacket.

Brussels, I think. So this is Brussels.

Luxembourg

A GIRL OF around two, wearing matching flowered shorts and top, chases a ball down a garden path. I watch her from the window of my room. Tonight's show has been canceled, poor ticket sales. Zach, Tom, and Boone have gone off to hang out with another band of Boone's, some bald guys out of L.A. Perhaps, I think, some exercise. Alicia and I lurk ineffectively around the equipment—two StairMasters and three molded plastic, polka-dotted hand weights—in the tiny hotel gym, then, wrapped in towels, we go to the steam room.

"Hey," she says. "Do you want to talk? I know it has to be hard."

I don't know where I would even begin, but who else do I have to talk to? Alicia, so pale she's almost transparent, rests one small, spectral foot against the tile wall. In repose in the steam, she looks angelic.

"I guess—I thought this was going to be a new beginning, but so far it's just been endings. And we're nearly done. I'm so tired, Alicia. My father. Other stuff. I shouldn't even be out here, this has to be some kind of sin. I feel like I've fucked up everything."

Alicia, eyes closed, angles her alabaster foot on the tile wall, angles it back. "No," she says. "It's just the whole weirdness. The way it gets. And then it all just stops, and it's worse. Right? Like Flatland."

"Exactly." To my surprise, I am comforted.

A silence falls. Then, "So, you know Ezra?"

"Yeah."

"He snaked my entire stash while I was sleeping. I wouldn't *mind,* you know, it's sort of an honor, but, like, wouldn't you think he could afford his own? What's that about?"

"He has issues."

The steam puffs loudly. Alicia's white foot on the wall begins to disappear, then her ankle. "Yeah, you could tell. The vibe was kind of weird." She yawns. "Tom's trying to get on that tour with Skullcrusher going out in the fall."

"He doesn't want to go back?"

"Nah. He had some sublet in San Diego, but he let it go, so now." Her calf disappears. "The guy pays. Wish they needed a cellist, I could use the money. You and Billy Q, you're friends?"

Basel

DIARRHEA: TWO DAYS. Chamomile tea. CNN. Europe: red with heat, pink even at the top of Norway. On the CNN weather map, the continent looks like an inside-out roast beef. Boone produces an afternoon for rehearsal from some hidden pocket of the budget (don't ask), in a well-appointed music room at the university, which is on the Rhine. In the music room, I settle myself into my guitar, tuning up, sing a note or two of "Wonderland." The acoustics are pristine, Swiss in their precision.

Boone says, "I'll leave you to it. Back in a few hours." He darts out.

Light falls from an oblong window high on the wall, illuminating the top of Tom's round head. He sits at the kit, adjusting the seat, running his hands over the drum skins, listening, tuning. "Dry in here," he says, standing up to turn the clasp on a drum. He rolls his shoulders as he sits down again, refitting himself to the kit, moving the seat a fraction of an inch here or there, up, then down. "I can't keep gaining weight," he says. "The kit is getting fucked. Anna, give me your diarrhea."

Alicia unbuckles the cello case and takes the cello out; it looks like Marlene Dietrich coming out of the gorilla suit in *Blonde Venus*. She buckles up the case and leans it against the wall, our audience of one. Unfolding the little folding stool, she sits down and positions the cello before her, then runs her hands up and down the strings, tuning. Her flip-flops have big plastic roses on them, blooming between her toes. Alicia has perfect pitch, which means that the tuning can go on for some time until she gets it exactly right. Zach, bent over and plugging things in everywhere, says, "Alicia, it's a rehearsal, okay? Let's not get all Yo-Yo Ma about it."

"Shut up," says Alicia softly, one hand high on the tuning pegs.

I feel strange and light from having been sick. The room is cool and superb. We can't see the river from here, but its brackishness comes in through the open window. The three others, weary-faced, move into position at their instruments. Like the hundred little girls with hammers, they look at me expectantly, waiting for the signal to begin. "Let's start from the top," I say. Alicia's low notes take us into "The Orchids."

After two lines, I say, "No, that's the problem." Alicia puts the cello bow down. "Zach, you're not listening to anyone else. We're already off." Because I don't read music very well, I have to say things like this: "You're being muddy while the rest of us are being sneaky. You have to get more sneaky."

Zach says, "Sneaky?"

"You know what I mean."

"Sneaky." He raises an eyebrow.

"Yes. Fucking *sneaky*. We've done this a thousand times. It's why we end up pulling in opposite directions by the middle of the set."

Zach shrugs. I remind myself that he went to Juilliard. It leaves its mark.

"Let's go."

Alicia lifts her bow, sounds those low notes, and Zach, not looking at me, sneaks through every window and down every chimney. Tom is the wind around the house. I sing the things I sing—"The Orchids" is about a murder—as plainly as I can. The others bring the complexity, turn day into night, night into day. I still feel a little queasy, my guts are roiling, but I ignore it, concentrating on how the light moves from the top of Tom's head to one rounded shoulder. In the song, blood moves over the floor.

Alicia puts down her bow. "No. I got that wrong. Can we start again?"

We pause. We start again.

The sound lifts. Although I wrote these words, this music, while sitting on the floor of my tiny apartment on 19th Street, sometimes with Jim eating a sandwich or typing on his computer next to me, they feel as if they came from somewhere else when the band is together like this. He shot his baby down (doesn't he always?), blood on the orchids, blood on the floor, and the sound is like that: the blood that moves through us all. *I wasn't there is what he said.* Alicia is the rain. Zach is the earth. The sound fills the room like the blood in our ears. The sound finds our pulse, the backs of our knees, the roots of our hair, our hearts, our lungs, the insides of our elbows. I can't really read music, but I can find it with my hands, groping blind. I can pull down the notes I want from the air, like stealing fruit from someone else's garden.

"Waiting for a Sign." "Smoke and Mirrors."

"Give the snare the finger, it has a throat to it when you hit it with the mallet."

"We're rampaging through the second verse."

"Alicia, stop cracking your knuckles."

"Tom, it's ganging up on the four on the floor."

Seven years of sound, of music only I could hear, now produced in the bodies of these strangers. I never imagined them, how could I have? I wasn't sure anyone else would ever hear that sound. The light touches Tom on the elbow. We all have our heads down, to listen. The awkward half-note — *never* ever, *bro* — shapes the door, and we duck, heads down, through the door, through the eye of the needle, to the place where the roads double back on themselves. Zach, Tom, Alicia, and, last, me. We are there.

"Wonderland."

I can't describe the next part. But however many times we do that song in the future, that's the one we'll be hearing in our heads, the one we'll be trying to get back to.

Circus Alberto

ON THAT LONG, hot afternoon in Berlin between sound check and the show, just before my father died in another country, without me, I walked past the catering room with its trays of pepperballs and catfish, the sun and the moon playing cards next to an open computer on whose screen men in green chased men in purple on a soccer field, down a corridor, up a back staircase, through an enormous, empty room that seemed to me like purgatory, and out to a wooden deck that looked over an abandoned train track on the left and, on the right, a collection of circus tents. On the deck it was extraordinarily quiet, save for the sound of the wind and the irregular clang of metal hitting metal somewhere. The heat seemed to have pressed all sound down to a sliver, to be bending light itself into a color that was almost purple. I felt buoyant in the heat, as if I could breathe underwater. The tiny muttonchop man hadn't appeared yet, so my face was bare, my hair was up in a plastic jaw-clip. I was wearing an old skirt, a tank top, sandals I bought once upon a time in Taormina. The leather strap on the left one was irretrievably loose. I walked to the deck rail on the right and looked over the circus. One big tent was striped, another was whitish gray, and a third, blue one appeared to be falling down on one side. On the roof of the striped tent was written *Circus Alberto*. A camper sat next to the whitish-gray tent along with a six-wheeled truck. In a round, cleared space in front of the whitish-gray tent was a two-story structure that looked partly like a cell phone tower and partly like the kind of diving board in a cartoon from which a donkey dives, ears flying, teeth bared, into a bucket of water. I was thinking about that circle Billy Q and I walked together earlier in the day, what its meaning could be, what powers it might possess, what his movie could possibly be about. I took my left foot out of the flapping sandal and drew a circle with my toe. The heat surrounded me, breathed me.

Down below, the sound of a door closing. A woman in a black leotard to the ankles, carrying a harness as big as a saddle, approached the tower and began, rung by rung, to climb it. When she reached the top, she threaded ropes around herself. I saw the glint of buckles as she tugged, pulled, leaned out perilously, then let go, turning over and over in the air, landing lightly on one pointed foot on the ground. For a second she turned there, pirouetting en pointe. Flatfooted, she went back to the tower and climbed to the top again. This time, instead of the harness contraption, she wound a rope around her waist, through her legs, back around her waist. She dove, swung out, hung for a moment, trussed, upside down, and then unraveled slowly, arms and legs spread wide, starfishing down point by point. When she reached the ground, she pranced, then tumbled backward and up, twining one leg in the hanging rope and swinging there for a minute, her ponytail brushing the ground. Like a woman in a swimming pool doing a flip-turn, she rolled right-side up, unwound the rope from her body, and went back to the tower, began climbing, hands and feet making of her a hieroglyph moving over the metal's geometry.

Leaning over the rail, I clapped, but she either didn't hear me or didn't want to be interrupted, her slender black form, like the itsy-bitsy spider, climbing steadily, undaunted, back up the tower. When I went inside, the tiny muttonchop man was waiting, armed with hairspray, brushes, bobby pins, false eyelashes, and all manner of creams and colors.

Letter to Lila

I MISS HIM, too. I'm back out here on the road with a suitcase full of clothes that are either too clean from hotel laundries or not clean enough because they should be dry-cleaned. (Why did I bring them?) I wash my bras in shampoo once a week, more for ritual purposes than anything that might produce actual cleanliness. They do smell nice, anyway. I thought I saw him limping down the street in Switzerland. I followed him for two blocks, just to see the face of a man who walked like him, but the man went into a store, so I turned around. I always thought he'd be back, didn't you? I mean: I thought he'd find it again, what got lost, his heart, his nerve, his honesty — I don't have a word for it, really. And maybe the payment was just. Lila, I know how brave you are. You planted a flag in Wyoming, evidence, trump card, immutable: thousands of acres of rock-solid, earthy, four-legged, muddy, pockmarked, furred and feathered and toddling proof of exigency. Countering everything our parents believed in — the dirty diapers, the animals that needed to be fed, the school year, the poverty everywhere, the diabetic cowboys, the winters, the unregenerate localness. In my seven years with the hundred little girls holding hammers, I felt that they were on your side, that they had, in some sense, been sent by you. Lila, I was true, too. I was. I stayed put for those seven years. I didn't complain. But now. Lila, now. Isn't it strange that neither of us ever truly imagined that he could die? It was as if, after he came back to life in Rome, he had been granted immunity to mortality. We were always mad at him and that was as if he could never die, too. You took Dad's glasses from Vermont. Ruthless, as much as it was intimate. You blinded him. But now. He isn't coming back. It was all sand. I don't blame the prison. Lila, didn't we both always know that? We're free.

Eurojet

I TAKE THE little twisted, pitted slug out of my pocket, feel its weight in my palm. The plane's oval window frames the powder-blue sky with metronomic regularity, recurrent beats of an ongoing wave. You, and you, and you, and you. The woman in the veil, Mads, Daisy and Vikram, William, little bird, and you, and you. Which mountain? Which field? Which music room? Which train? I run from door to door, window to window, some tiny, some huge, looking for you, and you, and you.

Latvia

LATVIA IS LIGHT filtered through trees. Just beyond the trees is the Baltic Sea. The sound of Portuguese rap music comes through the trees. Boone, God help us, is driving the rented van that we picked up at the frantic, hot little airport in Riga, jouncing over the dirt road to the entrance gate of the festival. Every time he has to shift gears, his hand flutters for a moment, with uncharacteristic indecision, over the gear stick before landing rather hard. I am leaning out the window, face to the sun, like a happy dog. In the back, Tom, Alicia, and Zach look frayed, a triptych of fatigue. Tom is wearing an Ace bandage on his wrist, because he slipped while climbing on-stage in Basel. He's been playing through the injury, packing his wrist in ice after each show. Alicia has unbuttoned the top button of her jeans. Zach, eyes closed, is working out chords on an imaginary guitar. Since Hamburg, the air among us has changed. Basel was more hospitable, which salved our egos; after the show, I treated them to a spectacular meal on my straining credit card, composed of elements none of us could identify, not even Boone – tree bark seemed to be a major ingredient, and sage, and something squid-like, and maybe some brick dust; but that's not what did it. What seems to have happened is more like a collective surrender, the tender openness of a long morning-after, or of sailors who now know for sure that they are lost at sea. Tom does sudoku. Alicia gazes out the window at the forest.

"There's a beach just through there," says Boone at the wheel, who has momentarily become our father. "We can swim."

"That would be *amazing*," says Alicia.

Zach shrugs, plucking at invisible chords with his long fingers.

We bump along. Latvia is soft, with soft, short trees, thin golden light. The festival is made of thin tents, a small stage. Boone pilots the van ever so slowly along a dirt road crowded with people. It looks something like 1968 here, warped and folded, colored-in slightly wrong. Low-slung, faded jeans, dreamy expressions, face paint. A young woman in a bikini top and tie-dyed cutoffs, wearing an orange lei around her neck, skips down the dirt road, arms extended. What does she think she's doing? Boone stops the van at the open gate of a chain-link fence. A burly, freckled man sits on a folding chair, holding a clipboard. On his black T-shirt in white letters is a phrase full of *b*'s and *l*'s and *v*'s. Boone leans out the window. "Brundage band." The back of Boone's neck is slightly sunburned; when did that happen?

"What does that mean, on that guy's shirt?" I ask Zach, who quickly types the phrase into his phone.

"Looks like it's Latvian for 'Behave well and everything will be fine.'"

The burly, freckled man, squinting, waves us in.

"Not bloody likely," says Tom, gamely giving Latvia the finger. The Portuguese rap music grows stronger. Boone downshifts into second, to nose delicately into the backstage area, a cluster of small red tents and tarp pavilions and two large white tents. He parks us next to a double-decker red-and-black tour bus. Standing outside the bus is a young man, shirtless, smooth-chested, muscular, blond, wearing what look like a baseball player's pegged white pants and flip-flops. A silver ring pierces his left nipple. He is lifting dumbbells, curling first one arm, then the other, his pectorals swelling each time. Next to him on the grass, on a little blue blanket, is a baby, perhaps eight months old, chewing on a ring of colored rings. Next to the baby is an African-American man with a serious expression, in chinos and a pressed white shirt, talking on a cell phone.

Boone leans out the window. "Hey, you bastards."

Both men look up, smile. The young man puts down the dumbbells, comes up to the van, and rest his forearms on the open window. "Oh, hallelujah. What the fuck is this place, *Hogan's Heroes*?" He gives a Nazi salute. "But the beach is great." He sticks his face farther in the window. "I'm Terry. Hello." He waves. It's odd to me how much sweeter-faced he is in person than he looked on the MTV Awards last year, when his band, Little Wars, won for this and that, Terry getting up from his seat in the audience several times in a sharp suit. Onscreen he looks ravaged and ravaging, although his music is dance-ready, peaches and cream and ass. But in person his eyes are wide, his face quite smooth and open.

"Is that one yours?" asks Boone.

Terry turns his head, laughs. "No. Jesus. That's Zelda, Kiki's kid. She's a total doll, we love her." Terry pulls himself up the side of the van, balances on straight arms. His pectorals bloom. "Anna. You don't know me, but I worship you. I just want to tell you that." He bounces up and back as if pulled on a string, lands soundlessly a few feet away. "Come hang out later. We have everything in the bus."

The man on the cell phone nods at us; the baby gurgles, wiggles her feet.

We wander around the festival, through the loping afternoon, because we don't go on until ten. How accustomed I have become to our band's particular forms, our shapes in crowds: the shine of Zach's head, his small ears; Alicia's way of walking on her toes; Boone attached to his iPhone by an earpiece and a cord; the roundness of Tom and his stiff-necked walk, in sunglasses, his fisherman's hat. I navigate by them, always keeping count: shine, toes, cord, hat. Our small, five-pointed constellation moves among the festival-goers, passing by the tennis courts, the Air Baltic tent where people are getting their hair done by orange-uniformed attendants, an exercise tent with hula hoops and treadmills, the Jägermeister tent, the Coco Loco tent, a small stage on which a woman sings in a long black dress with gold stripes, a flower in her hair. I don't know the language of the lyrics she is singing. A couple of thick, sunburned white guys play Ping-Pong under the trees. More people pass by wearing orange leis. What do these mean? Is it a cult? This festival looks as if it is made of paper, light and brightly colored.

At a smallish tent in the shade I find wooden trays of licorice set out on a long table covered in white paper: red-and-white striped, mint green, black, light purple, orange. The strands lie in slender loops like fresh pasta, dusted with – flour? cornstarch? I can't tell. An older man with a craggy face and a black mustache dozes in a folding chair behind the long table. Zach, smelling of sweat, hovers over my shoulder. "I love licorice," he says.

"Me, too."

"Those colors are awesome."

"Right? What do you think the purple is?"

The man with the black mustache raises his eyelids a fraction, closes them again.

We fill a white paper bag with multicolored strands, wake up the man with the mustache, pay in euros. He frowns at the euros but takes them anyway. We stroll on. I reach into the bag and pluck up a length of light purple: it is delicate, sweet, lavender and honey, and, unlike the waxy, tough licorice I'm used to at home – Red Vines – it is the consistency of homemade fettuccine.

"Taste this." I hand a skein to Zach.

"Whoa. That's some Willy Wonka shit right there."

"Let's try the green one."

We chew. "Wow," I say. "I could get addicted. Did you get the cinnamon hit?"

"How do they do that?"

"Latvian magic, I guess. What's the Latvian currency?"

Zach says, "I don't know. We're only here one night. Boone says we drive back to Riga after the show. That's going to be a bitch." He hands me a black strand. "You're not going to believe what this tastes like."

"God almighty," I say, chewing.

"Who needs infrastructure when you have this?" says Zach. "Licorice, opiate of the masses."

"Hey, Zach." I pause, embarrassed. "What's happening in the world?"

"Oh, you know. Disasters and miracles. The usual."

"Anything I need to know about?"

"Not here. Not today."

"Let's go to the beach."

We walk back down the honky-tonk and past the parking area, continue on the diminishing road through the dim, shady patch of forest, toward the light beyond the trees. The beach is fairly narrow, rock-strewn. Far to the left is a hut, and inside, the edge of a bar is visible. From the hut comes dance music, now in German? It must be German. Studding the beach, not far from the waterline, are blue, metallic cutouts of horses' heads, an orderly herd of them in two rows, the empty holes of their single eyes fixed to the right. Towels are hung on a few of them; on another, a string bag. People, towels, and umbrellas dot the beach. A few scruffy dogs scamper here and there. Zach and I, outfitted with nothing, sit down in the sand. I take off my sandals and he takes off the boots and socks he's wearing, revealing his long, slender feet, light hairs on the knuckles of his big toes.

"You're blond?"

"Was." He palms his head. "And curly. It was ridiculous. My bar mitzvah pictures would make you cry."

I lean back. Just below the top of Zach's pants I can see a bright yellow swath of his underwear. Canary yellow, in fact.

I puzzle over that. Zach getting up in whatever hotel room in whatever city, suitcase open on the floor, taking out a pair of canary-yellow briefs.

"Are you okay?" he asks.

"What?"

"You might be burning already. You're red."

"No, I'm all right. I should have brought a hat, I guess."

"Should we go back to the van and get one?"

"No, no. I won't fry all that fast." I sit up straight. "How's it going?"

He squints up at me in the sun. "How's it going? It's cool." He drizzles sand on his toes. "It's cool."

"What does that mean?"

"Touring is just, like, this constant sense of failure, you know? And then for like a few minutes"— he stretches out his hand —"you've got it, the thing is happening." He snaps his hand shut. "Next town. Next show. And if we *don't* do a show — like that one in Munich, the one that got canceled? — I feel like I'm going to jump out of my skin. I can't sleep that night. So it's just." He tosses a handful of sand up in the air. "Fucking Sisyphean. I'm so tired." He lies back in the sand, crosses one ankle over the other. I just barely keep from kissing him. I wonder if I ever saw him lying down in Göteborg; I only remember a stumble, the tangle of our legs, and then him sitting up.

"We're almost done. After Rome, it's over."

"Yeah."

I touch him on the forearm. "Want to go in?"

We strip down to our underwear and walk toward the water. His canary-yellow ass is high and firm, and his legs are lean, runner's legs. I wonder why no one ever corrected the duck toes, or, for that matter, his slight overbite. He is long-legged but short, compact in the body. His biceps are bigger than they need to be for playing guitar; clearly, they are like that for some other reason. Where is he from? Who are his people? He walks ahead of me into the water and the yellow turns darker, heavier, autumnal. The water, which is calm, just a few ripples, stops at his waist. "Come on," he says.

I know that my white cotton bra and underwear will become transparent in the water; I keep my back firmly turned to the beach, with its audience of people and one-eyed blue metal horses, and wade in. The floor of the Baltic Sea is soft, slushy; the water is a dull brown, warmish, not especially saline. I think, *We are swimming in the Baltic,* except that we're not swimming, we're wading, and as I reach Zach I realize that the water is only wading depth for quite a ways out. Fifty yards away, people stroll in water to their thighs. An empty, polka-dotted inflatable raft wafts along dreamily, heading for Sweden. Zach stoops, splashes his torso with water. The sea runs down over the taut curves and slopes of him, finds the hollows, the dips, the short, firm arcs. I see him see me watching him. He splashes his face, his lips, the back of his neck. I turn away, reddening.

We are swimming in the Baltic. Zach looks down at the placid sea around his waist, frowning. "Now what?"

"Float?"

He dips back and rests, elongated, on the surface, his long white feet waving gently underwater. "Okay."

I dip back and rest as well, my feet and hands rising, the water cooling my scalp, my ears. Weightless, I lie down between the sky and the sea, Zach quietly floating next to me. I feel my hair streaming and swirling above my head in the soft current. When I tear up, it feels oddly soft, too, not a full crying but a nearly unbearable tenderness that suffuses everything. When I open my eyes, the light is blurry. Zach is nearby, arms outstretched. The small ripples move over us.

He stands up first, holds out his hands; I take them and stand. We just skim one another, cooled by the sea. We don't let

go. *We are swimming in the Baltic.* Although we are not swimming, we are standing very close together, breath to breath.
His eyes are green.

It begins to rain around six, just as I've started on seconds of a
bland thing with noodles and vegetables in the catering tent.
The rain resounds against the canvas. "Oh, motherfuck," says
Zach, next to me.

Boone, chatting up a motley group of white people with
dreadlocks at a neighboring table, glances over at us, up, over
at us again, makes a face.

"I don't want to get electrocuted," says Alicia, hunched into
a shredding red turtleneck, smoking. "I'm not going on in this."

Zach shoots her a black look.

Tom holds up an unidentifiable piece of meat on his fork.
"This is a three-point-five," he says to Zach.

"I don't want to get electrocuted, either," I say to Alicia,
"but—"

Thunder sounds; rain guns down on the canvas roof. The
white and green paper lanterns strung along the ceiling bob.
A young woman with wet hair, a violin case clutched to her
chest, dashes into catering. "It's a monsoon!" she says. "The
tents are fucked!"

"Damn," says Tom. "Good thing we didn't unload the equipment yet. Is that mousse over there?"

"I don't trust that van," Zach says, zipping up his jersey.
"I'm going to check it out." He stands, looks at Tom. "Dude,
you coming?"

Tom, with a sigh, stands up. They leave the tent. The rain
guns harder, slams, thuds with a shocking determination. It is
not behaving well at all.

At the empty table, Alicia blows a smoke ring, eyeing me.
Her cuticles are ragged. "I hate Latvia," she says.

• • •

Standing in the opening of the catering tent, stronger and stronger waves of rain washing in on me, I can see Zach's bald head, Tom's hatted one, as they move around in the back of the van, stooping. The top of a guitar case bobs up in the long window, leans. One of the panel doors in the back opens, Zach squats there, pushing water onto the soaked ground. He turns his head to say something over his shoulder to Tom. Another guitar case appears to lean beside the first in the long window.

Ducking my head, I run out of the tent, splashing across the backstage area in my flapping Taormina sandals. Already the mud is rising, softening. My ankles are wet and cold. The color has gone out of everything; the music has stopped playing everywhere. I lose my left sandal, grab it with one hand, and orient it back in the vicinity of my foot, where it doesn't stay. The trees darken in the rain. Two guys with ponytails drag a big, black-and-silver trunk away from a small, red, half-collapsed tent. I splash up to the back of the van where Zach is crouching, bailing water with his hands. Behind him, Tom stoops, trying to maneuver Alicia's cello up on top of a pile of suitcases. The water seeps through a seam in one of the side windows, trickling in almost sweetly, so delicately that at first it's hard to connect it with the puddle on the floor of the van, cold water on cold, dirty metal.

"Oh, Jesus," I say to Zach, who grunts, bailing.

Splashing across to the double-decker tour bus, I pound on the closed door. "Hey! Hey! Terry!"

"They're not there!" shouts Zach.

"Not there?" I pound again. "Where could they be?"

"I don't know, Anna," he yells, "they're just fucking not fucking there."

I stand back from the door, peer up at the windows on the upper deck, getting drenched. "Do you think they're all sleeping?"

No answer. Boone dashes into view, holding his light jacket

together with one hand, hair plastered down on his chipped-plate face. "We can take it all into catering," he says. "Come on, Anna, get in." He climbs up into the driver's seat, Zach gives me his hand, and I step up into the back with him and Tom, who is holding the guitars upright by leaning against them, pudgy arms spread wide. It smells like wet dog back here – wet dog, wet fabric, wet skin. Zach and I perch on a duffel bag, which I think is his, damp shoulder to damp shoulder.

"Is anything ruined?" I ask Zach.

"I don't know. We have to lay everything out and look."

The van jounces Tom braces his feet and bends his knees to keep a grip on the guitar cases. "Slow down," he calls out, although we're barely moving, and in a minute or two we've arrived at catering.

"Oh, man," says Boone. When he comes around to open the van doors, I see the other bands who have come in vans or cars, lugging equipment through the rain to the relatively more substantial catering tent. One petite Asian woman, in curlers and black leather pants, carries an amplifier. I stand up, or crouch up, and take a guitar case from under Tom's left arm; Zach takes a guitar case from his right, along with another, smaller guitar case. I sling someone's backpack on my wet back. We clamber out of the van and lug the gear into catering, which, when we enter it, now looks like a triage center for musical instruments during some kind of war or natural disaster. All around the tent, cases are opened; drum kits and violins and horns and flutes and innumerable guitars are laid out on towels or tablecloths or bits of clothing – jeans, dresses, sweatpants – as musicians hover over them, wiping them down with paper napkins, paper towels, shirts, boxers, rags. The ferocity of the storm has taken everyone by surprise. Next to the soda machine, a black man with a long face and long arms crouches by a harp with a sprung string; the broken string tendrils along his back as he unwinds it from the base. His other hand fans out against the harp strings. Not far from the harp, three young men with full beards play guitars and sing in Spanish, occasionally thumping the bodies of the guitars. A lady is leaving, it seems, the heart is breaking. The heart is breaking, the lady is leaving. Thump of the heart, or is it the footsteps of the lady?

Zach unbuckles buckles, unzips zippers, bent over the gear. Tom and Boone and I lug pieces from the van into catering, going back and forth, soaked. Alicia shows up, her red turtleneck and pedal pushers going as soggy as everything else as she hauls gear into the tent. Her platinum hair sticks to her head. When the van is as hollow as it is cold, I close the doors, lock the wet lock, and put the keys in my pocket, next to what I realize is a sodden mass of licorice, now paste. I toss the brightly colored paste into a trash can, wipe my hands on my pants. Inside, in our rough square of triage, Zach has laid everything out with geometrical precision: neat rows of instruments, butterfly screws, cables, and cords on three tarps, and, carefully elevated above the floor on shoes, Alicia's cello, over which she hovers, wiping it down with a flowered blouse. She is crying. Tom, standing anxiously nearby, says, "I really think it's okay. It was hardly in there ten minutes." Alicia twists a bit of fabric around her index finger, runs her finger down each string. Tom kneels and steadies the cello for her as she tends to it. The cello case, empty on the ground, is spattered with rain.

Zach has torn a pair of his jeans into rags. He and Boone and I methodically move from guitar to guitar, cable to cable, drum piece to drum piece, each with a length of denim, drying as best we can. We look as if we're harvesting some invisible fruit or vegetable from a strange field. The hum inside the tent is sociable, the men with beards thump their guitars, the white and green lanterns sway as the storm continues full force. I reach over to put a hand on Tom's shoulder. "All of the kit looks good," I tell him. "I think it was far away from the windows."

He sighs, shaking his head. "It's my best kit. Everything else I have is junk."

"It's all right. Really."

"I'm going to have to retune all of it."

"Everything," says Alicia, tense-faced. "It's all going to be a mess."

The Spanish guys are singing something else now. What is that tune? Though they're singing it in Spanish, I recognize it, "Stormy Weather," at the same moment as others in the tent do; laughter rises from the musicians stooping and dragging and rubbing down their instruments. The mood is communal, but there is a palpable undertow of anxiety. Most of the people here can't afford to replace their instruments. Like Tom, like turtles, they travel with the only houses they have on their backs. Like me, selling my precious bit of rubble to get here, where I might never be again. I dry a guitar neck. It looks like I have the left ass cheek of Zach's jeans.

"What?" asks Boone.

"Nothing."

I scoot inch by inch across the tarp, drying curves and strings and pedals and plugs with Zach's back left pocket, his waistband. I put my hand in his pocket to get a better grip. Thus mittened, I make my way down the rows. Throughout the tent, men and women and even a few children do the same, stooping and standing and stooping again. Boone wipes his face with one of Zach's worn-out knees. "We might not make it back to Riga tonight. Terry's driver told me the roads are flooded. He thinks they have enough bunks on their bus for us."

Zach, inspecting an amp, winks at me, and I shoot him a look that means, *Don't even think about it,* although I am thinking about it, of course, crawling over the tarp. The narrow bus bunks with their little curtains in the middle of the night, shoes in the corridor outside each bunk, the sepulchral hush, the scattered laughter and sounds of gunfire from the movie a few people are watching, Terry and Tom racking up a lazy line or two, sprawled on the couches on the lower deck, the rain tapping the bus windows, tangled hair and warm skin, the turning toward each other. Let's just put it this way: it's not impossible.

Not impossible at all. Boys fall out of trees all the time. When I leave him, tripping over a high-top sneaker, to slip back into the bunk next to his, I find that it smells of him, because I smell of him. Lying down alone, I still feel as if I am floating with him in the parked tour bus.

In the morning, I pull on the skirt that's still damp, a sweatshirt Kiki lent me, the sandals that are now swollen, flaking, and also still damp. The rain has turned them definitively from provisional to notional. I make my way around the little staircase to the lower deck, where Kiki, in a head wrap imprinted with skulls, sits nursing the baby, breast modestly covered by a pretty little blanket imprinted with evergreen trees. On one of Kiki's fingers is a ring in the shape of an airplane.

"Hey," says Kiki. "It stopped raining, but it's a swamp out there."

In the tiny kitchen area I find a paper cup, cereal, milk, a plastic spoon. Also, blessedly, coffee in the large plug-in coffeepot. I pour coffee into a second paper cup and open the bus door with my foot. Outside, Terry and Zach stand smoking, both in hooded sweatshirts across the backs of which are written, in silver letters, *Suck It Twice*. It's the *Suck It Twice* tour of Little Wars.

"Morning," I say. I sit down on an upended cinder block, put my coffee cup on the wet ground, spoon cereal out of the other cup. It is cool, windy, gray. The festival now looks like a refugee encampment: people trudge by wrapped in mud-tipped blankets; a security guard walks around the backstage area with a mammoth plastic bag, spearing up the night's trash. The cereal is made out of marshmallows and chocolate chips and a few tasteless flakes that might be some kind of grain. Terry and Zach nod, Zach's gaze makes me blush. I poke around in the cereal with the plastic spoon. "Fucking Latvia," I say.

"They saw a tornado near Riga," offers Terry. "Since when does Eastern Europe have tornadoes?"

"How do we know they didn't before?" says Zach.

"Yeah, I guess," agrees Terry. "But still. That was intense."

"It was," Zach says, smiling. "Took me by surprise."

A tasteless flake gets stuck in my throat and I cough. "How does the gear look?" I ask.

"It's all there," says Zach. "But being in that tent over-night — we're going to hear that night all the way through Rome. I'm sorry, Anna." He taps his ear. "Hopefully we'll be the only ones who can really tell." He drags on his cigarette.

In the daylight, Zach is older, but also more handsome. In the night, he was tender, seeking, surprisingly joyous; at one point he murmured, "I feel like I'm seventeen and you're fif-teen," a comment I could have asked many questions about, but didn't. This morning, with the hood pulled up over his head, the long lines in his face, the bump in his nose, and the circles under his eyes suggest an inward, questioning man. He isn't brilliant. Maybe I can't read music, but I can hear what isn't there and never will be. And yet. He catches me looking at him and smiles, the smile of his fifty-two-year-old self, wait-ing for me one day at the back of the tour bus. It is a knowing smile. I smile back.

"This festival is busted," Terry says, stubbing out his ciga-rette in the mud. "We're in Stockholm tomorrow."

"Other way for us," I say. "I hope the flight still goes. How's the van?"

Zach shrugs. "Still has its wheels."

We all laugh. Zach shakes his head.

"Listen, Anna," says Terry, "do you guys want to open for us through Japan and Australia? Some shit went down last night, on top of everything else." He makes wavy hands, a horror face, then snaps back into beauty. "Mid-August to Thanksgiving."

I bite my knuckle. The hundred little girls holding hammers

pause at their tables, look at me goggle-eyed. I can't read their expressions. "Right. Can I—"

"It's cool. Just text me by, like, the end of the week? There are all these promoters and stuff." With his index fingers, Terry shoots himself in both temples. "Sometimes I just want to go back to the trailer park."

"The fuck you do," says Zach, and I feel that tug, the place where it tilts, wanting to be in his dreams. As if, once requested, it is a thing that could be willed.

"Let's go play Halo," says Terry, and Zach nods, stubs out his cigarette in the mud as well. The silvery *Suck It Twice* backs disappear up into the bus, Zach sneaking a tug on my hair as he goes by.

I remain on the upended cinder block, finishing the coffee as slowly as possible. The bus door whooshes open and Kiki comes out with Zelda, rosy and plump. "What was I thinking with this shit?" says Kiki, putting one of Zelda's hands in her mouth and opening her eyes wide. Zelda laughs. Kiki removes Zelda's hand, kissing it loudly. "What happens when she has to start school? There's no school on the road."

"The school of life."

"*Fffff.*" Kiki snorts. "The *alphabet*. Arithmetic. Social studies. Pilgrims."

"Here," I say, getting up from the cinder block.

Kiki sits down gratefully, stands Zelda between her knees, holding her under the arms. Zelda looks blue-eyed at the world. She sways and reaches wildly at the air, feet just grazing the mud.

My Apartment

MY TINY, TINY apartment at 19th Street and First Avenue is composed of two small rooms, an elbow of a kitchen, and an armpit of a bathroom. The smaller of the two rooms is my bedroom, which is painted sky blue. The unframed double mattress and box spring fill the width of the room from wall to wall. About two feet above the bed hangs a built-in storage cabinet; on the underside of the cabinet is a clever, subtle disk of light that I bought years ago in Paris. The light looks as if it flew there, spread its wings, and stuck. There are perhaps three feet of space from the foot of the bed to the wall opposite. In the corner of the blue bedroom is a rattan chair with a high, extravagant, rectangular back. The window in this room looks over a modest courtyard in which there is a table with an umbrella, which no one ever uses, and the building's trash cans, neatly enclosed in a wooden pen. The larger of the two rooms, which is painted burnt orange, is my living area. In this room there is a graceful wooden desk, a desk chair, a daybed/sofa, and a floor-to-ceiling wall of shelves filled with books, found objects, precious keepsakes, family photos, a punctured gourd shell in which reside several dusty vials of cocaine (does coke go bad?) and a few hits of ecstasy, violin strings, the cat's old collar, and, truth be told, in a white cardboard box, her ashes, which I somehow have never been able to scatter. In this room there is also an ingeniously partitioned closet, which holds, among many other things, my two pairs of Prada boots and the Lanvin dress, zipped into a Lanvin cover, that Simon bought me in Rome. It still fits.

I have lived in this apartment for fifteen years. Jim and I lived there together for six of those years, like two origami birds set beak to beak. All we could do there was eat, sleep, and fuck, which to Jim, in the early days of his sobriety, felt like sanity. When he left, it did not seem any bigger. If anything, it seemed smaller. The apartment is a good deal, and in recent years the landlord has painted the hallways, redone the entryway, installed new mailboxes, and put in a heavy, solid front door, the key to which cannot be duplicated. When I left to go on tour, I discreetly sublet my tiny, tiny apartment to a young Chinese woman, an NYU grad student in film who signed all her emails to me "with respect" and paid everything in cash, up front.

I imagine writing the Chinese woman: *Stay put. We are in wonderland.* Which is where, exactly? The same place, but it changes. *Suck It Twice.*

My tiny, tiny apartment, however, does not change. The blue does not change. The burnt orange does not change. The view out the window of the small courtyard does not change. It may seem as if that isn't much, not much to show for a life, but it's a lot, actually. A point of leverage. In New York, rent is everything. If I hadn't been able to trade my tiny, tiny apartment for Jonah's studio time all those years ago, that one week of sand, none of the rest would ever have happened. No *Whale,* no Simon, no chateau, no *Bang Bang,* no swifts, no electric blue, no Jim and his angelic fiddle, no circle with Billy Q, no Berlin, none of the large and small, generally unknown glories and betrayals that have composed my life. All that from two tiny rooms, a pop-up world. And a hundred little girls with hammers in there, waiting for me to come back.

Waiting on a bench in the crowded airport in Riga for our flight to be called, the three Spanish guys with full beards from last night playing cards and eating potato chips on the floor nearby, I miss my tiny, tiny apartment. I miss it like missing an animal, or maybe like I am the animal. On the television monitor above, sweat-soaked men in navy blue uniforms leap ecstatically around a soccer field. They have won the World Cup. I'm pretty sure the men in blue are Norway. Zach squats down by the three Spanish guys and they deal him in, crisp slap of the cards. Zach's life at the moment is in boxes in his parents' basement in Rockland County. Over his shoulder, I can see that he holds quite a few face cards, but since I don't know what game they're playing, I don't know if this means he is winning or losing.

Work

THE WALLS WERE impossible. Texas, unsurprisingly, isn't kidding when it comes to prisons. In the years since it had been abandoned, this prison, as my father told it, seemed to have become even denser, harder, more unyielding, a dark star. The electricity had been off for so long that the darkness within had grown in on itself, thickened, acquired a centripetal force. Worse still was the absence of scent: no sweat, no cooking smells, no cigarettes, no coffee, no rot of garbage. And, of course, no sound. No talk, no yelling, no rattle and bang of weights in the yard, no steel gates opening and closing, no footsteps, no cries of pain or pleasure or surprise, no television or radio. It was a fortress without a purpose: nothing to guard within, nothing to fend off without. Birds nested in the guard towers. The front door stood wide open to the black silence of the interior, but the walls refused to seam. Pockmarks dotted the walls from the morning's work, as if small fists had battered futilely at them from improbable heights. Titanic, expensive equipment lay shining in the weed-filled prison yard, motionless. The joke, for years after: that he couldn't break into that prison for love or money. It was a story he told us, because none of us were there when it was happening. I lived in New York by then. *Never* ever, *bro. Whale* had just begun whispering.

The three trucks gazed dumbly at the prison, which, with its black windows, gazed blindly back. The work, weightless, in the air between them, blowing away in the sunlight. The crew stood around smoking. With them, the film crew from Channel 4, also smoking. My father paced, peered, squinted, reassessed, studied the plans, felt the walls, tapped them. Where was the error? He might have wished his own father were still alive; his father, the engineer, had had a talent for the ways that matter moved, or didn't, and known how to make matter work, even against its will, for men. My father squatted in the dirt, looking at the placid field all around the prison, the long grasses on which birds alighted, flew, alighted. Flutter of butterfly wings. A slight darkening ripple as a cloud passed by overhead. Spots of periwinkle blue, of yellow, of magenta. A field cannot be cut, cannot be opened; it is already open. My father spit on the ground.

The prison was oblivious, eternal. The walls, merely scuffed, were cold.

The foreman squatted next to my father. "Roy," he said, "this is money down the drain every minute we sit here."

"What about blasting?"

The foreman shook his head. "We don't have a permit for that. And anyway, then what?"

"Then we'd get a space —"

The foreman shook his head again. "You can walk through that door there." He nodded toward the dark entryway. "That's about it."

"That's not the project."

The foreman shrugged. "Tell it to the State of Texas."

"Let's go up to the roof."

"We've been up there."

But they went up. The foreman smoked, leaning against a dead chimney. My father sounded the roof with a long metal bar, striking it in various spots, listening, striking, listening, striking. He heard no answer. The foreman balanced his boot heel on his booted toe, drawing on his cigarette, waiting. Below, the demo guys were playing Frisbee with the Channel 4 guys; the plastic, lemon-yellow disk spun through the air. My father, Roy Brundage, hurled the bar like a javelin into the field, where it dropped without a sound. And then he just stood there, on top of the silent, motionless concrete beast, his hands empty. The smoke from the foreman's cigarette could barely be seen rising into the light.

I cannot begin to understand what it is to feel the weight of the work drop away and be unable to retrieve it. Consider Norway, leaping streaks of blue: the winner is free, is weightless, has no work to do now and no reason to do it. I cannot understand it, I do not want to understand it. I see now that what I have been writing in my composition book is a catalog, a retrospective, of work that no one will ever see again, of work that existed for less time than it takes to play a song, or listen to one. Not long after my father's work was done, the photographers would pack up and leave and the bulldozers would arrive – except at the prison, which remains intact in the field to this day. He and I, makers of things that go away; these are the reverberations. I wasn't there when he cut open those buildings, that train. He didn't like my music all that much. How strange it is to have disappeared and to come back, years later, only to find that so many of the others have gone. They won't return. Sitting in the airport in Riga watching the men play cards, I draw a picture of that prison, that front door open into black, neither of which I have ever seen, in *Wonderland*. I write the date beneath it and close the book.

Rome, Morning

ZACH TAKES A picture on his cell phone of our band's poster, plastered onto a crumbling stone wall next to a poster of the Pope, his hand upraised to bless a group of dark-skinned children on a beach. "Sweet!" Zach says. The grainy, deliberately blurry image of the four of us standing in dark suits in the rain looks more ancient than the image of the Pope, apple-cheeked, in color, and shiny, beaming in bright tropical sun. Older than the others, I am also closer to the viewer, foreground left, looking ambivalent and existential. It's a good story, this visual modesty. It's becoming, but it isn't true.

"Catholics are shameless," I remark.

"No fucking kidding," Zach replies cheerfully. He left my room at six a.m. to pretend, I'm not quite sure to whom, that we aren't sleeping together, but returned at eight with coffee, two *cornetti,* and a hard-on.

"Do you think he's happy?"

"The Pope? I don't even think he's a person."

"What did the Queen of Denmark say to him?"

"'I'm sorry, Mr. Pope'?"

"No, before that. What was the insult?"

"Oh. Something about money. About the Church having a lot of it."

"But they do have a lot of it."

Zach shrugs. "I guess it's more polite to say he has a lot of holiness. Good *yontif,* Pontiff." He holds up the cell phone image, and it's very funny, the juxtaposition of us with the Pope, a rainbow of ironies. Zach's fingers are long, his fingertips callused. "I'm going to post this onto our site."

Rome is hot and still today. A striped cat lies on top of a parked car not much bigger than a shoe, cleaning itself. Zach hits buttons, squinting, grinning. His duck feet, in sneakers, splay outward. We amble on and the narrow street opens up into a bright piazza.

"Is this the one from before?" I ask.

Zach eyes it. "Maybe?"

"Did we ... Wait, I'm—" I take out the map we got at the hotel, but it's only half a map, studded with stores and restaurants that are apparently the size of the Roman Forum. "I'm confused."

"Rome is confusing," says Zach.

"It is." Which postcard rack is that? Which church? Which man? "But pretty."

Zach looks around. "It's okay. I think I like Jerusalem better."

"Those are the two cities? Rome and Jerusalem?"

"You're so sassy, Anna. Just, you know, in terms of shit being old. I like the old shit in Jerusalem better. I guess because it's old Jewish shit."

"There are plenty of Christians in Jerusalem," I point out, still trying, and failing, to read the cartoon map. "What's the name of that street over there?"

Zach shrugs. "I'm hungry." He palms his head. "And horny."

Even as I light up, it occurs to me, not for the first time, that this is a bad idea, and a cliché to boot. Who doesn't know the next part of this movie? It ends with bizarre yet inevitable abruptness, I am rueful, he says he's sorry, but he isn't, really. He feels clean and free, and I know this, but I don't say so, because it's more becoming to be rueful and wise and bite my lip in the last scene, waving a small wave at the station as his train pulls out, flicking my cigarette butt onto the tracks. No regrets, coyote.

I sigh. It's not my song. Plus, I don't smoke.

"What?" says Zach. "Come on. We have a whole *day*."

"Do you think we're a cliché?"

Zach laughs his squinty-eyed laugh. "What, like 'Maggie

May' or something? I don't know." He pauses, frowns. "I might be. I have a little thing for –" He shakes his head.

"Older women?"

"Sad women. Like Alicia. They always dump me."

"I'm not anything like Alicia. That is hilarious."

Zach looks me in the eye. "Not in your story, maybe. And you're my boss – you know, boss?"

"Well –"

He opens his palms. "I know I keep you amused." He winks. He takes the map and turns it around. "The museum is that way."

And, in fact, it is. It's a small museum, the long-ago folly of some count who fancied himself a connoisseur of art. It still has the air of a crazy rich person's house, with multiple staircases and heavy drapes on the windows. The marble floors are scuffed. Zach steers us up the correct staircase and along several hallways into the main exhibition room, which must have once been the house's ballroom. Hanging in surprisingly unforced groupings, the unfinished sketches of the master are seamed, stained, interrupted by second thoughts and afterthoughts, ghostly, half-realized possibilities. Next to the precisely drawn curve of a man's back, a pair of legs, upside down, plunge toward the bottom edge of the yellowed sheet. The side of a woman's face interrupts the front view of the same woman's face, snub-nosed, round-cheeked. A boy has three left arms, in various positions.

"They look like the hands of a clock, don't they?" says Zach. "Like time-lapse photography of waiting. I feel like that."

"Like what?"

"Like that boy. I'm always *waiting*, you know? On edge."

"For what?"

"Something. Everything. It gets annoying. It's like spiritual ADD."

I regard him, peering at the boy with three left arms. Zach stands so close to the sketch that he's almost touching it, as if he is trying to learn something by smelling it. There is no guard in this room, no one else but us, so he could touch it, but he doesn't, although he holds his palm quite close.

"That doesn't change," I say.

He glances up at me but doesn't reply. We walk on, making our way slowly around the walls hung with indecision. It's ironic, or something, because we both know that I haven't texted Terry yet. It's up to me. The hundred little girls with hammers furrow their brows. They will not wait for me. And though they might not seem important, all the determined little rich girls, I see now that they are. Will I say no to her again, all hundred of her, all her arms?

Zach takes my hand. "That doesn't really make sense," he says. "People slow down."

"Today is my birthday," I tell him. "I'm forty-five."

"Congratulations."

We go back to the fairly ratty hotel to make love, laughing as we walk down the dank corridor. The lights, on a timer, click on for a moment, then as quickly go off again. Against the closed door of someone else's room, in the penumbra of midmorning, I press against Zach and open his mouth with mine. He tastes of coffee, pastry flakes; his lips are soft. His hands are strong, his arms are strong, but alone in my room a few minutes later, I notice again that he is a smaller and more compact man than he seems when he's clothed. His nakedness always happens in an instant, quick as a thought, while I am still unbuttoning. He is so easy to fuck. It is like being in water. We twine and push; he is muscled everywhere, firm and rounded and curled so tightly that he seems like a creature that might be on the verge of turning into another creature altogether, sprouting wings or fins. He comes fast, silently, eyes closed. I don't entirely know him in that moment, I don't know where he goes. He is more than his animal then, and this is why, I see, that I am falling in love with him. I want to know his remainder that I can't ever know, a remainder that is only broadened by the difference

in our ages. Curled against him when we're still, my leg over
his hips, I know that he is thirty-two, maybe thirty-three. The
years between us feel like another person, a being with its own
personality, tastes, interests. I don't feel younger with him; on
the contrary, I feel exactly and fully forty-five, every minute of
it, every frame; it feels something like wealth. I am not sure I
have ever felt as completely my age as I feel with Zach. He is a
true clock to me, like one of those mirrors that doesn't reverse
your image. Left is on the left, right is on the right. These are
the actual years of my life.

"Have you done this before?" I ask him.

"Um, yeah."

"No, I mean, been with someone older."

"Well. Yes. Just once. It was kind of a messed-up thing. But
you must have had a boy toy or two—"

"No. Never."

"Really? So how is it?" He smirks a little.

"I'm not sure yet." I run my hand over his beautiful leg.
"Rome is a weird place for me. People in my family don't have
good luck with it. A lot happened here."

"Good or bad?"

"Oh"—I shake my head—"you know." I pull the thin sheet up
to cover us. We sleep awhile.

"Anna? Do you have your ears in?"

I nod. Zach's chord pings clearly in my ear.

The lanky sound guy at the back of the house says, "There's
a buzz on the left channel."

We are at the venue, which is midsized but well known. It
is in the center of Rome, in the center of a labyrinth of gardens
that open unexpectedly into small seating areas, squares of
lawn, leafy bowers. The last time I played here, I fell over one
of the knee-high hedges; Simon had ended it, again, for the last
last time. I wasn't sure I believed him, although it turned out
to be true. In retrospect, it seemed the beginning of a longer

fall, all the way back to my sky-blue bedroom on 19th Street, my dying cat. The labyrinth looks the same to me, although possibly the hedges are higher. I'm not sure. The venue smells exactly the same, stale beer and cigarette smoke.

Boone is pacing back and forth, biting his thumb, ears in. He is clean-shaven now. When did that happen? And why? His skin is exceptionally clear and soft-looking. Zach, a few feet away to my right, runs his hand across the electric acoustic, pressing the foot pedal on the floor. "Wow," says Boone, "that was worse." He signals to me. I sing a few bars of "Waiting for a Sign," like running up a short stair. Boone shakes his head. The open double door of the dim, cool venue is a square of light. My throat is stiff. I cup my hand around it. I do not want to sing today. Tom and Alicia materialize in the square of light, both in wraparound sunglasses. Alicia, in Rollerblades and a white jumpsuit, glides in, taller. Tom walks beside her, talking. They take seats at the empty bar, their heads together in conversation, Alicia's skates surreally big on her feet.

"Hey," I say from the stage, and they briefly turn their insect faces toward me, Tom lifts a hand, and they turn back to each other. Australia. Japan. Who would we all be by the end of that? Everyone knows about Terry's offer, of course, but no one is asking me what I'm going to do. Boone, over drinks in the hotel lobby last night, ran the numbers for me on a cocktail napkin. They were Janus-faced numbers. He tap-tap-tapped them with a forefinger. He has other people he has to go out with in the fall, he'd be sure to drop in to check up on us but . . . Zach noodles a few chords, stretching them, like licorice, with the foot pedal. They tickle my ears.

The lanky sound guy at the back of the house says, "There's a buzz on the right channel."

Boone looks at the ceiling in exasperation. His naked chin is delicate, like a small white arrow pointing up. He wants to be gone, I think. He's done with this now. That's why he shaved. He runs a hand over his eyes. "I'm so fucking tired."

"Let's take a break," I say, pulling the small plastic buds out of my ears.

The Via Condotti, at any time of the day or night, is packed with shoppers shopping. This is the narrow, twisting street of high-end stores, window after window of mannequins draped in silk, in fur, in ropes of gold. The shoppers display their bags, the celebrated names written across the shiny white or black surfaces, loving to be laden down, to have to dodge and weave as they walk in the street. Efficient forward progress is not only rude but sad; no one on the Via Condotti has, or should have, any place to be but here, tacking from window to window on gusts of desire. I pass the windows of Lanvin, of Prada. If you have to ask what it costs, as they say, you can't afford it. It cost a bit of rubble, pitted from salt and weather. My transparent reflection shadows me, flash of red, disappears as I pass. It occurs to me that just now I looked, in the glass, like one of my mother's pieces, one of her evanescent women. She had to wear special glasses to paint on glass, because the paint could move so fast.

I drift. I've always loved the Via Condotti, its mad, nouveau riche shamelessness, its ridiculous excess. Who needs ermine socks? A bikini made of strands of diamonds? It's a continuous impromptu show composed of shoppers' fantasies, a show that never ends. When my father was in the hospital, my mother and Lila and I used to sit on the Spanish Steps for hours, watching the crowd, doing crossword puzzles, and eating warm chestnuts, cracking the skins quickly to get at the pale knot of meat inside. Lila and I took turns braiding each other's hair. That was the time of the punks, who busked ineptly at the foot of the steps, singing parts of songs off-key and holding out their dirty hands. Lila was fascinated. "Where do they sleep?" she asked.

They're gone now. In their place, a few folky street musicians, tourists on cell phones. I take a picture of the scene on my phone, send it to Lila, captionless. She'll know what I mean. I zigzag through the Piazza di Spagna, buy a bag of chestnuts. I enter a smaller street where the linen shop I like might still be, and there, standing before me, is Billy Q. He is wearing lacy cream-colored leggings, short black leather boots, and suspenders, with no shirt. His chest is smooth.

"Anna," he says, as if we had agreed beforehand to meet on this very corner, on this very day, at this very time, 14:17. We kiss on both cheeks.

"Sir," I say. "What are you disguised as?"

"A younger, better-looking man than I am."

"Chestnut?"

"Love these." He cracks it in one hand, pops the meat into his mouth. "Do you believe in God?"

"I never thought about it, I guess. Do you?"

"I might. I really might." He looks pensive, chewing the chestnut.

"Are you making another film here?"

"No, no. Vacation. Let's walk around. There's a designer a few streets over you should see." From I'm not sure where, the air maybe, he produces an exceptionally thin white cotton scarf, which he ties around his head, pirate fashion. Instantly, although he looks like he might be someone in that outfit, he doesn't look especially like Billy Q anymore.

"How do you do that?" I ask.

"My head was cold."

We talk about Ezra a little as we walk, the same conversation we had in Göteborg, in Berlin the morning after the show, before Alicia staggered over, still in the catsuit; the same conversation we will have in other cities, at other times, for many years to come. We agree, and, after all, Ezra is still alive. That seems to signify something, though whether it's for or against isn't clear. Billy Q has a few facts to offer that I didn't know about, facts about money that make me wonder what, at the end of the day, Ezra's true habit is. Susie's role, of course, is more complicated than it seems. She's already back in Berlin. His heart, his eyes, his hands: no one knows what holds him together, whatever has done; perhaps it's the memory of fire. His given name probably wasn't Ezra, but does it matter? We'll never know that, either. Billy asks about my father, he heard what happened, and I try to explain at least part of it. I show him the little twisted slug, which he examines carefully, almost scientifically.

I like Billy Q. He peers intently into every window; he drags us into shops where he engages the shopkeepers in long conversations in Italian about items that look like nothing much to me – a cut-glass pitcher, an oddly shaped clay bowl – but that clearly have great resonance for the two of them. When Billy Q asks questions, the shopkeepers back up warily, narrow their eyes, answer *sotto voce,* spy to spy. He buys nothing. I feel that I am witnessing some sort of devastation, like Sherman's March, and I try to look at the shopkeepers sympathetically when we leave each store.

We stop for an espresso and are standing at the bar. "Hey," I say, "what do you think of Little Wars?"

"They blew up kind of fast on that first record. They're on a big label – I know there are certain expectations there, could be good or bad for them. Everything is so rough now, it's hard to say. It's like . . . climate change. No one knows where it's all going. Nowhere good, I guess."

The espresso is bracingly bitter. A group of Italian workmen in green jumpsuits tumble in, ranging in age from lithe youth to craggy elder, faces brown from the sun. They jostle and push for midafternoon coffees, laughing and talking. "They asked if we want to open for them in Japan and Australia this fall."

I study Billy Q's face for a sign, but he is studying mine. "Do you want to do that?"

"I would lose my job."

"You have a job? What kind of job?"

"It's – it doesn't matter – it's a job. It pays the rent. They're not that nice there, they would feel betrayed, and they wouldn't have me back."

"Could you get another job?" I wonder if Billy Q has ever said the word "job," it sounds so strange when he says it, as if he's saying, "Could you get another yellow-bellied platypus?"

"I don't know. I guess. I never really, you know, looked for a job. This is the only one I've ever had."

"Do you like it?" Billy Q, bless him, looks deeply interested, as if this is a fascinating conversation. Maybe for him it is. The Italian workmen all leave as quickly as they came in, and the bar goes quiet again.

I frown. "Sometimes. We build things. I like that, I guess."

"Uh-huh." Billy nods, and I can tell he is confused, although he is trying to be helpful.

"The point is, well, the point is that – I mean, look, it's been a while. For me. Let's be honest. It's been a while. This tour has done okay, but it hasn't shattered any records, and I don't know if the Little Wars audience is our audience, if we even have one. When I've looked out at the crowd these past few weeks, I don't recognize those people. I don't know who the hell they are. And then with everything else – I'm kind of a mess."

Billy Q squeezes the lemon rind between his fingers. "Terry knows that band is getting old. They only had hits that one time – that was two records ago. He has to suss out a different crowd, pop is too brutal. That's why he wants you. He wants the people who remember you, that whole *Whale* moment. He wants your . . . your trace, your vibe. I'm sorry, am I being too blunt? My Queens side is showing. I am *so* my mother." He smiles. "Anyway, listen, we all think you're genius, the admiration is real, but I'm just talking demographics. Do you know who they were going to go out with before it fell through? Whether." He sips his espresso. "I thought that was a bit VH1, but anyway, they split up or something. I'm not sure I love Little Wars as a band, but Terry is a smart dude. He's thinking of his future." Billy Q looks at me with the sharp gaze I just saw him turn on the shopkeepers. "I don't know if that helps. I guess it doesn't answer the job question." He leaves the lemon rind in the empty espresso cup. "Tokyo is lovely in the fall."

Back at the venue, the problems with the channels must have been resolved, because I find everyone at a table in the garden out back, eating a leisurely Italian lunch. I sit down next to Zach, who pours me a glass of red wine. Alicia, barefoot now, says, "Anna, this risotto with the peas is *gorgeous*. You have to try it."

Some performers say that at every show they pick out a person in the audience, one face, and do the show for that person, who will never know that the entire show was for him or her. Others say that they try to blur the faces behind the stage lights as much as possible and concentrate on who's on the stage with them, playing for family. Others stay high. Who are you out there in the dark? Where do we meet? To whom is our love addressed? I run from door to door, some tiny, some huge, looking for you. I was playing, that night in Rome, at the venue in the middle of a labyrinth of gardens, for you and you and you. The house was packed. We wrecked it. We went too far, really, we were almost bullying, but the audience loved it. They wanted to be wrecked, maybe it was the full moon. After five encores, shaky-legged and gasping for breath, we stood in silence in the green room, which was an aluminum hut at the back of the garden. Tom took off his hat and poured a bottle of water over his balding head. Boone wept. Alicia grinned. Zach sat down on a bench. "Jesus Christ," he said. "Jesus fucking Christ."

Flicker, flicker. Out, later, champagne and gelato, it flashes in the long mirror over the bar. Then gone.

Rome, B-Side

IN THE OTHER ROME, that didn't happen: Simon and I walk through the Roman Forum on a hot July day with Maya, who is thirteen, and often dour in a way that mystifies both of us. She is a tall girl with his dusky skin, his hawkish features, and my mother's flowing way of moving, a grace of which she seems to be entirely unaware and which she doesn't value. At school in Zurich, where we live, she's at the top of her class in nearly everything. She's especially brilliant at mathematics. She says she wants to be an engineer.

Simon pauses, face turned up. He says, "Maya, look at this. This was a temple." The three broken columns remain, with nothing to hold up but the sky. She takes his hand unselfconsciously, squinting up at the ruin through her glasses.

"It's still so symmetrical," she observes. "Were there ... eight columns?"

Simon, beaming, gesturing, still holding her hand, explains what was there once, what crumbled, what was rebuilt. Sweating in the heat and the rubble – why didn't I put on sunscreen? – I check the calendar on my phone; Analiese has managed some clever way of color-coding that lets me know at a glance that this is a school event, that an evening event of mine and Simon's, this an appointment of mine at the dentist, that my swimming class (deep aqua). The surface of my phone looks like Tibetan prayer flags, a brightly colored string of pleasantly productive days and nights. It occurs to me that I have nothing whatsoever to worry about, all the wars are over. This is the prosperous peace. I doubt I'll ever love Zurich – who could? – but Maya is worth it, I knew that all those years back, lying on the bed that stretched from wall to wall on ratty 19th Street with nothing to my name, but still, *I cannot give you up. Darling, stay.* Sacrifices had to be made, but those sacrifices were long ago. I suppose I have become European. I know all about Janáček now, and Smetana, too.

I walk over to them and take Simon's other hand, rub my thumb on his in the gesture that means *I love you.* He kisses my surely reddening forehead. The three of us walk through the ruins, hand in hand in hand, talking about finding a cool spot for lunch.

East 79th Street

I CAME IN from the rain, annoyed and wet, my thumb pinched from trying to chain my bike up with the heavy, wet lock, because it hadn't been raining when I'd left home that morning. It was 7 a.m.; grade school starts early. Stu, at the Arts and Crafts front desk, nodded me in, along with four incandescent sixth-graders in multicolored wellies riding a giggle all the way up the carpeted stairs, past the oil paintings of the school's founders. I wondered which one might look like me.

"Wet one," said Stu, our elderly stone lion, in his suit and tie, his milky gaze fixed briefly, sharply on each small person coming in, as if he could actually distinguish one from another.

"Yup."

"You need an umbrella."

"I know. I forgot."

"Weather always changes, Miss Brundage."

"It does that."

I pushed open the heavy oak door to the teachers' lounge with my hip, trying simultaneously to zip up my wet backpack, unclip my jeans leg, and text Jim to meet me at the gate after school if it was still raining in the afternoon. I realized that I'd also forgotten the lunch he'd packed me. "Motherfuck," I mumbled, tossing the entire wet mess of clip, open lunchless backpack, and phone onto a sofa.

Jamal, the art teacher, drinking coffee by the stained-glass window, said, "Mercy, Anna. Already that bad?" Jamal had several skin tags on his face, a visible paunch, and nearly always wore the same jeans and button-down striped shirt to school, but there was nevertheless something sexy about him, something knowing. I'd been thinking about Jamal a fair amount recently. But what was a thought? Just a thought.

"It wasn't raining when I left."

"Sounds like a song." He smiled at me over his half-glasses.

"Stop." I poured myself some coffee in the clean, generous, bone-white mug that was waiting for me in the cabinet, added warm milk from the thermos, indulged in a pecan muffin from the ribboned basket on the table. Thursday was pecan muffin day, a treat made by the headmaster's wife, and they were truly spectacular, dense yet lofty spheres of butter, sugar, and nuts. Since the headmaster's wife was the heiress to a tire fortune, one didn't have to feel guilty about gender politics, etc.; the pecan muffins were clearly a ceremonial curlicue, a gift from the Queen to her loyal subjects. I sat down by the fire, took my wet shoes off, and bit in. "These. Are. So. Brilliant."

"Are you going to the brown bag today?"

"Well, I forgot my brown bag. But who is it again?"

"That violinist, what's his name, the big Russian guy — Sasha's father. Just tell Holly in the kitchen —"

"Right." I wiggled my toes toward the warmth of the fire, took a sip of coffee. "Oh, this helps. This is good. Hey, what happened with your back?"

"Reply hazy, try again later," Jamal said. "They maybe want to fuse the disk, but I don't know. I need to read more about it. Apparently a lot of people have problems even after the surgery."

"Surgery, Jesus. That's no fun."

"I've been a back person all my life. You know." Jamal waved a hand. He had beautiful, tapered brown fingers, one with a single, slender gold band. "What?"

"Nothing." My own fingers — one banded in Oaxacan silver — were sticky from the muffin. I wiped them with a napkin, considered eating another muffin, but, just barely, didn't. Today was jigsaw day, and I didn't want to have a sugar crash at the machine. Jamal did have beautiful hands; he often slept in his studio on Canal Street, worked in metal, paper, and string. How long had it been since I'd written a song? I quietly counted on my clean fingertips. Five years, three months. "Did you finish that thing?"

"Which thing?"

"The one with the spinning part."

"Not yet." He reached for a muffin, ate it slowly. "I'm still working it out. Damn, these are good."

The rain pattered against the stained-glass window, leaving the light blue glass sky, the white glass knights, and the dark blue glass river untouched. Onward the glass knights went in their quest, on a perpetually bright day, forever about to pass the same light green and dark green glass tree. A log in the fireplace opened, sparking. My socks were almost dry.

"How old do you think those windows are?" I asked Jamal.

"These?" He touched the one near him appreciatively. "A century or so. Imagine living with this kind of thing, having it in your house."

"They were rich."

"Yeah," said Jamal, "and then they were all dead." He shrugged. "Do you want to get a drink later?"

I looked at Jamal. He looked at me over his half-glasses. His eyes were brown. The rain rained, but the knights didn't know it. I put my feet back in my wet shoes. "No," I said. "I have something I want to work on." Which is how it is, really—throw the rope out into nothing, hope it holds, starfish down.

On the Bullet Train to Kyoto

WE TAKE UP an entire Green Car compartment. Zelda alternately walks and crawls up the aisle, teeter-tottering in her corduroy overalls. Her curly hair is exclamatory. She tips from Terry's outstretched hand to Kiki's to Luther's to Badge's meaty fingers; when she tumbles, Grant, Terry's bodyguard, leans from his seat to right her; the guitar techs, Red and Fred, call to her, and she almost runs before, butt high, returning to crawling. Terry's trainer, José, has taken up two seats to sort out everyone's respective protein snack; he smiles as Zelda tugboats past. Alicia, coming down the aisle with a violet cardboard bento box, scoops Zelda up and the child burrows into Alicia's neck.

"She's in love," comments Kiki.

Alicia settles with Zelda in a seat, and they share a rice ball that has something purple inside. Zelda turns her small head toward the window, her hands full of rice and purple. The sea appears, disappears behind trees, appears again. "Fish!" says Zelda.

"In the sea," Alicia agrees.

"Maybe," murmurs Zach, next to me. "Might glow a little."

"Shhhh." I close the composition book, open the footrest, lean back. "This first-class thing is working for me."

"But we really have to talk to Terry—"

"I know, I know. When we get to Kyoto. I know Tom fucked up. I hate having to fire people."

"But, you know," Zach continues, tilting his seat back, "Tokyo kind of blew my mind. It felt like Tomorrowland."

"And it was so quiet, did you notice that? I've never been in such a hushed city."

"All that light," Zach says. "It's like the sound was in the light."

"I want to go back. I'm not finished."

"No," says Zach. "Me, neither." He taps his feet together restlessly.

I don't know what we are yet. I suppose that's always the case, the unknowing, but I feel between us a continual shifting, sliding motion, like a ball rolling first one way then another, the weight tipping unpredictably. In the years between us are worlds of echoes that are different to me than they are to him, different to him than they are to me. *Whale* is one of his, huddled with his bad stoner high school friends in the wrecked house that smelled like gas back in the woods. He spray-painted the lyrics on the walls: "When the wolf found her / she was already waiting . . ." He wanted to get to that planet as fast as possible, and he did. He dropped out of Juilliard to go on the road, which is the kind of choice we have in common. He's been in those vans, slept on those sofas, gotten clawed by those untamed egos.

He's been making me playlists, sonic valentines that are also helping me catch up, although I'm not sure that I'll ever quite catch up now. Once you step away, you will always be at least a breath behind. The beat moves on. Was the world this tender, this open before? Is it love or is it real, my sense from what he plays for me that he comes from a lighter, faster, more fluid generation where melancholy is the aquifer? When did this happen? He listens to music from Thailand, from Zimbabwe, to 1930s gospel. Time is negotiable for him; history pleats easily. His biceps, handsome though they are, remain a mystery to me, because he never muscles his way into anything. It isn't his youth that throws me off balance, it's his lightness. He zips across the world, the worlds, a glowing streak of ambition. He aspires to a kind of frictionless hypermobility I don't truly understand. "I go deep with you," he has said to me. "I get the bends." I think this is a compliment, but it might also be a warning. And, of course, it's true. Something has happened.

The bullet train flies on. I touch the little twisted slug in my pocket. The sea is steady outside the windows, done with hide-and-seek for the moment. Zelda is sleeping in Alicia's lap, one of her curls wrapped around Alicia's finger. Zach yawns, palms his head. "Are you hungry? I'm hungry."

"You're always hungry."

He gnashes his teeth. "I am." He propels himself up out of the seat, duck-foots up the aisle, stopping by Terry to lean down, confer, laugh.

Out the window on our side of the train, houses begin to appear, first many beats apart, then just a few, then in a rhythm too fast to feel as separate notes. They become a long chord. Before too long, the chord rises, punctuated by taller buildings, glimpses of highway, power lines. The train slows. As we approach a nondescript apartment building, someone flings open a double set of windows, breaking the structure's gray surface: within, light and movement, rooms opening into other rooms, flash of sun from the windows on the wall perpendicular to the façade. I can't make out much more than that, and then we're past it, although the image remains – a blur, a bit of movement – pressed into my memory.

Zach returns with several elaborately painted bento boxes full of brightly colored food I don't recognize, sits down, and begins spreading it out on our little table. I am happy to see him.

He smiles at me. "Almost there," he says.

Acknowledgments

I am grateful to the Guggenheim Foundation, Beatrice Monti della Corte and the Santa Maddalena Foundation, Columbia University, the American Academy in Rome, and the MacDowell Colony for the gift of time and space. I was also fortunate to have the company of the Bartlett family, with special thanks to Gunner Caldwell, who named the band. I owe a particular debt of gratitude to Thomas Bartlett, also known as Doveman, for his advice and support. Without his unparalleled generosity of mind and spirit, this book could not have been written. Nor could it have been written without the support and intelligence of Maud Casey, Jennifer Charles of Elysian Fields, the incomparable Bill Clegg, Larry Cooper, Ephen Glenn Colter, Pat Dillett, Jeanne Fury, my wonderful editor Jenna Johnson, William Kentridge, Daiken Nelson, Christopher Potter, Elizabeth Povinelli, Alicia Jo Rabins, Frances Richard, and Jason Sellards and Scissor Sisters. I also thank Martin Glaz Serup and his poem "Marken," or "The Field," for the image of a field in crisis.